the Reckoning

DARKEST POWERS
•Book Three•

the Reckoning

KELLEY ARMSTRONG

HARPER
An Imprint of HarperCollinsPublishers

Library of Congress Cataloging-in-Publication Data

Armstrong, Kelley.

The reckoning / Kelley Armstrong. — 1st ed.

  p.   cm. — (Darkest powers ; bk. 3)

Summary: Fifteen-year-old Chloe, a necromancer, struggles to understand her feelings for werewolf Derek and his sorcerer brother, Simon, while seeking a way to enter the headquarters of the sinister Edison Group and rescue her aunt Lauren and friend Rachelle.

ISBN 978-0-06-166283-6

[1. Supernatural—Fiction. 2. Magic—Fiction. 3. Werewolves—Fiction. 4. Ghosts—Fiction.] I. Title.

PZ7.A73369Rec 2010   2009044008

[Fic]—dc22   CIP

                                                                          AC

Typography by Larissa Lawrynenko

10   11   12   13   14   LP/RRDH   10   9   8   7   6   5   4   3   2   1

❖

First Edition

To Julia

one

AFTER FOUR NIGHTS ON the run, I was finally safe, tucked into bed and enjoying the deep, dreamless sleep of the dead . . . until the dead decided they'd really rather have me awake. It started with a laugh that slid into my sleep and pulled me out of it. As I rose on my elbows, blinking and struggling to remember where I was, a whisper snaked around me, words indistinguishable.

I rubbed my eyes and yawned. Dull gray light shone through the curtains. The room was silent and still. No ghosts, thank God. I'd had enough in the last few weeks to last me a lifetime.

A scrape at the window made me jump. These days, every branch scratching the glass sounded like a zombie I'd raised from the dead, clawing to get in.

I went to the window and pulled back the curtains. It'd

been nearly dawn by the time we got to the house, so I knew it had to be at least midmorning, but the fog outside was so thick I couldn't see anything. I leaned closer, nose pressed to the cold glass.

A bug splattered against the window and I jumped a foot in the air. A laugh sounded behind me.

I whirled, but Tori was still in bed, whimpering in her sleep. She'd thrown off the covers and was curled up on her side, her dark hair spiked across the pillow.

Another chuckle erupted behind me. Definitely a guy's laugh. But no one was there. No, strike that. I just couldn't *see* anyone. For a necromancer, that doesn't mean no one *is* there.

I squinted, trying to catch the flicker of a ghost and saw, off to the left, the flash of a hand that was gone before I could see more.

"Looking for someone, little necro?"

I spun. "Who's there?"

A snicker answered me—the kind of snicker every fifteen-year-old girl has heard a million times from jerk boys.

"If you want to talk to me, you have to show yourself," I said.

"Talk to you?" he said in an arrogant high school quarterback voice. "I think you're the one who wants to talk to me."

I snorted and headed back to bed.

"No?" His voice slid around me. "Huh. I figured you'd

want to know more about the Edison Group, the Genesis experiments, Dr. Davidoff . . ."

I stopped.

He laughed. "Thought so."

The four of us—Tori, Derek, Simon, and me—were on the run from the Edison Group after discovering we were subjects in the Genesis project, an experiment for genetically modifying supernaturals. My aunt Lauren had been one of the doctors involved, but she'd betrayed her colleagues by helping us get away. Now she was being held captive. Or so I hoped. Last night, when the Edison Group tracked us down, a ghost had tried to help me . . . a ghost who had looked like Aunt Lauren.

We were supposedly in a safe house owned by a group opposing the experiments. Now a teenaged ghost showed up, knowing about the project? I wasn't about to banish him, however tempting it might be.

"Show yourself," I said.

"Bossy little necro, aren't you?" His voice slid behind me. "You just want to see if I'm as hot as I sound."

I closed my eyes, pictured a vague male form, and gave a mental tug. He began to materialize—a dark-haired guy, maybe sixteen, seventeen, nothing special, but with a smarmy smile that said he thought he was. I could still see through him, like he was a hologram, so I closed my eyes to give him another pull.

"Uh-uh," he said. "You want more, we gotta get to know

each other a little better." He disappeared again.

"What do you want?" I asked.

He whispered in my ear. "Like I said, to get to know you better. Not here, though. You'll wake your friend. She's cute, but not really my type." His voice moved to the door. "I know a place we can chat in private."

Yeah, right. Did he think I'd just started talking to ghosts yesterday? Well, close—two weeks ago, actually. But I'd already seen enough to know that while there were some ghosts who wanted to help and some who just wanted to talk, there were more who wanted to cause a little trouble, spice up their afterlife. This guy definitely fell in the last category.

Still, if he was another Edison Group subject, one who'd presumably died in this house, I needed to find out what had happened to him. But I wanted backup. Tori had no experience helping me with ghosts and, while we were getting along better, she still wasn't anyone I wanted watching my back.

So I followed the ghost into the hall, but stopped at Simon and Derek's door.

"Uh-uh," the ghost said. "You don't need to bring a guy along."

"They'd like to talk to you, too." I raised my voice, praying Derek would hear me. He usually woke at the slightest noise—werewolves have superhearing. All I could hear, though, was Simon's snores. There was no one else upstairs. Andrew, the guy who'd brought us here, had taken the downstairs bedroom.

"Come on, necro girl. This is a limited-time offer."

You know he's up to no good, Chloe.

Yes, but I also needed to know if we were in danger here. I decided to proceed with extreme caution. My subconscious voice didn't argue, which I took as a positive sign.

I started walking.

We'd gone straight to bed after we got here, so I hadn't gotten a good look at our new place. I only knew that it was huge—a rambling Victorian straight out of a Gothic horror movie.

As I followed the voice down the hall, I had the weird sense I was in one of those movies, caught in an endless narrow corridor, passing closed door after closed door until I finally reached the staircase . . . heading up.

From what I'd seen of the house as we'd driven up, it was three stories. The bedrooms were on the second floor, and Andrew had said the third was an attic.

So the ghost was leading me to the dark, spooky attic? I wasn't the only one who'd seen too many horror films.

I followed him up the stairs. They ended at a landing with two doors. I paused. A hand appeared through the door in front of me, beckoning. I took a second to prepare myself. No matter how dark it was in there, I couldn't let him see my fear.

When I was ready, I grabbed the doorknob and—

It was locked. I turned the dead bolt latch and it clicked free. Another deep breath, another second of mental preparation, then I swung the door open and stepped in—

A blast of cold air knocked me back. I blinked. Ahead, fog swirled.

A dead bolt on an attic door, Chloe?

No, I was standing on the roof.

TWO

I WHEELED AS THE door swung closed behind me. I caught the edge, but something hit it, hard, and it slammed home. I grabbed the handle as the dead bolt clanked shut. I twisted the knob, sure I was mistaken.

"Leaving so soon?" he said. "How rude."

I stared down at the handle. Only one very rare type of ghost could move stuff in the living world.

"An Agito half-demon," I whispered.

"Agito?" He twisted the word with contempt. "I'm top-of-the-line, baby. I'm a Volo."

Which meant nothing to me. I could only guess it was a more powerful type. In life, a telekinetic half-demon could move objects mentally. In death, they could move them physically. A poltergeist.

I took a careful step back. Wood creaked underfoot,

reminding me of where I was. I stopped short and looked around. I was on a kind of walkway that circled the third floor—the attic, I presumed.

To my right was a nearly flat section littered with rusty bottle caps and beer cans, like someone had used it as a makeshift patio. That calmed me down. I wasn't stranded on a roof, just a balcony. Annoying, but safe enough.

I rapped on the door, lightly, not really wanting to wake anyone, but hoping Derek might notice.

"No one's going to hear you," the ghost said. "We're all alone. Just the way I like it."

I lifted my hand to bang on the door, then stopped. Dad always said the best way to deal with a bully was not to let him know you were frightened. At the thought of my father, my throat tightened. Was he still looking for me? Of course, he was, and there was nothing I could do.

Dad's advice for bullies had worked with the kids who mocked my stutter—they gave up when they couldn't get a reaction from me. So I took a deep breath and went on the offensive.

"You said you know about the Edison Group and their experiments," I said. "Were you a subject?"

"Boring. Let's talk about you. Got a boyfriend? I bet you do. Cute girl like you, hanging out with two guys. You've gotta have hooked up with one of them by now. So which one?" He laughed. "Dumb question. The cute girl would get the cute guy. The chink."

He meant Simon, who was half Korean. He was baiting me, seeing if I'd leap to Simon's defense and prove he was my boyfriend. He wasn't. Well, not yet, though we seemed to be heading that way.

"If you want me to stay and talk, I need some answers first," I said.

He laughed. "Yeah? Doesn't look to me like you're going anywhere."

I grabbed the doorknob again. A bottle cap pinged off my cheek just below my eye. I glowered in his direction.

"That was only a warning shot, little necro." A nasty tone edged his voice. "Around here, we play *my* game by *my* rules. Now, tell me about your boyfriend."

"I don't have one. If you know anything about the Genesis experiment, then you know we aren't here for a vacation. Being on the run doesn't leave much time for romance."

"Don't get snarky with me."

I banged on the door. The next bottle cap hit my eye, stinging.

"You're in danger, little girl. Don't you care?" His voice lowered to my ear. "Right now, I'm your best friend, so you'd better treat me good. You've just been led into a trap and I'm the only one who can get you out."

"Led? By who? The guy who brought us here—" I thought up a fake name fast. "Charles?"

"No, some total stranger, and Charles just happened to bring you here. What a coincidence."

"But he said he doesn't work for the Edison Group anymore. He used to be their doctor—"

"He still is."

"H-he's Dr. Fellows? The one they were talking about at the lab?"

"None other."

"Are you sure?"

"I'd never forget that face."

"Huh, well, that's weird. First, his name isn't Charles. Second, he's not a doctor. Third, I know Dr. Fellows. She's my aunt, and that guy downstairs looks nothing like her."

The blow hit me from behind, striking hard against the back of my knees. My legs buckled and I fell on all fours.

"Don't toy with me, little necro."

When I tried to rise, he hit me with an old plank swung like a baseball bat. I tried to twist out of the way, but he got my shoulder and knocked me into the railing. A crack, and the railing gave way. I toppled, and for a second, all I could see was the concrete patio two stories down.

I caught another section of railing. It held and I was steadying myself when the plank swung straight for my hand. I let go and scrambled onto the walkway as the board hit the railing so hard that the top rail snapped and the plank snapped, too, splinters of rotting wood flying.

I ran toward the flat section of roof. He whipped the broken board at me. I stumbled back, bumping into the railing again.

I caught my balance and looked around. No sign of him. No sign of anything moving. But I knew he was there, watching to see what I'd do next.

I ran for the door, then feinted toward the flat part of the roof. A crash. Shards of glass exploded in front of me and the ghost appeared, lifting a broken bottle. I backpedaled.

Sure, that's a great idea. Just keep backing into the railing, see how long it'll hold.

I stopped. There was nowhere to run. I considered screaming. I've always hated that in movies—heroines who scream for help when cornered—but right now, caught between a broken-bottle-wielding poltergeist and a two-story fall, I could survive the humiliation of being rescued. Problem was, no one would get here in time.

So . . . what are you going to do? The superpowerful necromancer against the bullying poltergeist?

That was right. I did have a defense, at least against ghosts.

I touched my amulet. It'd been given to me by my mother. She'd said it would ward off the bogeymen I'd seen when I was little—ghosts, as I knew now. It didn't seem to work that well, but clutching it helped me concentrate, focus on what I was.

I pictured giving the ghost a shove.

"Don't you dare, little girl. You'll only piss me off and—"

I squeezed my eyes shut and gave him a huge mental push.

Silence.

I waited, listening, sure that when I opened my eyes, he'd be right there. After a moment, I peeked and saw only the gray sky. Still, I gripped the railing tight, ready for a broken bottle to fly at my head.

"Chloe!"

My knees shook at the shout. Footsteps thudded across the roof. Ghosts don't make footsteps.

"Don't move."

I looked over my shoulder to see Derek.

three

DEREK MADE HIS WAY across the flat section of the roof. He was dressed in jeans and a T-shirt, but his feet were bare.

"Watch out," I called. "There's broken glass."

"I see it. Stay where you are."

"It's okay. I'll just back up and—" The wood creaked under me. "Or maybe not."

"Just stay there. The wood's rotting. It's holding your weight as long as you stand still."

"But I walked out here, so it must be—"

"We're not testing that theory, okay?"

There was none of the usual impatient snap in his voice, meaning he was really worried. And if Derek was worried, I'd better stay right where I was. I gripped the railing.

"No!" he said. "I mean, yes, hold on, but don't put any

weight on it. It's rotted through at the base."

Great.

Derek looked around, like he was searching for something to use. Then he stripped off his shirt. I tried not to look away. Not that he looked bad without his shirt. The opposite, actually, which is why . . . Let's just say friends are really better when they're fully dressed.

Derek got as close as he dared, then knotted a corner of the T-shirt and tossed it to me. I caught it on the second throw.

"I'm not going to pull you in," he warned.

A good thing, because with his werewolf strength, he'd probably wrench it from my hands and I'd tumble off the roof backward.

"Pull yourself along—"

He stopped, seeing I was already doing that. I made it onto the flat part, wobbled a step, then felt my knees start to give way. Derek grabbed my arm—the one without stitches, bandages, and a bullet graze—and I lowered myself slowly.

"I—I'm just going to sit for a minute," I said, my voice shakier than I liked.

Derek sat beside me, his shirt back on. I could feel him watching me, uncertain.

"I—I'll be okay. Just give me a second. It's safe to sit here, right?"

"Yeah, the slope's only about twenty-five degrees, so—" Seeing my expression, he said, "It's safe."

The fog was lifting, and I could see trees stretching into the distance on all sides, a dirt road winding through them to the house.

"There was a ghost," I said finally.

"Yeah, I figured that."

"I—I knew I shouldn't follow, but—" I paused, not ready for the full explanation, still shaky. "I stopped outside your door, hoping you'd hear me. I guess you did?"

"Kind of. I was dozing. Woke up confused, so it took me a while to get out here. Got a touch of fever."

I saw it now, the flushed skin and glittering eyes.

"Are you—?" I began.

"I'm not Changing. Not for a while. I know what that feels like now, and I've got a ways to go. Another day, at least. Hopefully longer."

"I bet you'll Change completely this time," I said.

"Yeah, maybe." His tone said he doubted it.

As we sat there, I snuck a look at him. At sixteen, Derek was more than a foot taller than me. Solidly built, too, with broad shoulders and muscles he usually kept hidden under baggy clothes, so he wouldn't look as intimidating.

Since he'd started Changing, Mother Nature seemed to have cut him some slack. His skin was clearing up. His dark hair didn't look greasy anymore. It still hung in his face— nothing emo, just like he hadn't bothered to get it cut in a while. Lately, that would have been the last thing on his mind.

I tried to relax and enjoy the fog-laced view, but Derek

fidgeted and squirmed, which was more distracting than if
he'd just been his usual self and demanded to know what had
happened.

"So there was this ghost," I said finally. "He said he was
a Volo half-demon. Telekinetic, but a stronger type than Dr.
Davidoff. Probably the same kind Liz is. He lured me out
here, locked the door, then started pelting me with stuff."

Derek looked over sharply.

"I banished him."

"Good, but you shouldn't have followed him at all,
Chloe."

His tone was calm, reasonable, so un-Derek-like that I
stared at him, the weird idea that this wasn't Derek creeping through my head. Before I'd escaped the Edison Group
laboratory, I'd met a demi-demon, chained there as a power
source. She'd possessed someone but only a ghost. Could
Derek be possessed?

"What?" Derek said as I stared.

"Are you okay?"

"Yeah, just . . ." He rubbed the back of his neck, wincing and rolling his shoulders. "Tired. Feeling off. Really off.
Too much . . ." He struggled for the word. "Being here. Being
safe. I'm still adjusting."

That made sense. Derek's werewolf protective streak
had been in hyperdrive for days, keeping him awake and on
guard. Having someone else to watch out for us now would be
weird. Still, not blasting me for blithely following a random

ghost onto a roof was so totally not Derek that I knew there was more to it.

When I asked what was bothering him, he muttered that it was nothing. I backed off and was about to explain more about the ghost when he blurted, "It's Tori. I don't like her story about how she got away."

When the Edison Group had almost captured us last night, they'd nabbed Tori. Yet when they'd refocused their efforts on the biggest threat—Derek—they'd left the young witch with only a single guard. She'd locked him in a binding spell and escaped.

"You think they let her get away?"

"I'm not saying . . . It's just . . . I don't have any proof."

And that's what was making him uncomfortable, that his misgivings were based on nothing but a gut feeling. The math and science whiz really preferred dealing in facts.

"If you're thinking she's been a plant from the start, she hasn't." I lowered my voice. "Don't tell her I told you this, okay? When she helped me escape, she only wanted to get away from the Edison Group and run back to her dad. So she called him. Instead he sent her mom—the woman we'd just escaped. Tori was hurt, really hurt. In shock even. She couldn't have faked that."

"I didn't figure she was in on it from that far back."

"Just that she cut a deal last night?"

"Yeah."

"Would Tori turn us in for the promise of getting her old

life back? It's possible, and we should be careful, but I *do* buy her story. Unless her mom told them Tori was figuring out how to cast spells—which I doubt—then, as far as they know, she just has random outbursts of power. Her binding spell could have taken out a single guard. I've seen her use it. She doesn't even need to say an incantation. It's like, if she thinks it, she can do it."

"No casting? No practicing?" He shook his head. "Don't tell Simon that."

"Don't tell Simon what?" said a voice behind us.

We turned to see Simon step out of the doorway.

"That Tori doesn't need to use incantations to cast," Derek said.

"Seriously?" He swore. "You're right. Don't tell me." He picked his way across the roof. "Better yet, don't tell her that I need incantations and weeks of practice, and I still suck."

"You were good with that knock-back spell last night," I said.

He grinned. "Thanks. Now, do I dare ask what you guys are doing hiding out up here? Or is it going to make me jealous?"

Simon was smiling as he said it, but Derek glanced away with a gruff "Course not."

"So you weren't having another adventure?" Simon lowered himself on my other side, so close he brushed against me, hand resting on mine. "It sure looks like a good spot for one. Rooftop hideaway, old widow's walk. That is what that is, huh? A widow's walk?"

"Yeah. And it's rotting, so stay off it," Derek said.

"I did. So, adventure?"

"A small one," I said.

"Oh, man. I always miss them. Okay, break it to me gently. What happened?"

I explained. As Simon listened, intent and concerned, he cast glances at his brother. Foster brother, I guess you'd say—one look at them and you knew they weren't related by blood. Simon is fifteen, a half-year older than me, slender and athletic, with dark, almond-shaped eyes and spiked blond hair. When Derek was about five, he'd come to live with Simon and his dad. They were best friends and brothers, blood tie or not.

I told him as much as I'd told Derek so far. Then he looked from me to Derek.

"I must have been sound asleep if I missed all that shouting," Simon said.

"What shouting?" Derek said.

"You mean that Chloe just told you that she followed a ghost onto a roof, and you didn't blast her all the way to Canada?"

"He's a little off this morning," I said.

"More than a little, I'd say. Aren't you going to ask her for the rest of the story? The part where she explains *why* she followed the ghost? Because I'm sure there was a reason."

I smiled. "Thank you. There was. It was a teenage guy

who knew about the Edison Group and the experiments."

"What?" Derek's head whipped around, the sound more growl than question.

"That's why I followed him. There's a dead kid here who might have been another subject, and if he died here . . ."

"Then that's a problem," Simon said.

I nodded. "My first thought, naturally, was 'Oh my God, we've been led into a trap.'"

Simon shook his head. "Not Andrew. He's one of the good guys. I've known him all my life."

"But I haven't, which is why I prodded the ghost, and it was clear he hadn't recognized him. Andrew said this place was owned by the guy who started his group and was involved in the experiments. If there's a link to this kid, I think we'll find it there."

"We can ask Andrew—" Simon began.

Derek cut him off. "We'll find our own answers."

Simon and Derek locked gazes. After a second, Simon grumbled something about making things difficult, but he didn't argue. If Derek wanted to amuse himself playing detective, then fine. We'd be gone soon anyway, back to rescue those we'd left behind and take out the Edison Group . . . or so we hoped.

four

WE WENT DOWNSTAIRS SHORTLY after that. Derek headed straight for the kitchen to scrounge up breakfast. We might have gotten only a few hours sleep, but it was already almost noon and his stomach was, predictably, growling.

While he searched for food, Simon and I poked around our temporary new home. I read a book once about a girl in a huge English mansion with a secret room no one had found in years, because a wardrobe had been pulled in front of the door. I remember thinking that was ridiculous. My dad had friends with really big houses, and there was still no way you could lose a room. But with this place and a little stretch of the imagination, I could see it.

It wasn't just big. It was set up weird. Like the architect just slapped rooms onto a blueprint, with no thought to how they connected. The front was simple enough. There was a main hall connecting the doors, the stairs, the kitchen, a living room, and dining room. Then it got confusing, branching into a couple of back halls, with rooms that only joined other rooms. Most were really tiny, not even ten feet square. It reminded me of a rabbit's warren, all these little rooms going off in all directions. We even found a separate set of stairs back there, ones that looked like they hadn't been cleaned in years.

As Simon went to see if Andrew was up, I wandered into the kitchen, where Derek was eyeing a rusty can of beans.

"That hungry?" I asked.

"I will be soon."

He prowled the kitchen, flipping open cupboards.

"So you don't want me asking Andrew about that kid," I said. "You trust him, though, right?"

"Sure."

He took down a box of crackers and turned it over, looking for a "best before" date.

"That didn't sound convincing," I said. "If we're here with someone you don't trust . . ."

"Right now, the only people I really trust are you and Simon. I don't think Andrew is up to anything. If I did, we wouldn't be here. But I'm not taking a chance, not if we can find our own answers."

I nodded. "That's fine. Just . . . I know you don't want to spook Simon, but . . . If you're worried . . ." My cheeks heated.

"I don't mean you need to confide in me, just don't . . ."

"Blow you off when you know something's wrong." He turned and met my gaze. "I won't."

"Is he drinking the ketchup yet?" Simon swung into the kitchen. "Ten minutes, bro. Andrew's on his way and—"

"And he's apologizing profusely for the lack of food." Andrew walked in. He was about my dad's age with really short gray hair, square shoulders, a stocky build, and a crooked nose. He clapped a hand on Derek's shoulder. "It's coming. One of the group is bringing breakfast and will be here any minute."

He kept his hand on Derek's shoulder, giving it a squeeze. It was an awkward gesture, maybe because he was a half-foot shorter than Derek, but it seemed more than that. Last night, when he'd first seen Derek after a few years, a pulse of surprise and wariness crossed his face. Derek had seen it, and I knew he'd felt it—the jab of having a guy he'd known most of his life reacting like he was some teenage thug you'd cross the road to avoid.

Like Simon, Andrew was a sorcerer. He was an old friend of their dad's, and a former employee of the Edison Group. He was also their emergency contact. Andrew and their dad had some kind of falling out a few years ago, but they'd stayed in contact, so when we'd been stuck, we'd come to him.

Andrew gave Derek's shoulder one last squeeze, then he bustled about the kitchen, getting out plates and rinsing them off, wiping dust from the counters and the table, asking how we'd slept, apologizing again for the lack of preparation.

"Hard to prepare when you don't know anyone's coming," Simon said. "Is this going to be okay? You staying here with us? I know you've got work . . ."

"Which I've been doing from home for two years now. Finally built up the seniority to start telecommuting, thank God. The daily trips into New York were killing me. I go once a week now for meetings."

Simon turned to me. "Andrew's an editor. Books." He glanced at Andrew. "Chloe's a screenwriter."

I blushed and stammered that obviously I wasn't a real screenwriter, just a wannabe; but Andrew said he'd love to hear about what I was working on, answer any questions about writing. He even sounded like he meant it, unlike most adults, who just say things like that to humor you.

"Right now, she's working on a comic with me," Simon said. "A graphic journal of our adventures. Just for fun."

"Very cool. I take it you're doing the art? Your dad told me you're—"

The doorbell rang.

"And that would be breakfast," Andrew said. "Chloe? I know Tori's probably exhausted, but she should be here for the meeting."

"I'll go wake her up."

So the mysterious resistance group was here. It didn't look like much: three people plus Andrew.

There was Margaret, who looked like a lot of the women my dad worked with—a corporate business type, tall with graying brown hair cut short. She was a necromancer.

Gwen wasn't much taller than me and barely looked out of college. As for supernatural type, with her short blond hair, turned-up nose, and sharp chin, I started wondering if there was such a thing as a pixie, but she said she was a witch, like Tori.

The third newcomer was Russell, a bald grandfatherly guy who was a shaman paramedic, in case we needed medical attention after our ordeal. With Andrew and Margaret, he was one of the group's founding members and had also once worked for the Edison Group.

Andrew said there were another half-dozen members in the New York City area, and twenty or so more across the country. Under the circumstances, though, it didn't seem safe to have them all trooping up here to meet us. So they'd sent the ones who could help us the most—a necromancer and a witch. Derek was out of luck. There weren't any werewolves in the group, not surprising given that there were maybe a couple dozen in the country, compared to hundreds of necromancers and spell-casters.

The supernaturals who joined the Edison Group weren't evil. Most were like my aunt, who offered her services as a doctor because she wanted to help people like her brother, a necromancer who'd either committed suicide or been driven off a roof by ghosts when he was still in college.

The Edison Group believed that the answer was genetic manipulation—tweak our DNA to minimize side effects and improve our control over our powers. Things started going wrong back when we were little, and three of the werewolf subjects attacked a nurse. They were "eliminated." Killed, by the same people who swore they were trying to help supernaturals. That's when Simon's dad and others, like Andrew, left.

But leaving wasn't enough for some. Concerned about what they'd seen, they'd monitored the Edison Group, making sure they didn't pose a threat to other supernaturals. Now we were bringing news of exactly what they'd feared most. For many of us, the genetic modification had backfired, producing kids with uncontrollable powers—witches who could cast without incantations and necromancers who could raise the dead by accident.

When those failures hadn't proved as easy to control as the Edison Group had hoped, they'd done the same thing they'd done to the werewolf boys. Killed them.

Now, we'd come to Andrew's group for help. We were in mortal danger and we'd left behind another subject, Rachelle, and my aunt Lauren, who were in even greater danger. We were asking this group to rescue them and end the threat against us. Were they up to it? We had no idea.

Gwen had brought the breakfast: donuts, coffee, and chocolate milk, which I'm sure she thought would be the perfect treat for teenagers. It would have been . . . if we hadn't been living on junk food for three days and if one of us wasn't diabetic.

Simon picked out a donut and a half-pint carton of chocolate milk, joking about having the excuse to eat stuff that was normally off his diet. It was Derek who complained. Andrew apologized for forgetting to warn the others about Simon and promised more nutritious food for our next meal.

Everyone was really nice and sympathetic, and maybe I was just being paranoid—Derek rubbing off on me—but behind those smiles and kind eyes, there seemed to be a touch of unease, like they couldn't stop thinking about our messed-up powers. Like they couldn't help but think that we were all ticking time bombs.

I wasn't the only one who felt uncomfortable. When we moved to the living room, Derek staked out a corner and retreated there. Simon barely said a word. Tori, who normally wanted nothing to do with us, stuck so close to me that I thought she was trying to swipe my donut.

Us versus them. The genetically modified freaks versus the normal supernaturals.

Simon and I did most of the talking. That was weird for me, the kid who always sat in the back of a group, hoping she wasn't called on to speak because she might start stuttering. But the burden of proof lay with me and what I'd seen: the ghosts of the other kids and the files on Dr. Davidoff's computer.

As we explained, I saw sympathy in their eyes but doubt, too. They believed that the experiment had gone wrong for some subjects—that was exactly the kind of thing they'd feared when they quit. They also believed us about Lyle House, the "group home" where the Edison Group had kept us. When the experiment screwed up, naturally the Edison Group would try to cover their tracks.

But the rest of it? Hunting us down when we escaped? Shooting at us, first with tranquilizer darts, then real bullets? Locking us up in the laboratory? Killing three kids who'd failed rehabilitation?

That sounded like something from a movie. No, strike that. As an aspiring blockbuster screenwriter/director, if I'd heard this pitch, I'd have dismissed it as too outrageous.

I could tell that Andrew believed us. Gwen did, too. I could see it from the horror in her face. But Gwen was the youngest, and her opinion didn't seem to count for much. Russell and Margaret couldn't hide their skepticism, and I knew convincing them to help us wasn't going to be as easy as we'd hoped.

Finally, I blurted, "Rachelle and my aunt are in *danger*. They could be killed any day now, if they haven't already been."

"Your aunt is a valuable member of the team," Margaret said, her severe face unreadable. "They won't kill her. Nor does your friend seem in imminent danger. She's happy and compliant. That's all they'll ask for now."

"But if she finds out the truth, she won't be nearly so compliant—"

Russell cut in. "Your aunt and your friend made their choices, Chloe. As harsh as that seems. They both betrayed you. I didn't think you'd be so eager to rescue them."

"My aunt—"

"Helped you escape, I know. But you wouldn't have been there if it wasn't for your friend's betrayal."

Rae had told Dr. Davidoff about our escape plans, so they'd been ready when we tried to make a run for it. She'd believed their lies about wanting to help us and thought I'd been brainwashed by the boys.

"She made a mistake. Are you saying we should let her die for it?" My voice was rising. I swallowed, trying to stay calm, reasonable. "Whatever she did, she thought it was the right thing at the time, and I won't abandon her now."

I glanced at the others. Simon agreed quickly and vehemently. Derek mumbled a gruff "Yeah, she screwed up, but stupidity isn't a capital crime."

We all looked at Tori. I held my breath, feeling the weight of the adults' gazes on us, knowing we needed consensus on this.

"Since we're already going back for Chloe's aunt, then Rae should be rescued," Tori said. "And they *both* need to be rescued ASAP. The Edison Group might not be a bunch of vindictive homicidal maniacs, but my mother is the exception, and when we left, she really wasn't happy with Dr. Fellows."

"I don't think—" Russell began.

"Now it's time to move on to the boring discussion part," Andrew interjected. "Why don't you kids go upstairs and check out the other rooms. I'm sure you'd each like one of your own."

"We're good," Simon said.

Andrew looked at the others. They wanted us out of the room so they could discuss whether they were going to help us or not.

I wanted to scream, *What is there to discuss? The people you used to work for are killing kids. Isn't this your mission—to make sure their work doesn't hurt anyone? Stop chowing down on donuts and do something!*

"Why don't you—?" Andrew began.

"We're good." It came out as a growl. That was just Derek's *I'm serious* tone, but the room suddenly went very still. All eyes turned toward him, every gaze wary.

Derek glanced away and mumbled, "You want us to leave?"

"Please," Andrew said. "It would be easier—"

"Whatever."

Derek led us out.

five

IN THE HALL, DEREK turned. "You guys go see about finding a new bedroom for Tori. I'm getting more donuts."

Simon and I exchanged a look. As much as Derek
loved to eat, the last thing on his mind right now would be
filling his stomach. What he meant was *take Tori and get out
of here, so I can listen in on the meeting.* Werewolf hearing
meant he could eavesdrop from the kitchen.

"Save me a chocolate dipped," Simon said, leading Tori
and me to the stairs.

"You aren't supposed to have—"

"Just winding you up," Simon tossed back. "Come on,
Tori. Let's get you a room of your own."

As it turned out, Tori wanted to stay with me. Not that she said
that, of course. She checked out the other options, bitched

and moaned about how dusty they were and how it seemed she was stuck with me after all. I offered to take another one. She lit into me about being too nice and how I had to learn to stand up for myself. I decided it was time for a shower.

A shower would also give me a chance to wash the temporary dye from my hair. When we'd run away from Lyle House, my dad was told I'd done just that—run away. He had no idea I'd been caught almost immediately and taken to the Edison Group lab. He didn't know what the Edison Group was or what a necromancer was. To him, his schizophrenic daughter had run away from her group home and was now living on the streets of Buffalo. So he'd offered a reward. A half-million-dollar reward.

I wanted to let him know I was okay. God, I wanted to. But Aunt Lauren said he was safer not knowing the truth and Derek agreed. So, for now, I tried really hard not to think about how worried he must be. I'd get a message to him as soon as it was safe. In the meantime, his reward was a problem.

My strawberry blond hair was distinctive, even more so with the red streaks I'd added before I got shipped off to Lyle House. So Derek bought me temporary dye. Black dye. I was way too pale for black, and now I looked exactly like you'd picture a necromancer: white skin and harsh black hair. Uber-Goth. But now, thankfully, the color was fading. Or so I thought.

Tori followed me down the hall, offering tips about how to get the dye out, being Miss Helpful two minutes after calling me a wimp. These days, that seemed par for the course with Tori. She'd start inching toward friendship, then remember we were supposed to be mortal enemies.

Now she was in friendly mode. "Don't wash it more than three times or your hair will be like straw. I saw conditioner in there. Make sure you use that and let it sit."

"Right now, dry hair is better than black hair."

Simon poked his head out of his room. "You're washing out the color?"

"As fast as I can."

He hesitated, the look in his eyes telling me he was about to say something he really didn't want to. "I know you want it gone, but . . . Well, if we go out . . ."

"At this point, I'll take house arrest over black hair."

"It's not that bad."

Tori mock-whispered, "Simon's thinking the Goth girl look is kinda hot."

He glowered at her. "No. I just want—" An impatient look at Tori, telling her to get lost. When she stood her ground, he leaned down to my ear, his fingers entwining with mine. "I know you want to get rid of it. I'll ask Andrew to get you a better color. I don't care what your hair looks like; I just want you to be safe."

"That's so sweet," Tori said.

Simon moved to stand between us, his back to her. "You can check with Andrew. Maybe I'm overreacting—"

"No, you're not. I still need that shower, but I won't try washing out the color."

"Good. Oh, and Derek said you were asking about self-defense lessons. How about we try that after?"

I wasn't really in the mood for that, but he was smiling, obviously eager to do something nice for me after vetoing my hair fix. It wasn't like we had anything better to do, so I said, "Sure."

"Sounds good," Tori said. "Yes, I know, you weren't inviting me, but we could both use the training. And, no, I'm not trying to get between you guys. I'm over you, Simon. I think you and Chloe make the most nauseatingly cute couple ever. But you can gaze soulfully into each other's eyes another time. Right now, I need self-defense lessons. So I'll meet you out back."

She started for the stairs, calling, "And it wouldn't have been one-on-one for long anyway. I'm sure Derek will join in as soon as he's done eavesdropping."

I ran into Derek as I came out of the bathroom.

"Meeting over?" I asked.

"Yeah."

Simon popped his head out of their room and Derek motioned him into the hall.

"Where's Tori?" he asked.

"Outside. She's waiting for us, though, so we can't be long."

"And the verdict is?" Simon prompted.

"Gwen and Andrew believe us. Margaret suspects we may have misunderstood the situation and jumped to the wrong conclusion about Liz, Brady, and Amber being killed. Only Russell thinks we're intentionally lying."

"Jerk. Where does he get off—?"

Derek gave him a look. Simon zipped it and gestured for Derek to continue.

"They teleconferenced with a couple of the other senior members and—" Derek looked at me, and I read the answer in the way his gaze dipped from mine. "They want to slow down, get more information first. They're going to send a team to Buffalo to do recon work."

Simon glowered. "Sure, take the slow and steady path while Rachelle and Dr. Fellows could be—" He looked at me. "Sorry."

We all stood there for a minute, simmering.

I turned to Derek. "What do you think we should do?"

"For now? Play it out." His voice was gruff with frustration. "Nothing else we can do. We've got the Edison Group gunning for us. We have to stay put."

We found Tori out back. I apologized for taking so long; they didn't. Simon had barely begun showing us a wrist hold when Andrew summoned us inside.

Russell had already left. "Fled," Simon muttered, "so he wouldn't have to look us in the eye after telling the others he thinks we're lying."

Gwen was gone, too, but only to grab groceries and take-out for dinner. Yes, it was dinner time already. Having gotten up so late, we were skipping lunch.

We ate with Andrew, Gwen, and Margaret. They couched the plan in optimistic terms, of course—they were just doing a quick bout of reconnaissance work in preparation for the rescue operation.

"So, guys," Andrew said, "over the next few days, your job will be threefold. Rest up. Tell us everything you can about the lab. And get some training."

"Training?" That perked Tori up. Me, too.

Gwen smiled. "Yep. That's what Margaret and I are here for."

"And I'll be working with Simon," Andrew said, "though I know your dad's been training you for years."

"I'm sure he can use the practice," Tori said.

Simon flipped her off. Andrew pretended not to see it.

"As for Derek . . ." Andrew said.

"Yeah, I know. No werewolf teachers for me."

"True, but we do have someone. Tomas, a half-demon member who lives in New Jersey. You may remember him from when you lived at the laboratory. He was a member of the team responsible for the werewolf section of the project."

Did I imagine it or did Derek flinch? I wouldn't blame

him if he did. Derek had lived in the lab until Simon's dad took him and that section of the experiment had been abandoned. The other three werewolves had already been killed. Meeting one of his "keepers" certainly wouldn't be a happy reunion.

"Tomas quit before you left the lab, primarily because he disagreed with the way you boys were treated. But he knows more about werewolves than anyone I know. Your dad used him as a resource for raising you."

Derek's shoulders relaxed. "Yeah?"

"He's away on business, but he'll be back next week. If we're still waiting to act—which I hope we won't be—it'll give you someone to talk to, answer any questions you might have."

six

FTER DINNER, ANDREW WARNED us it would be lights-out at ten. Until then, he was going to get caught up on some work and we could amuse ourselves.

Problem was, we didn't want to amuse ourselves. Or get a good night's sleep. We wanted our lives back—stop the Edison Group, free Aunt Lauren and Rae, find the guys' dad, and let my father know I was safe. Sitting around playing board games would be torture . . . and that's exactly what Andrew suggested, the house being otherwise diversion free.

Tori and I were heading up to our room when Gwen popped into the hall to say good-bye.

"Can I ask you a couple of things before you go?" Tori said to Gwen as she hurried down the stairs. "I'm new to all this witch stuff and I know we're starting lessons tomorrow, but if you have time for a few questions . . ."

Gwen grinned. "Always. I'm usually the student around here, so I'm looking forward to this. Come on in the living room and we'll chat."

I felt a pang of envy. I had questions, too. Tons of them. And who did I get for a teacher? Margaret, who wasn't exactly the *let's hang out and chat* sort. Not to mention the fact that she was one of the doubters.

I trudged up the stairs and didn't notice that the guys' door was open until Derek reached out, fingers brushing my elbow.

"Hey," I said, struggling for a smile.

"You busy?" he said, voice barely above a whisper.

"I wish. What's up?"

He glanced back at the bathroom door. Light shone under it. He stepped closer, voice dropping even more. "I thought, uh, if you weren't doing anything, maybe we could—"

The bathroom door swung open and Derek jumped. Simon walked out.

"Good, you found Chloe," he said. "So what're we doing? This time, I'm not missing the adventure."

"All our adventures are accidental," I said, "and we'd be happy to miss most of them." I looked up at Derek. "You were saying?"

"Nothing. Just that we shouldn't do too much."

"Okay. So what *are* we doing?"

"Nothing tonight. Just . . . whatever." He retreated into their room.

I looked at Simon.

"Yeah, he's weird. I'll talk to him. Catch up with you in a few minutes."

I was heading into our room when Tori came up. We went in and talked, awkward conversation, thankfully interrupted when Simon rapped at our door.

"Everyone decent?" he called, and started opening it.

"Excuse me?" Tori said. "Could you at least give us a chance to answer?"

"It was a warning, not a question. I was being polite."

"Being polite would mean waiting for—"

I held up my hand. That was all it took to stop the bickering.

"I found something," Simon said as he walked in. He whipped an old-fashioned key from his pocket and grinned at me. "It was taped to the back of my dresser drawer. What do you think? Buried treasure? Secret passageway? Locked room where they keep crazy old Aunt Edna?"

"It probably unlocks *another* dresser," Tori said. "One they threw out fifty years ago."

"It's tragic, being born without an imagination. Do they hold telethons for that?" He turned back to me. "Chloe, help me out here."

I took the key. It was heavy and rusting. "It's definitely old. And it *was* hidden." I glanced up at him. "Bored, aren't you?"

"To death. So will you come exploring?"

Tori rolled her eyes. "I think I'll lie down and dream of being home, with kids who don't think hunting for a locked door is fun."

"Hey, I told you we were uncool," Simon said. "The more time you spend with us, the more it rubs off." He looked at me. "Coming?"

When I didn't answer right away, he said, "No?" Disappointment dragged down his voice before he propped it up with a forced smile. "That's cool. You're tired—"

"It's not that. It's just . . . we need to ID that kid I saw and figure out if he has a connection to this house."

"What kid?" Tori asked.

I explained about the ghost, then said, "I know Derek said we shouldn't do too much tonight, but . . ."

"But, apparently, that warning only applies to us, because he's off right now, hunting for clues about that kid. He doesn't want us pitching in. He says it'll look suspicious if we're all poking around."

So Derek was searching without me? I felt a pang of . . . I don't know, disappointment, I guess. Then I thought about earlier, in the hall. Had he been trying to invite me along? The disappointment grew.

"How about those self-defense lessons?" Tori said.

"Sure, I guess . . ." Simon said. "Better than nothing."

"Actually, there's something else I should do," I said. "You guys go on."

They looked at me like I'd suggested they swim with

sharks. Not a bad analogy, really. Simon and Tori doing self-defense together was bound to result in bloodshed.

"What did you have in mind?" Simon asked.

"Just . . . Well, my aunt . . . What I saw last night . . . I'd like to . . ."

"Try summoning her," Tori finished for me. "See if she's dead, right?"

Simon shot her a look for being so blunt, but I nodded. "Right. And Liz. I want to try contacting Liz. She'd come in handy searching for clues. The problem is that, if I summon, I might call up that other guy."

"Which is why you shouldn't do it alone," Simon said. "I'll stay."

"Me, too," Tori said. "If you do summon the demon kid, maybe I can get him to talk."

She put out her hand. A ball of energy started to swirl.

"All right," I said.

seven

SUMMONINGS AREN'T NEARLY AS cool as they look in the movies. Basically, it's the reverse of how I banish a spirit. I close my eyes and picture pulling a ghost out instead of shoving him back in.

Ideally, I'd have something that belonged to the deceased. I'd been using a hoodie of Liz's before Tori's mom confiscated it. I didn't have anything of my aunt's. So the only way this would work was if they were hovering around, waiting to make contact.

I suspected one spirit *was* hovering around—the jerk from this morning. While I was tempted to question him further, a voice in my head—which sounded suspiciously like Derek's—warned me against it. He hadn't been forthcoming before, and I'd pissed him off by banishing him. So as I sat on the floor in our room, I was careful to keep very clear pictures of my aunt and Liz in my head, alternating between them.

While I hoped I wouldn't see my aunt, I really did want to contact Liz, my former roommate at Lyle House. She had been killed the night I arrived. It'd taken time for her to believe she was dead, but once she did, she refused to go to the other side. She'd stayed and helped.

Not only was a ghost the perfect spy, but Liz was the same type of half-demon as that kid from this morning—telekinetic, meaning she was a poltergeist. So, yes, Liz would be very useful right now; but, more than that, I just wanted to see her, make sure she was okay.

"That necklace is supposed to prevent you from seeing ghosts, right?" Tori asked after a few moments of unsuccessful summoning.

Simon opened his mouth to tell her off for interrupting, but I cut him short.

"Obviously I still see them," I said. "Either it doesn't work or things would be a lot worse without it, something I'm sure I'll test eventually. I want to talk to Margaret about it."

"Okay, but if it keeps ghosts away, maybe that's why Liz isn't coming."

She had a point. And yet . . . I fingered the necklace. If it did work, what else was it keeping at bay? Something worse than that telekinetic half-demon kid?

"Why don't you take it off?" Tori began.

"Because she—" Simon snapped, then caught himself. "Let her try a bit more with it on. These things take time, and we're not in any rush. If you're bored, our room's empty."

Tori looked like she wanted to snap back, but couldn't, not when he'd said it reasonably.

"I'm good," she said, and I resumed the summoning.

Because Liz was the one I really wanted to see, she was the one I concentrated on, throwing out only the occasional calls to my aunt, praying they wouldn't be answered. Finally, when Liz didn't respond, I ramped up the appeals to Aunt Lauren. If I wanted reassurance that she was still alive, I needed to know that I'd tried as hard as I could to summon her.

"Don't," Tori whispered.

My eyes snapped open. "Don't what?"

She frowned.

"You said 'don't,' " I prompted.

"Um, no, I didn't open my mouth."

"She didn't," Simon said. "You must be hearing a ghost."

I closed my eyes and concentrated on Liz.

"Don't," the faint female voice whispered. "Please, baby."

My gut seized. That wasn't Liz. But it wasn't something Aunt Lauren called me, either. Or did she? I wasn't sure.

"If you're there, whoever you are, please show yourself."

Nothing.

"The amulet," Tori whispered. "If she can't get through, that must be stopping her."

I reached for my necklace.

"No!" the voice whispered. "Not safe."

"You don't want me to take it off?"

No answer. My hands shook so badly the amulet knocked against my neck.

"Go on," Simon said. "We're right here. Anything happens, I'll get it back on you."

I started lifting it.

"No! Please, baby. Too dangerous. Not here. He'll come."

"Who'll come?"

Silence. Then I thought I heard her whisper, but it was too faint for me to make out.

"She's trying to warn me about something, but I can't hear it," I said.

Simon gestured for me to take off the necklace. I raised it over my head—

"What the hell are you doing?" a voice roared.

Derek strode into the room and yanked the amulet back down. "You're summoning without your amulet? Are you crazy? A ghost lured you onto the roof this morning, could have gotten you killed."

Simon got to his feet. "Ease off, okay? We were trying to get hold of Liz. Then a spirit wanted to warn Chloe about something, but she couldn't hear her, so we suggested she take off the necklace, see if that would help it materialize."

Derek's trademark scowl didn't waver. "Just because

you suggest it doesn't mean she needs to listen. She knows better."

"No, but the suggestion made sense," I said. "I was being careful. If you had stopped to watch instead of charging in here, you'd have seen that."

Derek kept glowering, looming over me. No one looms like Derek, but I'd had enough experience to stand my ground.

"I'll leave the necklace on," I said, "but I'm going to try again. If she's still here, then I might take it off."

"Who is it?"

"I—I—" I faltered, chest seizing. "M-maybe my aunt. I—I—don't think so, but . . . I should try again."

Some of the anger drained from his face then. He ran a hand through his hair, sighed, then nodded. "Okay. You should. If she comes back and she seems to be trying to warn you, then . . . we'll see what we can do about the necklace."

I could point out that it was really my decision, but he was calming down, and I wasn't about to crank him up again.

So I tried one more time. No luck.

"She didn't want me summoning here," I said.

"Yeah? Probably because you could call up that half-demon jerk." Derek paused, then took the sarcasm down a notch. "We'll go for a walk tomorrow, get farther from the house, and try again."

"I'll come," Tori said. "And if the idiot shows up?"

She lifted her fingers. A ball of energy appeared, whirling over the tips. She grinned and whipped her hand back, throwing it like a softball. It hit the wall and exploded in a shower of sparks, scorching the faded wallpaper.

"Whoops," she said.

Derek spun on her. "What the hell do you think you're doing?"

"Showing off. I didn't know it'd do *that*."

He strode over and wiped the wall. The marks stayed.

"No one's going to notice it," Tori said. "And if they do, they sure aren't going to blame my spells."

"I don't care. Someone could have seen you."

"So I'll get in trouble for marking the wallpaper. I'll survive."

"You don't get it, do you? We can't do things like that. They're already worried about how powerful we are. We need to tone it down or we're going to make them so nervous they might decide we really *should* be locked up in a lab."

"Now that's going a bit far," Simon said. When Derek turned on him, he lifted his hands and lowered his voice. "Look, I know why you're freaking out—"

"I'm not freaking out."

"Okay, just . . . I think we have to be careful, but they already know about the experiments. They don't expect us to be normal supernaturals. Yes, you probably shouldn't go throwing furniture and Tori should nix the fireballs, but in general . . . well . . ."

"They should know," Tori said. "If we're trying to convince them that the Edison Group messed us up, then they need to see the proof. They should know I can do stuff like that. They should know you can toss a couch across the room. They should know Chloe can raise the dead."

"No." When no one answered, Derek looked from face to face, then settled his glower on me. "Absolutely not."

"Um, I was the one keeping my mouth shut," I said.

"I'm just saying, for all of us, we need to tone it down. We can't give them any reason—" He glanced up sharply. "Andrew's coming." One last glare at the scorched wallpaper, and he hustled us out of the bedroom.

Andrew wanted us in bed, so Simon left to check his blood sugar for the night. I went downstairs for some water and was getting out a glass when Andrew popped in.

"Simon tells me you've been having trouble sleeping, so I'm going to give you this." He laid a small pill on my palm. "It's a half dose of an over-the-counter sleep aid. I'm not telling you to take it. I'm not going to ask if you did. I'm sure you got enough sleeping pills at Lyle House. I just think it's important for you to get a good night's rest. If you decide to take it, there's water in the fridge."

He left. I stared down at the pill. Taking it seemed like a cop-out. I had to learn to deal with ghosts because they weren't going away anytime soon. But he was right—I needed sleep. Being rested would help me train better tomorrow. And yet . . .

"Take the pill."

I jumped. Derek walked over to the counter and grabbed two apples from the bowl.

"You need your sleep. Toughing it out isn't going to impress anyone. It's just stupid."

Ah, Derek. Always so encouraging.

"How about you?" I said. "You thought you were close to your Change again."

"It won't happen tonight. But if it does, I'll . . ." He shrugged and bit into an apple.

"Come get me?"

"Yeah," he mumbled through a mouth full of apple.

I filled my glass from the pitcher in the fridge. "So what do you think—?"

I turned midsentence and found I was talking to myself as the kitchen door swung shut.

eight

I TOOK THE PILL and fell right to sleep. When I woke up, I did feel refreshed, but the room was dark. I'd left the window shade open last night, like I always did. Tori must have pulled it down. I yawned, rolled over to check the clock . . .

3:46 A.M.

I groaned, tried to sleep, and won again, only to wake to the sound of crying.

I sat up and looked around. The clock said 5:28.

At a snuffle to my right, I glanced over at Tori, curled up in her bed. Crying in her sleep? She mumbled, then resumed snoring, but still I heard the soft whimper of stifled crying. I peered at her. She was sound asleep.

I heard another wet snuffle, ending in a gasp, definitely coming from Tori's bed. I went over. Her cheeks still looked dry. I even touched one to be sure.

A long, low whimper made the hair on my neck stand up. It came from under the bed.

I backed up.

Um, what do you think is down there? The bogeyman?

Yes, a monster under the bed was a terrible cliché . . . but that didn't mean I was looking.

I thought you were going to stand up to ghosts from now on?

Maybe tomorrow . . . preferably during daylight hours.

My inner voice gave a deep, put-upon sigh.

You know who it is. Same jerk; second verse. He's trying to trick you with the crying. You can't go back to bed now or he might smother you with a pillow.

Gee, thanks. That'll help me sleep.

Open the shade. The worst thing that'll happen is you'll wake up Tori. Serves her right for closing it.

True. As I walked over, I noticed a dark oval next to Tori's bed. Figures. One throw rug in the room and she pulls it over to her side.

I had the shade halfway up when I caught a flicker of movement. Something was dripping off the side of Tori's bed, but there was no soft leaky-faucet plop—the carpet must be soaking it up.

I tugged the shade again, moonlight filling the room, illuminating—

The shade slid from my fingers, flying up with a *flap,*

flap, flap. I staggered into the nightstand. The clock crashed to the floor.

The dark oval beside Tori's bed wasn't a rug; it was a pool of blood. My gaze rose to the blood-soaked sheets, then up to . . .

The body on the bed was covered in blood, the head bashed in, the face a bloody—

I tore my gaze away, stomach heaving, Tori's name coming out in a whimper. Then I saw the rest of the body: blood streaked but whole. It wore only pajama bottoms, bare chest leaving no doubt that it was male. A kid, maybe thirteen, fourteen, with dark blond hair streaked with blood and dotted with—

My gorge rose. I blinked hard, and the boy vanished. In his place lay Tori, sound asleep, still snoring. My gaze flew to the floor. Bare. No blood. No rug.

As I stared at that empty spot on the floor, I remembered the dripping blood. It hadn't made any sound. A ghostly memory, like the girl at the truck stop and the man in the factory. Horrible deaths endlessly replaying like silent films.

So it can't hurt you, right?

No, it couldn't hurt me. It could scare me. It could upset me. It could be seared into my brain forever. But it couldn't physically hurt me.

The moment I got back in bed, the sobbing started again. Then something that sounded like a laugh. I sat up, but the room went silent. I looked around. Another noise, this time somewhere between a sob and a laugh.

It might have been just the death scene replaying, but I didn't usually get a soundtrack with that. I wouldn't put it past that half-demon kid to be the director of this little scenario. If I wasn't spooked by his poltergeist stunts, maybe a gruesome death scene would work. I started to lie down again, then stopped. Derek had given me crap earlier for toughing something out on my own. I'd already let this ghost play me for a fool. I wasn't doing it again. I got out of bed and headed for the guys' room.

I stopped at their not-quite-closed door. I could hear Simon's snoring. Derek, as always, was silent. I made some noise in the hall, coughing and stamping my feet as I walked. I felt like a kid throwing pebbles at a friend's window, seeing if he'd come out and play. No answer.

I tentatively pushed the door open a few inches and stood there, waiting. Barging into the guys' room while they slept . . . well, not something I cared to do, not when I knew Derek slept in his shorts.

I coughed and shuffled a little more. When Derek still didn't wake, I peeked inside. Simon lay on the bed closest to the door, sheets tangled around him. Derek's bed was empty.

I checked the bathroom, but the door was open, the inside dark. I thought about the roof, but after the other night, I was saving that for last. Downstairs, then. First stop? The kitchen, naturally. I found an empty milk glass and a crumb-spotted plate neatly placed in the sink.

As I walked through the rooms on the first floor, I kept glancing down the hall at the rear door. He had said he'd call me if he went out to Change, hadn't he? Did he go alone? A stab of hurt zinged through me.

So what if he had? That was his right. He didn't need me to help. Except he'd seemed to appreciate having me there, and I'd liked that, being able to do something for him.

I went to the back door. Sure enough, it was unlocked. I stifled the fresh stab of disappointment and opened it. The house backed onto a tiny rear yard surrounded by forest. The sun was rising over the trees. I stepped out and peered around.

"Derek?" I called.

No answer.

I took a few more steps, then called a little louder, "Derek? Are you out here?"

A branch snapped in the woods. I pictured Derek, in the middle of a Change, unable to respond, and hurried toward the forest's edge. The noise stopped and I paused at the end of the path leading in, peering into the dark woods, listening. Another snap. Something like a groan.

"Derek? It's me."

I stepped in. It took only a few paces for the morning light to fade and darkness to envelop me.

"Derek?"

I jumped as he rounded a corner down the path. I didn't need full daylight to see the expression on his face. I didn't even need to see his face at all to know I was in trouble, just the set of his shoulders and the long strides as he bore down on me.

"I—" I began.

"What the hell are you doing, Chloe? I said we'd come out here later and try to contact that ghost. Key word? *We.* If you're here—"

I lifted my hands. "Okay, you caught me. I was sneaking out on my own, hoping no one would notice. That's why I've been calling your name."

That gave him pause.

I went on. "I had another early encounter in my room and thought, after yesterday, I'd better get backup. Tori and Simon are sleeping, but you're up, so I was looking for you."

"Oh." He rubbed a hand over his mouth and muttered what could have been an apology.

"Are you Changing?" I asked.

"Hmm? Nah. I would have come to get you if I was."

"Good. These days, the buddy system is a smart idea for both of us."

I walked back into the yard. Derek followed. The path was narrow, but he walked beside me, so close his hand brushed my elbow a few times before he mumbled something and pulled back, letting me go ahead.

"So what were you doing?" I asked. "Early morning hike?"

"Looking around. Just . . . restless."

I glanced back at him, seeing the tightness in his face, the way his gaze darted about. More anxiety than restlessness. I stepped from the forest into the yard and turned to face him.

"Something bothering you?"

"Nah." A pause, then, "Yeah. I couldn't sleep so I went up on the roof and thought I saw something down here. A light in the woods. I couldn't find anything, though."

His gaze returned to the forest, fingers tapping his thigh, like he was eager to get back in there.

"You want to keep looking?" I asked.

"Yeah, maybe."

"I'll leave you to it, then." I started for the door.

"No." He said it quickly, and reached for my arm, but stopped before he touched me. "I mean, if you're tired, sure. But you don't have to."

"Okay."

He nodded. Then we stood there. After a moment, he rubbed the back of his neck and rolled his shoulders.

"So, uh, you said something about a ghost?"

"Right." I told him what happened.

"You okay?" he said when I finished.

"Spooked, but sure, I'm fine." He kept looking at me, like he didn't believe that, and I hurried on. "So did you find anything last night when you searched the house?"

He shook his head. "I tried getting into the basement, but

it was locked. There should be a key somewhere."

"Old-fashioned lock, needing an old-fashioned key?"

"Yeah, how . . . ?"

"You and Simon need to communicate better. He's already found it. Well, a key anyway. We should see if it works before everyone else gets up."

We were almost at the back door when it opened. Andrew glanced out, frowning. He didn't say anything, but the look he gave us was a lot like the one we'd gotten from the staff at Lyle House when they found Derek and me climbing out of the crawl space together. Andrew's was more uncertain, like he hoped he was wrong. Considering he'd seen me holding hands with Simon the other night, I didn't blame him for that.

The last time Derek and I had been caught together, I'd stammered excuses. He'd said nothing, and that had pissed me off. But he'd been right—my excuses only made it seem like we'd done something that needed excusing. Andrew hadn't caught us making out or holding hands or even coming out of the forest. We were in the yard together, in daylight, walking and talking. Nothing wrong with that. So why did he keep looking at us like he expected an explanation?

"Getting warmer out," I said. "Might even see the sun today."

A very mature, casual thing to say. Derek even rumbled, "Hope so." Andrew's expression didn't change.

"Are the others up?" I asked. "They were dead to the world when we left."

"Not yet. I was about to make breakfast when I noticed the back door open."

"I figured we shouldn't close it," I said. "You probably want to know where we are, right?"

He nodded and waved us through, waiting until we were inside, then turning to look out at the woods, frowning, before closing and bolting the door.

Derek went upstairs for a shower. I was going to check on Tori, but Andrew wanted my help in the kitchen, asking me to set the table while he fried bacon.

"You're a writer, so I presume you like to read," he said. "Who're your favorite authors?"

I rattled off a few names.

He laughed. "Simon was right. No society-girl princess books for you. I have something you might like, lots of action and adventure. It's still in manuscript form, but if you want a sneak peek, I'll let you borrow my laptop. I'd love to get your opinion"—he grinned over his shoulder at me—"if you don't mind playing test audience."

"No, that'd be cool. What's it about?"

He certainly made it sound good, and we talked books a bit. Then he asked me how I liked my eggs and when he was cracking ours, he said, "How much do you know about werewolves, Chloe?"

"Just what I've learned from Derek."

"Well, I'm hardly an expert myself. But Tomas told me

years ago that there is one thing you always need to remember when dealing with a werewolf. They may look like you and me, but they aren't. They're only half human."

I bristled. I'd heard enough of that crap at the laboratory.

"And half monster?" I said, my voice cooler.

"No, half wolf."

I relaxed. "Derek's dad raised him to understand that."

"I'm sure Kit did, but . . . To Kit, Derek is his son, as much as Simon. There are things parents gloss over for their children. Being half wolf doesn't just make Derek a little different. Half of him is an animal ruled by instinct. There are some instincts . . ." He cleared his throat. "Derek seems very attached to you, Chloe."

"Attached?" I couldn't help laughing at that. "Sure, he feels some responsibility for me. It's like you said about being part wolf. I'm temporarily in his pack, so he has to watch out for me, whether he wants to or not. He feels obligated—instinct."

For a moment, Andrew said nothing, just flipped the eggs.

"Do you want me to start the toast?" I asked. "I can—"

"When the Edison Group first planned the Genesis project, Dr. Davidoff wanted to include werewolves and vampires."

"V-vampires?" There were *vampires*? I was still getting used to the idea of werewolves.

"The others outvoted him on that point, but he got his way with werewolves. With all of you we were messing with things we knew nothing about, but more so with werewolves."

He handed me the bread and pointed at the toaster. "Werewolves and vampires are different from the other supernatural races. They are much, much rarer and we consider them—as they consider themselves—a breed apart. You won't find a single werewolf or vampire in our group or the Edison Group. The Cabals won't hire them. Our special hospitals won't treat them. I know that sounds like segregation, but it goes both ways. Our doctors don't know enough about werewolves to treat them. And they aren't interested in coming to our doctors or working alongside us. We are as alien to them as they are to us. That doesn't mean there's anything wrong with them. They're just better off—and happier—with their own kind."

I shook my head. "Derek's happy where he is."

"Derek's a good kid, Chloe. He always has been. Responsible, mature . . . Kit used to joke that, some days, he'd rather have a dozen of Derek than one of Simon. But the wolf is coming out now, and he's struggling with it. I always told Kit . . ." He exhaled and shook his head. "The point I'm making is that I know Derek seems like a normal kid."

Normal? I could have laughed at that. I don't think anyone ever mistook Derek for a normal kid.

"But you need to remember that Derek is different. You need to be careful."

I was sick of hearing how dangerous Derek was. Different, yes, but no more than a dozen guys I knew from school, guys who stood out, didn't act like everyone else, followed their own rules. He *could* be dangerous, with his superhuman strength. But how was he any worse than Tori, with her uncontrollable spells? Tori had a track record of trying to hurt me, but no one except the guys had ever warned me away from her.

Unlike Tori, Derek was struggling to control his powers. But no one even recognized that. They didn't see Derek. All they saw was the werewolf.

nine

GWEN ARRIVED FOR TRAINING after breakfast, and Margaret was supposed to show up at any moment. Simon and I were in the hall when Gwen popped in, cell phone in hand.

"Is Tori with you guys?" she asked.

"I think she's still in bed," I said. "She didn't want breakfast. I'll go get—"

"That's okay. I just got a call from work. Someone called in sick and they need me to mind the gallery. Tell Tori I'll be back around four." She started to leave, then stopped and turned to Simon. "Yesterday, when Andrew said I was a witch, you looked surprised. You couldn't tell?"

"Uh, no."

"Cool. Guess that part of the modification worked."

"Huh?"

She smiled and waved us into the parlor, then she plunked into an oversized armchair, kicked off her shoes, and tucked her stockinged feet under her, obviously in no hurry to get to work.

"I can tell you're a sorcerer just by looking at you. It's a hereditary trait. Sorcerers can recognize witches and vice versa. Andrew said they wanted to get rid of that when they tweaked your genes."

"Why?"

"Political correctness run amok. They say witches and sorcerers developed the trait as a defense mechanism." She grinned. "Know thy enemy."

"Enemy?" I said.

She looked at Simon. "What have you heard about witches?"

"Um, not much."

"Oh, don't be polite. You've heard we're inferior spell-casters, right? We hear the same about sorcerers. It's a silly rivalry, rooted back in the Inquisition. Both races are good spell-casters, with their own specialties. Anyway, Andrew says the Edison Group got the idea that if they could do away with that internal radar, we'd all just get along."

She rolled her blue eyes. "Personally, I think they made a big mistake. That recognition serves a perfectly good evolutionary purpose—to prevent accidentally interbreeding."

"Between witches and sorcerers?" I said.

"Right. It's a volatile mix and—" She stopped short,

cheeks coloring. "Enough of my blathering. Work calls, however much I might like to avoid the summons." She started to stand, then stopped. "You guys like pizza?"

"Sure."

She asked us what we wanted. "I'll bring dessert, too." She looked at Simon. "Can you eat dessert?"

"I can have a little of whatever you get."

"Good." She lowered her voice. "Anything I can get you guys, just let me know. This isn't exactly a teen-friendly house, and you must be going nuts, worrying about your dad, Simon, and your aunt, Chloe. I'm really hoping—" Another glance, another notch lower on the voice volume. "They'll come around. Andrew will push them in the right direction and I'll do what I can to help."

We thanked her. She asked us what magazines we read, so she could grab some. Then Andrew called for Simon—it was time for his lesson. He told Gwen he'd love some comics, whatever she could find, and he took off. I asked for a copy of *Entertainment Weekly*, which I figured would be easy to find.

Then, before she left, I asked, "What you said about mixing witch and sorcerer blood, is it dangerous?"

"Do you mean . . . ?"

"Someone I know might have both."

She smiled. "Something tells me we're both talking about the same person, but neither wants to be the one to say it in case the other doesn't know. Is this someone named after a dead queen?"

I nodded, and Gwen breathed an exaggerated sigh of relief. "Andrew wasn't sure if you guys knew, and I didn't want to be the one caught gossiping."

I tried to tell her that Tori didn't know, but she kept going.

"Yes, mixed blood presents some challenges. It adds an extra boost, and you guys, from what I've heard, don't really need that. But the group says neither Diane nor Kit was a particularly powerful spell-caster, so—"

"K-Kit? S-Simon's dad?"

We stared at each other. Gwen's lips formed a soundless curse and she winced.

"Guess I really *am* spreading gossip. Typical." She gave a shaky laugh as she busied herself checking her cell phone. "It probably isn't true. Even the part about her dad being a sorcerer might not be true. Not like I'd know—I never worked for the Edison Group and I don't know either Kit or Diane. Anyway, sorcerer blood or not, I'm sure Tori will be just fine. I'll tell her—"

"No! I mean, she doesn't know the rumors. Any of them. Her dad being a sorcerer was just something I overheard at the lab."

"Well, then, I won't tell her. You shouldn't either."

Was Kit Bae Tori's father? He couldn't be. Kit Bae was Korean, and you could easily see it in Simon. Not so in Tori.

Sure, genetics did some wonky things—like Simon's dark blond hair. But if Diane Enright intentionally got herself pregnant with a sorcerer's child—as the demi-demon claimed—picking Kit Bae would be like choosing a red-headed father when neither you nor your husband had red hair. There was a good chance Tori's dad would know the baby wasn't his.

So, no, Tori and Simon didn't share a father. But if everyone else believed they did, Tori and Simon might hear the rumor, and that was a complication no one needed.

TEN

MARGARET ARRIVED SHORTLY AFTER Gwen left. When Tori came down and heard Margaret was taking me out for my lesson, she decided to join us. Tori might be good at hiding it, but I knew she was just as anxious and restless as we were. The last thing she needed was to spend the morning in our room. Derek and Simon sure wouldn't invite her to do anything with them.

When Margaret hesitated, I said I'd be more relaxed with Tori along. Complete crap, but I can't help it. Derek isn't the only one to suffer from overwhelming instincts. I have the unshakable urge to be helpful, which I usually end up regretting. I only hoped I wouldn't this time.

Before we left, Andrew gave Margaret a bunch of tips about touring with a half-million-dollar runaway. It was clear he didn't want us to go out at all, but Margaret insisted. I was a long way from Buffalo, she said, and with my black hair, I didn't look like the girl in the poster. Besides, what kidnap victim would be driving around with a woman who could pass for her grandmother?

So we left. Margaret's car was some fancy European model, like the kind my dad always leased, which made me think about him. Dad and I had never been real close. I was Mom's baby, and after she died, well again, it was that instinct thing. Some people have the instinct to be parents and some don't, and Dad didn't, though he tried his best.

He traveled a lot, which didn't help. He did care about me, though. More than I realized. After my breakdown he flew from Berlin to stay at my bedside until I went to Lyle House. He only went back when he had to, and he thought I was safe in Aunt Lauren's care.

"So this necromancer stuff," Tori said from the backseat. "Chloe doesn't know a lot about it."

She motioned for me to start asking questions. I'd fantasized about meeting another necromancer, and here I had one and hadn't asked a single thing. Worrying about Dad wasn't going to help me any.

I started by asking Margaret about the ghostly reenactments I'd seen. Residuals, she called them, but she didn't tell me anything else I hadn't already figured out. They were leftover energy from a traumatic event that played over and over again, like a film loop. Harmless images, not ghosts. As for how to block them . . .

"You won't need to worry about that for a few years. Concentrate on ghosts for now. Deal with residuals when you're old enough to see them."

"But I am seeing them."

She shook her head. "I suspect what you're seeing is a ghost reverting to his death form—how he appeared at the moment of his death. Ghosts can do that, unfortunately, and some like to do so to intimidate necromancers."

"I don't think that's what this was." I told her about residuals I'd seen—a man jumping into a saw in a factory and a girl being murdered at a truck stop.

"My God," Tori said. "That's . . ." When I glanced at her, she'd gone pale. "You *saw* that?"

"I've heard you like movies, Chloe," Margaret cut in. "I suspect you have a very good imagination."

"Okay, so can you tell me how to block them when I *do* start seeing them?"

I must have let a little sarcasm sneak into my tone, because Margaret looked over sharply. I fixed her with my best wide-blue-eyes look and said, "It helps if I know what's coming. So I'll feel ready to handle it."

She nodded. "That's a good attitude to take, Chloe. All right then. I'll let you in on the trade secret. When you see a residual, there's a surefire way to deal with them. Walk away."

"Can I block them?"

"No, but you don't need to. Simply walk away. They aren't

ghosts, so they can't follow."

I could have figured that out by myself. The problem was: "How do I know it's a residual? If it looks real, how do you know it *isn't*? Before you see . . . the dying part."

"One sign is that residuals don't make any noise."

I knew that.

"Another is that you can't interact with them."

Knew that, too.

So if I noticed a guy about to jump into an industrial saw, I should stop and listen for any noise? Yell at him and see if he answered? By then, if he was a residual, he'd have already jumped, and I'd see exactly what I'd been trying to avoid. And if he was real, I could let him die while trying to spare myself an ugly sight.

If I could tell it was just a ghost—residual or not—I'd know the person wasn't in danger and I could get out of there. So, while she drove through a small town, I asked how to do that.

"Excellent question," Margaret said. "Now the real lessons begin. There are three ways to tell the ghosts from the living. First, clothing. For instance, if a man is wearing a hat and suspenders he's a ghost, likely from the nineteen fifties."

"I've seen guys wearing hats and suspenders," Tori said. "Young guys, too. It's retro."

"A Civil War uniform, then. If he's wearing that, he's a ghost."

No kidding.

"Second, as you may have noticed, ghosts can pass through solid objects. So if he walks through a door or a chair, you can be sure it's a ghost."

Even someone who wasn't a necromancer could figure that out.

Margaret turned the car onto a road leading out of town. "And the third . . . Any ideas, Chloe?"

"If they don't make noise when they walk?"

"Excellent! Yes. Those are the three ways to tell ghosts from the living."

Great. So if I saw a guy standing still, and he wasn't wearing an old uniform, I just had to ask him to walk through furniture. If he stared at me like I was crazy, then I'd know he wasn't a ghost.

I hoped that the practice part of the day would go better. When I saw where she was taking us, though, that hope faded fast.

"A c-cemetery?" I said as she pulled into the parking lot. "I c-can't— I shouldn't even be here."

"Nonsense, Chloe. I certainly hope you aren't afraid of cemeteries."

"Um, no," Tori said. "It's the bodies buried in them that worry her."

Margaret looked from me to Tori.

"Uh, dead bodies?" Tori said. "Potential zombies?"

"Don't be silly. You can't accidentally raise the dead."

"Chloe can."

Margaret gave a tight smile. "I've heard Chloe is quite powerful, but I'm sure she doesn't need to worry about raising the dead yet."

"She already has. I was there."

"I-it's true," I said. "I raised subjects of Dr. Lyle's experiment, buried in the basement at Lyle House. Then I raised dead bats in a warehouse, and a homeless guy in a place we tried to spend the night."

"Bats?" Tori said, nose wrinkling.

"You were asleep. I didn't want to wake you up."

"And I thank you for that," she said. She turned to Margaret. "I was there for the homeless guy. I saw him crawling across Chloe—"

"I don't doubt you did, but I'm afraid you girls have been the victims of a cruel trick. There are members of the Edison Group who have a very big stake in this experiment and would love to make it appear that the subjects' powers were vastly increased by the modification. One of their staff necromancers apparently wanted to make the group believe Chloe could raise the dead. That's absurd, of course. Not only do you need years of training, but it requires rituals and ingredients you don't have."

"But I raised the homeless guy *after* we got away."

"That's what they wanted you to think. Obviously, they were on your trail, which is how they intercepted you at Andrew's house. It doesn't matter. Even if you could raise the dead"—a twitch of her lips, clearly humoring me—"I'm here and I'll make sure we take the proper precautions. Learning control is the best way to overcome your fears."

When I tried to protest again, Tori asked if we could have a minute. We got out of the car and she led me to a spot under a maple tree. My stomach clenched every time I caught a glimpse of the gravestones, imagining accidentally slamming ghosts back into the corpses buried under them.

I only had to glance at the cemetery walls and I could see Derek's scowl, hear him snap, "Don't even think about training in there, Chloe."

"She's jealous, you know," Tori said.

"What?"

"You can raise the dead. If she admits that, then she has to admit you're a better necromancer than she is."

"I don't think being able to raise the dead makes anyone *better*."

"In their world it does, because it means you're more powerful. Everyone wants to be more powerful." She looked around the cemetery, her gaze going distant. "It doesn't matter if it's good power or bad. I lived with my mom long enough to see that. Margaret might not want to raise the dead, but she wants to be able to, and she doesn't want some kid to be better at it than she is. So she's telling herself you can't."

"Okay, but I'd rather *not* prove her wrong."

Tori's lips pursed. "Actually . . ."

"Uh-uh. I'm not returning any poor ghost to its rotting—"

"Only temporarily."

I gave her a look.

She sighed. "Fine. But whatever that chick's hang-ups, her job is to train you, and you need training. We all do. It'll be fine as long as you take it easy, right?"

True. While I couldn't help remembering Derek's suspicion that Tori was betraying us, I could see no nefarious advantage to encouraging me to raise the dead.

"Look, do what you want," she said. "I'll back you up. As cliché as it sounds, we're in this together. You, me, the guys. Not exactly the gang I'd pick—no offense—but . . ."

"You're stuck with us."

"My advice? Take her lesson and be careful."

I imagined what Derek would say. He wouldn't like the situation, but I think he'd eventually agree.

I went back to Margaret and said I was ready.

eleven

MARGARET LED US INTO the cemetery. There were some mourners under a temporary canopy, huddled around a casket. We steered clear of them.

The only graveyard I'd ever been in was the one where my mom was buried. Dad and I went every year on her birthday.

This one was bigger, with new graves at the front, where the mourners were. Margaret led us to the back, which had the old graves. It was empty there—the dead having been dead so long there was no one left to visit them.

As cemeteries went, I supposed it was nice, with lots of trees and benches. Take away the headstones and it would make a decent park, especially with the sun warming up the cold April morning. I tried to focus on the sun and the scenery, not on what lay under my feet.

Margaret stopped at one of the more recent graves in the

old area. It was of a woman who'd died in 1959 at the age of sixty-three. Margaret said that was ideal—someone who hadn't died so long ago that she'd be spooked by our modern clothes, but long enough ago that she wouldn't have a lot of loved ones left and want messages passed on.

She told us to kneel like we were the family of this woman—Edith—come to pay our respects. Most necromancers avoided daytime summoning, but Margaret thought that was silly. Coming at night only called more attention to yourself. In the daytime, if you brought a friend—a supernatural of course—it was easy, because you could kneel at a grave and talk and no one would look twice.

"Or you could use a cell phone," Tori said.

"That's hardly respectful in a cemetery," said Margaret with a sniff.

Tori shrugged. "I guess. But she *could*. And she should probably have a cell anyway, for when a ghost tries talking to her in public."

Margaret rolled her eyes. I thought it was a good idea and appreciated it.

It would be great to think Tori was starting to like me, but, as she said, she'd realized how alone she was. Everyone needs an ally and I was the only choice.

I sighed. I'd never realized how good I'd had it, back in my normal life, where if a popular girl talked to me, the worst thing that could happen was she was planning to mock my stutter to get a laugh from the popular guys.

Margaret opened her briefcase and took out baggies of herbs, a piece of chalk, matches, and a little saucer. Ritual material to help necromancers summon, she explained. Tori suppressed a snort, as if to say I didn't need that. I said nothing.

"Should I remove this?" I asked, pulling my pendant from under my shirt.

Margaret blinked. "Where did you get that?"

"My mother, when I was little. I was seeing ghosts, and she told me this would keep them away. So it's for real?"

"Real, yes—real superstitious nonsense. I haven't seen one since I was about your age. Necromancers don't use them anymore, but they were once quite the hot fashion item for our kind. It's supposed to reduce a necromancer's glow."

"Glow?" Tori said.

"That's what ghosts see that marks us as necromancers, right?" I said.

Margaret nodded.

"And if this necklace makes it dim," I said, "then the necromancer won't attract ghosts."

"Well, then Margaret's right," Tori said. "It's definitely not working. But that's not the same one you were wearing at Lyle House. That was red and on a chain."

"It *was* red." I fingered the blue stone. "The chain broke. But if it is real, then changing color could mean it lost its power."

Margaret stared at the pendant. "It changed color?"

I nodded. "Does that mean something?"

"They say—" She shook it off. "Superstitious nonsense. Our world is full of it, I'm afraid. Now let's get started. The first thing I need you to do, Chloe, is read the woman's name, and keep that in your mind. Then, aloud, you'll repeat what we call an entreaty. Say the spirit's name and respectfully ask her to speak to you. Try that."

"Edith Parsons, I'd like to speak to you please."

"That's it. Next we light the . . ."

As Margaret explained, a plump woman in a blue dress appeared behind the gravestone, her wrinkled face frowning as her bright blue eyes peered around. When those eyes swung my way, the frown vanished in a wide smile.

"Hello," I said.

Margaret's gaze followed mine and she jumped.

Tori snickered. "Guess Chloe doesn't need that stuff after all."

Margaret greeted the woman, who glanced her way, but her gaze—and smile—swung back to me.

"Aren't you a sweet little thing," she said. "How old are you, doll?"

"Fifteen."

"And you can see ghosts. I can tell by the glow. I've never met one of you, but I've heard the others tell of such things. They call you a . . ." She struggled for the word.

"Necromancer," I said.

Her face screwed up, like she'd bit a lemon. "In my day,

they called people who talked to ghosts spiritualists or mediums. Much nicer words, don't you think?"

I agreed.

She looked from me to Margaret and laughed. "All these years of not believing folks when they talked about you people, and here I meet two in one day."

She reached out and tapped the air around me, my glow, I guess.

"So pretty," she murmured. "It draws the eye . . . Yours is so bright, dear. Much brighter than hers. I suppose that's because you're younger."

I'd heard that the stronger the glow, the stronger the necromancer, and it must be true, because Margaret's lips tightened.

"C-can I try something?" I asked.

"Of course, doll. No need to be shy. This is a special day for me." She lowered her voice. "It can get a bit dull on the other side. This will be a lovely story to tell my friends."

"I'm going to take off my necklace, and I'd like to know if it changes my glow."

"Good idea," Tori murmured.

Margaret harrumphed, like it was a waste of time, but didn't stop me. I lifted the ribbon over my head and handed it to Tori.

The old woman gasped. "Oh my."

I turned to see her staring, eyes like saucers. Then there was a shimmer to my left . . . and one to my right.

Margaret let out an oath. She lunged over, snatching the necklace from Tori and pressing it into my hand. The air continued to shimmer, shapes taking form as I yanked the necklace back on.

Edith vanished and in her place appeared a young woman in a pioneer outfit. She knelt in front of me, sobbing.

"Oh, praise God. Praise *God*. I have been waiting so long. Please, help me, child. I need—"

A young man in a ripped and filthy denim jacket grabbed her by the shoulder and yanked her back. "Listen, kid, I've been stuck here since—"

A heavyset man gave the young guy a shove, sending him flying. "Have some respect for your elders, punk."

"Thanks." I looked past him to the pioneer woman, cringing and sobbing. "How can I—?"

"I was talking about *me*," the man said. "I was here first."

"No, you weren't. I'll get to you." I tried leaning around the man.

"You want me to take a number? Fine." He grabbed the pioneer woman and threw her. She disappeared. "Whoops. Guess she left. My turn."

I leaped to my feet. "Don't you—"

"Don't I what?" He lunged forward. His face went purple, swelling to twice its size, eyes bugging out, black tongue lolling. I reeled back. The guy in the dirty jacket jumped behind me. I spun out of his way.

"Sorry, kid." He smiled, showing rows of rotting teeth. "Didn't mean to spook you. Spook you. Get it?" He laughed. I backed away, but he closed the gap between us. "Got a problem you can help with, kid. See, I'm stuck here in limbo, on account of a few things I didn't do. Bum rap, you know? So I'm trapped here, and I need you to do something for me."

"And me!" a voice behind me shouted.

"And me!"

"Me!"

"Me!"

I turned slowly and found myself surrounded by ghosts of all ages, at least a dozen of them, pressing closer; eyes wild; hands reaching for me; voices rising, shouting, demanding, snarling. The heavyset guy who'd flashed his death mask planted himself in front of me.

"Don't just stand there, brat. This is your job. Your duty. To help the dead." He shoved his face down to mine, purple and swollen again. "So start helping."

"We will," said a voice to my left.

I turned. The mob of ghosts parted. Margaret stood there, a saucer filled with dried plants in one hand, a burning match in the other.

"You're scaring the child," she said calmly. "Come over here and speak to me instead. I can help."

The ghosts swarmed her. Then they screamed. They howled. They cursed. And they began to fade, fighting and struggling and cursing some more, but continuing to vanish until only Margaret was standing there, blowing smoke from the burning plants in the saucer.

"Wh-what is that?" I asked.

"Vervain. It banishes ghosts. Most of them, anyway. There's always a stubborn one."

She strode past me and I turned to see a grandfatherly old man backing away.

"No, please," he said. "I wasn't bothering the child. I was only waiting my turn."

Margaret kept advancing. Tori scuttled out of her way, looking around in confusion, only able to see and hear us.

"Please," the man said. "This might be my only chance. It's just a message."

He looked past Margaret to me and his eyes glistened with tears. "Please, dear. Just one moment of your time."

A creepy, queasy feeling snaked through me. This felt so wrong—a grown man begging me for a favor.

"Hold on," I said to Margaret. "Can I hear what he wants to say? Please? He wasn't one of the ones scaring me."

Margaret hesitated, then waved for the man to continue quickly.

He took a moment to compose himself, then said, "I died two years ago. I fell asleep in my car and it went off a cliff. They never found it and they said . . . they said I took off, left my wife, kids, grandkids. All I need for you to do is send them a letter. Just tell them where they can find the car."

"I have to write this down," I said, turning to Margaret. I

was sure she had paper in the car. Even a cell phone would do—I could text in a message—but she shook her head.

"Wait," Tori said. She pulled a few pieces of folded paper and a pen from her pocket. "I was going to make a list of stuff we need. Andrew said someone would go shopping for us later."

I took down his wife's address and the location of the car. It didn't make sense to me—roads and landmarks I wouldn't know—but the ghost said his wife would understand. He said to add a note from him, that he loved her and would never have left her.

"She might not believe I sent a message from the grave, but she'll look anyway. I won't take up any more of your time. Thank you."

Before I could say a word, he disappeared.

"Now that was cool," Tori said, taking the pencil and extra paper from me.

As I folded the page with the information, Margaret reached for it.

I handed it over. "I guess it'll have to be mailed from someplace far from here, huh? Just in case."

"It's not being mailed."

"What?" Tori and I said in unison.

"You never promise to deliver a message for a ghost, Chloe. *Never.*"

"But—"

Her hand cupped my elbow, voice going gentle. "You

can't. If you do, then what you saw today will be only the beginning. Word will get out that you're willing to help, and while there are perfectly good requests, like this one, you heard some of the others. Most of those ghosts were in limbo. *Sentenced* to limbo. You can't help them, and you don't want to, but that won't keep them from hounding you day and night. So you have to ignore both: the good and the bad."

I looked up into her face and briefly saw someone else there, a younger, sadder woman. I realized that what seemed like cold efficiency was self-preservation—the tough, no-nonsense necromancer, her heart hardened to the pleas of the dead. Was this my fate? Toughen up until I could throw that note in the trash and never think of it again? I didn't ever want to be that way. Ever.

"Are you okay?" Tori whispered.

Margaret had moved away and was dumping out the ashes of the vervain. Tori touched my arm. I realized I was shaking. I wrapped my arms around myself. "I should have brought a sweater."

"It's still chilly when the sun goes in, isn't it?" Margaret said as she came back to us.

She held up a baggie of dried stuff.

"Vervain," she said. "I'll give you some back at the house. Obviously you could use it."

She tried to smile, but she was out of practice and only managed a twist of her lips.

"Thank you," I said, and surprised myself by meaning it.

"Are you up to some more work?" she asked.

I glanced down at the bag she held, like it was a prize for a lesson well done, and as much as I wanted to quit, that eager-to-please part of me blurted, "Sure."

twelve

"I T'S EASY TO SUMMON ghosts who want to be called," Margaret said, "but sometimes you need to speak to a reluctant one. While we try to respect the wishes of the dead, you've just seen the importance of maintaining the upper hand in the necromancer-ghost relationship. Some really believe we exist only to help them, and we must quickly disabuse them of that notion. Being firm in your summoning is one way to establish the proper reputation."

Margaret took the lead, going from grave to grave. We visited four ghosts, chatting with them for a minute, before she found one that didn't want to answer her summons.

She let me try. The ghost didn't answer me either.

"Do you know how to increase the power of the summons?" Margaret asked me.

"Concentrate harder?"

"Exactly. Slowly increase your concentration and sharpen your focus. Start doing it now. Gradually, gradually . . ."

We kept on like this for a while, Margaret getting frustrated by how slowly I was ramping up the juice. Finally, I felt an inner twinge that said "that's enough," and I said so.

She sighed. "I understand you're nervous, Chloe. Whoever raised those bodies has frightened you."

"*I* raised—"

"That's not possible. Yes, you are clearly a powerful young necromancer, but without the proper tools and rituals, you just can't do it. I don't even have the ingredients with me."

"But what if that's one of the modifications they made? Making it easier for me to raise the dead?"

"There would be no reason to—"

"Why not?" Tori interjected. "Raising the dead must have some use."

Armies of the dead, I thought, and tried not to remember the old pictures I'd seen, crazy necromancers raising undead hordes.

"All right," Margaret said. "You girls are worried because you don't know what's been done to you. But the only way to overcome that fear is to understand the extent of your powers and learn control. I'm not asking you to give it everything you have, Chloe. Just a little more."

I did, and caught the first shimmer of an appearing spirit.

"Wonderful. Now, just a little more. Pace yourself. That's it. Slowly, but firmly."

That inner alarm clanged louder now.

"No more," I said. "It doesn't feel right."

"But you're making progress."

"Maybe, but I'm not comfortable with going further."

"If she doesn't want to—" Tori began.

"Victoria?" Margaret held out the keys. "Please go sit in the car."

Tori stood. "Come on, Chloe."

I got to my feet. Margaret's fingers wrapped around my leg. "You can't walk away and leave a spirit like this. Look at him."

The air shimmered. An arm poked through. A face began to take form, then faded before I could make out any features.

"He's caught between limbo and the world of the living," Margaret said. "You need to finish pulling him through."

"Why don't *you*?" Tori said.

"Because this is Chloe's lesson."

Tori started to argue again, but I silenced her with a shake of my head. Margaret was right. I had to learn to fix this problem. I wouldn't be responsible for trapping a ghost between dimensions.

"I'll push him back," I said.

"Banish? That doesn't work on trapped spirits."

I shook my head. "I mean *push* him. Like summoning,

only in reverse. I've done it before."

The look she gave me reminded me of when I was seven and I'd proudly informed our housekeeper that I'd donated half my clothing to a charity drive at school. It had seemed perfectly sensible to me—I didn't need so much stuff—but she'd stared at me like Margaret was now, with a mix of horror and disbelief.

"You never, ever push a ghost back, Chloe. I've heard it's possible, but—" She swallowed, like she was at a loss for words.

"I think it's a bad thing," Tori whispered.

"It's a terrible, cruel thing. You have no idea where you're pushing them. They could be lost in some—some . . ." She shook her head. "I don't mean to alarm you, but you can never take that risk again. Do you understand?"

I nodded. "So I keep tugging this one . . ."

"That's right."

I knelt and kept at it until sweat trickled into my eyes. I went past the mental alarms and finally the ghost began to materialize.

"That's it, Chloe. You're almost there. Give him one last—"

Tori yelped. My eyes flew open. She was staring at a nearby oak tree, her eyes wide. Something was moving under the tree—a shapeless mat of blackish gray fur stretched over bone.

"Send it back," Tori whispered. "Quick."

"Ignore that and finish summoning this spirit," Margaret said.

I turned on her in disbelief.

"Are you nuts?" Tori said. "Can you see—?"

"Yes, I can," Margaret's voice was eerily calm. "Apparently I was mistaken about the extent of Chloe's powers."

"You think?" Tori said.

I stared at Margaret. Her face was expressionless. In shock? She had to be. While she didn't seem like the type to freak out, she'd just seen me raise a dead animal—without rituals, without ingredients, without even trying. Gaping in horror like Tori would be a perfectly reasonable response. But she only watched the thing, creeping toward us, pulling its mangled body along.

Its head lifted, as if it could sense me watching. It had no eyes, though, no snout, no ears, just a skull covered in bits of tattered fur and skin. Its head bobbed and wobbled, like it was trying to see who had called it forth.

"Chloe," Margaret said sharply. "As horrible as that thing is"—did her voice quaver a little?—"your priority is this human ghost. Pull him through quickly."

"B-but if I—"

She clasped my arm, panic edging into her voice. "You need to do this, Chloe. *Quickly*."

The creature was closing the gap between us. It was a squirrel; I could see tufts of long, gray fur left on the ratlike tail.

It started to chatter, a horrible squeaking, rattling sound. It lifted its head, then turned its empty eye sockets my way and continued creeping forward, leaving a trail of fur and bits behind, the wind bringing the stink of rotting flesh.

Tori clapped her hand over her mouth. "Do something," she whispered.

I shored up my nerve, closed my eyes, and plowed forward, throwing everything I had into one massive pull, imagining myself yanking the ghost—

The ground under us shook. Tori shrieked. Margaret gasped. My eyes flew open. The earth quavered and groaned and then, with an earsplitting crack, ripped open right in front of us.

Tori grabbed my arm and yanked me to my feet. We backpedaled as the ground yawned open with a thundering roar, dirt spilling into the crevasse and flying up, the musty stink of it billowing out.

The chasm split wider and deeper, an avalanche of dirt rushing in from all sides, tombstones swaying and rumbling. One toppled in, and still the earth split, until the top of a coffin appeared, shaking and rattling.

"Oh no," Tori said. "No, no, no."

She grabbed my arm again and tried to yank me backward. I brushed her off, walked to a place far enough away to be safe, then closed my eyes and concentrated on releasing the spirits. And if that sounds incredibly calm of me, let's just say the earth wasn't the only thing shaking. I had to drop to my knees before they gave way.

I squeezed my eyes shut and kept at it even when Margaret grabbed my shoulders. She shouted for me to get up, but I concentrated on releasing. Release, release, release . . .

Someone screamed. Then someone else. I leaped up and looked around, but there was no one near the crack in the earth, now at least twenty feet long, a half-dozen coffins exposed.

The ground had gone still. All I could hear was the rustling of leaves. I looked up. The tree branches were covered in tiny, new buds. That wasn't what was making the noise.

I followed the sound to the coffins. Not a rustling, but a scratching, nails raking the inside of the caskets. Then came the faint, muffled cries of ghosts trapped in those bodies, trying to claw their way—

I dropped to my knees again.

Release them. That's your job now. Your only job. Release those spirits before the zombies—

Another scream, this time from behind me. A group of newly arrived mourners was coming our way, the pallbearers carrying the casket toward an open grave on the edge of the old section.

They'd stopped and were staring down at the casket. I started toward them, slowly, cautiously, gaze fixed on that coffin, telling myself they'd stopped because of the earth tremors.

A gasp from the crowd. Then I heard what they did—a

bump-bump from inside the casket.

Relax. Relax and release. Release, release, re—

A low moan came from the casket, and every hair on my body rose. Another moan, louder. Muffled. Then a strangled cry from within.

Two of the pallbearers dropped their handles. Their end of the coffin tipped and the other four, startled, let go. The casket plummeted, hitting a gravestone as it fell, lid popping open with a crack.

The knot of mourners blocked my view, everyone grabbing the person nearest them—some for support and others to push them out of the way as they ran.

When the throng cleared, I saw an arm on the ground, the rest of the body still hidden behind the gravestone. It just lay there, hand palm downward, arm encased in a suit sleeve. Then the fingers moved, curling clawlike, gripping the ground as the corpse pulled himself forward, turning my way, toward the one who'd summoned him and—

And the one who'll send him back. Now!

I squeezed my eyes shut and imagined the man, a vague figure in a suit. I imagined setting his soul free, sending up an apology with it, releasing him—

"Good," Tori whispered beside me. "It's stopped moving. It's— No, wait. Keep going. Keep— Okay, it stopped." A pause. "Still stopped." Her voice was breathless with relief. "You did it."

Maybe so, but I didn't open my eyes to check. As Tori

went to assess the situation, I kept releasing spirits, picturing people in suits, people in dresses, people of all ages, animal spirits, spirits of every kind; and while I did, I listened, not just for the shouts and shrieks of the living, but the thumps and cracks and scratches of the living dead.

When I opened my eyes, Tori was coming along a path toward me, keeping back from the edge of the crevasse. People lined both sides now, eyeing it warily, waiting for the earth to move. But it didn't.

"The dead are dead again," Tori murmured as she came up beside me. "Everything's quiet."

Margaret stood along the chasm with the others. When I called to her, she turned slowly, eyes meeting mine, and in them I saw fear. No, not fear. Horror and revulsion.

You aren't like her. She sees that now, what you are, what you can do, and it scares her. Scares and disgusts.

She waved us back to the car, but didn't move herself, like she couldn't bear to walk with me.

"Stupid bitch," Tori muttered. "Oh, let's take the necromancer with superpowers to the cemetery. Of course you aren't going to raise the dead, you silly girl."

"I'd say I showed her, but I really would have rather not."

Tori's laugh quavered. "We should probably get out of here before anyone starts asking questions."

"Not too fast," I said. "We don't want to look like we're running from the scene."

"Right."

As we walked, we gawked—it would seem weird if we didn't. We gaped at the crevasse. We squinted up at the sky. We pointed at the fallen casket and whispered, all the while walking as fast as we dared, trying to look like we were as shocked and confused as everyone else.

"Girls!" a man called. "Hold on."

I turned slowly and saw a middle-aged man bearing down on us. I tried to get Margaret's attention, tell her we might have trouble, but she was looking the other way, leaving us to deal with it.

Thirteen

"ARE YOU GIRLS OKAY?" the man asked.

Tori nodded. "I think so."

"Wh-what was that?" I said. "An earthquake?"

He nodded. "Seems so. We haven't had even a tremor in twenty years."

A young woman in a long leather coat came up behind him. "And we wouldn't have had one now, if it wasn't for the quarry reopening last summer."

"We can't go pointing fingers until we're sure," the man said.

"Oh, I'm sure. There's a reason those environmentalists wanted to keep it closed, and a reason it shut down in the first place . . . after the *last* tremors, twenty years ago. Do you think that's a coincidence? All that digging, knocking around the Teutonic plates. Now look—" She gestured at the chasm and scowled. "The quarry's going to have to pay for this."

"Is everyone okay?" I asked. "I thought I heard a scream."

"Oh, that was just—" She waved at the casket, still upended on the ground, surrounded by mourners who were all hoping someone else was going to volunteer to return the body. "My great-uncle was being buried today; and when the ground shook, he started bumping around in the coffin, scared the guys, and they dropped it."

The man cleared his throat, warning her that we didn't need the gory details, but she carried on.

"The coffin busted open, Uncle Al fell out, the ground shook again, and—" She tried to suppress a snicker. "They thought he was, you know, moving."

"Eww," Tori said. "I'd have screamed, too."

"Anyway," the man cut in, "I see your grandmother wants you girls in the car. I don't blame her. Mother Nature might not be done with us yet."

We thanked them and headed to the parking lot, Margaret still keeping pace twenty feet behind us.

"Teutonic plates?" Tori said. "Do they bury German pottery with the dead around here?"

I had to laugh at that, but it was a bit shaky.

She continued, "To cause an earthquake the *tectonic* plates need a fault line, which are, like, on the other side of the country."

"It sounded good. And that's all that matters. Derek

and Simon say that's what people do if they see supernatural stuff—make up a logical explanation. If you didn't know about necromancers and you saw what just happened, what would you think? A freak earthquake? Or someone raising the dead?"

"True. Still, Teutonic plates?"

This time I sat in the back with Tori. When we reached the highway, Margaret finally spoke.

"Who taught you to do that, Chloe?" she said.

"What?"

Her eyes met mine in the rearview mirror. "Who taught you to raise the dead?"

"N-no one. I—I've never even met another necromancer before you." Not exactly true. I'd briefly met the ghost of one, but he hadn't been much help.

"Did the Edison Group give you books? Manuals?"

"J-just a history book that I—I skimmed through a bit. Th-there wasn't anything on rituals."

A moment of silence as she studied me through the mirror. "You were trying to make a point, weren't you, Chloe?"

"Wh-what?"

"I said you couldn't raise the dead; you proved you could. You visualized returning a soul—"

"No!" My stutter fell away. "Return a ghost to a rotting corpse to make a point? I'd *never* do that. I was doing exactly what you asked—trying to pull that spirit through. I was summoning. But if I do that with bodies around, I can raise the dead. That's what I tried to tell you."

She drove for a minute, the silence heavy. Then her gaze rose to the mirror again, meeting mine.

"You're telling me you can raise the dead simply by summoning?"

"Yes."

"My God," she whispered, staring at me. "What have they done?"

Hearing her words and seeing her expression, I knew Derek had been right last night. I'd just done something worse than raising the dead—I'd confirmed her worst fears about us.

When we got to the house, Andrew was the only one around. Margaret called him into the kitchen, closing the door behind them.

There wasn't much point in shutting that door. Margaret didn't yell, but her voice took on a strident note that echoed through the house.

The upshot of her tirade was that I was the devil's spawn and should be locked up in a tower before I unleashed hordes of the living dead to slaughter them all in their sleep. Well, maybe that's an exaggeration, but not by much.

Tori smacked open the kitchen door and marched in, with me close behind. "Excuse me. Who took the genetically modified necromancer into the cemetery?"

Andrew turned to her. "Tori, please. We don't need—"

"Chloe didn't want to go there. Did Margaret tell you that? Did she tell you we warned her that Chloe could raise the dead? That I'd seen it? That she didn't believe us?"

I swore I could see sparks flying from Tori's fingertips as she waved her hands.

"Did she tell you Chloe asked over and over to stop? That Margaret *made* her keep going? Even after Chloe raised a dead squirrel, Margaret forced her to keep summoning."

"I did not force—"

"You told her she'd trapped a ghost between dimensions."

"All right," Andrew said. "Clearly, we need to discuss—"

"Oh, we need to discuss a lot of things," Margaret said.

Andrew shooed us out. As soon as we were gone, the fight started up again. Tori and I listened outside the door.

"We weren't prepared," Margaret said. "Not at all."

"Then we need to *get* prepared."

"She split open the ground, Andrew! The very earth opened to free the dead. It—it—" She took a deep, ragged breath. "It was like something out of the old stories my grandfather used to tell. Terrible stories that gave me nightmares about necromancers so powerful they could raise entire cemeteries of the dead."

I remembered what the demi-demon said. *You called to your friend and the shades of a thousand dead answered, winging their way back to their rotted shells. A thousand corpses ready to become a thousand zombies. A vast army of the dead for you to control.*

"She can raise the dead at fifteen," Margaret continued. "Without training. Without ritual. Without intention."

"Then she has to learn how to—"

"Do you know what Victoria told Gwen? She's never learned a single spell, but she can cast them. If she sees it, she can do it. No training. No incantations. Naturally, we thought she was telling stories, but now—"

She sucked in air. "We can't handle this. I know they're just children, and what has happened to them is terrible and tragic. But the greater tragedy would be to tell them they can expect to lead normal lives."

"Lower your voice," Andrew said.

"Why? So you can keep assuring them everything will be all right? It won't. Those children are going to need to be monitored for their entire lives. It's only going to get worse."

Tori tugged me away. "She knows what happened was her fault, so she's covering her butt as fast as she can. We don't need to listen to this."

She was right. Margaret had screwed up and she'd been scared. She wasn't the kind of person who could easily accept either, so she had to lay the blame elsewhere—make us out to be so bad that she couldn't have been expected to control the situation.

And yet . . .

These were our allies. Our only allies. We knew that Margaret and Russell had already been second-guessing Andrew's decision to take us in. Now I'd given them exactly the ammunition they needed.

fourteen

TORI AND I WERE heading for the stairs when I heard the thud of heavy footfalls. I hoped it was Simon. Prayed it was. But I knew it wasn't. I turned to see Derek bearing down on us, scowling.

"I'll handle him," Tori said.

"I've got it." I raised my voice as he drew near. "We had a problem—"

"I heard." He parked himself three feet in front of me, like he was trying not to loom, but it didn't matter. Derek could loom from across a room.

"Then you also heard it wasn't her fault," Tori said.

He didn't even glance at her, the full weight of that scowl pinning me. "Did you summon in a cemetery?"

"Yes, I did."

"You knew that was a problem?"

"Yes, I did."

"She didn't have a choice," Tori said.

"She always has a choice. She can say no."

"I tried," I said.

"You can't *try* to say no. Either you do or you don't." He lowered his voice, some of the fury evaporating, but the hard edge lingering. "It's not enough to say the word, Chloe. You need to follow through and that's the part you can't seem to manage."

"Whoa," Tori said. "You're out of line."

"He has a point," I murmured.

"What? You—" She struggled for a word. "Don't put up with that, Chloe. I don't care how big or how smart he is, he has no right to talk to you that way. You did your best."

I'd allowed myself to be pushed into something I'd known was wrong.

"What do you think they're talking about in there?" he said. "How to help us control our powers?"

"We know what they're talking about, Derek. And I know what I did. Exactly what you warned us against last night. I gave everyone who doesn't want to help us a reason not to."

He opened his mouth. Closed it. You'd think that I'd get some credit for realizing this before he told me. But he had a point to make; and all I'd done was throw up a temporary obstacle, one that barely checked his speed before he barreled right through it.

"The word is *no*, Chloe. *No*, I will not do that. *No*, I don't think it's safe. And if you push me, well, sorry, but I just can't seem to summon right now."

"I—"

"What if they asked me how strong I was? Do you think I'd walk in there and pick up the sofa for them?"

"That's not what I was trying—"

"But it's what you did. You gave them a full-out demonstration of just how powerful you are, and now they're going to be wondering if the Edison Group had the right idea, locking us away—even killing us."

"Oh, come on," Tori said. "They wouldn't—"

"Are you sure?"

I shook my head. "If you believed that, Derek, you wouldn't still be here. You'd be upstairs with Simon, packing his bag for him."

"Yeah? And where would I go? The Edison Group tracked us to Andrew's cottage and we still have no idea how they managed it. And what did they do to us there? Ask us to come along nicely? Fire a few tranquilizer darts? No, they shot at us. Bullets. We're stuck here, Chloe."

"Whatever happened today, she didn't do it on purpose," Tori said.

His jaw worked, then he spun on Tori. "Why are you suddenly defending her? Trying to win her over for a reason?"

"What's that supposed to mean?"

"I don't trust you, Tori."

"Um, yeah, I got that message loud and clear long ago."

Simon appeared in the doorway behind Tori and Derek. He waved to me and mouthed "run while you can."

Not a bad idea. I snuck around them and zipped out the door to where Simon waited. Then I glanced back at Tori.

"Don't worry about her," he said. "Probably the most fun she's had in days." He led me into the next room. "Sadly, I can't say the same for Derek, and as soon as he stops arguing long enough to notice you're gone—"

"Hey!" Derek called. "Where are you two going?"

Simon took my elbow and steered me at a jog through the house as Derek's footsteps pounded behind us. Simon kept going until we were outside.

He led me to a garden bench and we sat. I glanced toward the house.

"Relax. He won't pull that crap in front of me."

He eased back on the bench, arm going around my shoulders, gaze slanting my way, checking to make sure of his welcome. I moved closer and he smiled.

"Okay, so what happened with your lesson?" he said. "I know it wasn't good, but I missed the details."

I told him, and when I was done, he shook his head. "What was she *thinking*? Taking you to a cemetery for necromancy lessons?"

That was exactly what I wanted to hear, but I knew this was the easy way out. Blame someone else, like Margaret had done. Yes, she'd played her part, but so had I.

Derek was right. I should have refused. I had to take

responsibility, even if it meant saying no to an authority figure, because I was the authority on me.

"Do you like ice cream?"

"What?"

Simon smiled. "That got your attention."

"Sorry, I was just—"

"Worrying. Which is why I'm taking you out for ice cream. Derek and I went for a jog earlier and saw a service station about a half-mile that way." He pointed. "There was a sign for ice cream in the window, so that's where we're going after dinner."

"I don't think they're going to let me go anywhere now."

"We'll see. So . . . ? Yes? It's not exactly what I had in mind for a first date, but we're kinda stuck here and I'm kinda tired of waiting."

"D-date?"

He glanced over. "Is that okay?"

"Sure. Yes. Definitely." My cheeks heated. "Okay, let's try that again, with a little less enthusiasm."

He grinned. "Enthusiasm is good. It's a date then. I'll talk to Andrew."

I was about to go on my first date. Not just my first date with Simon. My first date ever. I wasn't telling him that of course. Sure, he'd be cool with it, probably joke about the pressure. Being fifteen before my first date wasn't that weird, but it felt weird, like being fifteen before my first period, and

I certainly hadn't told anyone about *that*.

A date, with Simon. I'd agreed quickly enough, but after we went inside for lunch, I realized what I'd done.

It felt like standing at those cemetery gates again: my gut was telling me this was a really, really bad idea. Dating while on the run for our lives? Dating one of the guys I was on the run *with*? What if it went badly? How would we—?

But it wouldn't go badly. It was Simon and everything would be okay.

I just had to relax. Unfortunately, lunch didn't help with that.

Margaret was gone, but she must have told Russell what happened, and he'd swooped in like a vulture, hoping to catch us in some terrible display of uncontrollable power.

Andrew should have shown him the door. He didn't, probably thinking it was better to let him see that we were just normal kids. But it made all of us miserable, me most of all, feeling Russell's gaze on me as I struggled to eat, that faint look of distaste on his face. The kid who can raise the dead. The necromancer freak.

After lunch, I fled to my room. Simon tried to lure me out, but I said I was tired and joked that I didn't want to fall asleep on our date. Around three, Derek rapped on the door, calling a gruff "You should come out. Simon's worried." When I said I was napping, he went silent and I thought I heard him sigh and scuff his feet, like he wanted to say something else, so I got up and went to the door, planning to walk out and say,

"Oh, I didn't know you were still here."

I'd hoped he did have something to say. Not an apology for chewing me out—that would be expecting too much—but an excuse to talk to him about what had happened at the cemetery, consider our options if things got worse . . .

Mostly I just wanted him to stop being mad at me and go back to being the other Derek, the guy I could talk to, could confide in. But when I opened the door, the hall was empty. I went back to bed.

fifteen

TORI CAME IN AT four and seemed surprised to find me still in bed.

"You've been in here all afternoon?" she said. "I thought you were outside with the guys."

"What'd I miss?"

"Me mopping floors."

That made me smile.

"You think I'm kidding?" she said.

"No, I guess we'll have to pull our weight around here. We can't expect Andrew to clean up after us."

She rolled her eyes. "Can you really see Andrew assigning us chores? The guy apologized for the place not already being cleaned and ready for guests. I offered to clean for him, just to be nice."

When I didn't say anything, she shook her head. "That

last part *was* a joke, Chloe. Andrew's paying me the same amount he would for the housekeeper, though it'll probably take me twice as long. Not like we're overscheduled, I figured, and I could use the money. So now I'm the official housekeeper, and if I find wet towels on the floor, I'll hide them between your sheets."

Two weeks ago, if someone had told me Tori would willingly clean a house—even for money—I'd never have believed it. I couldn't imagine her wielding a mop. But I'd also seen how hard it had been for her when we'd been on the run, not having any cash of her own. While I was sure this wasn't her ideal way to earn it, apparently she'd rather scrub toilets than ask for handouts.

That made me realize something. What would happen to Tori when this was over? Did she have relatives she could live with? Was she thinking the same thing? Frantically making money just in case?

"Gwen's back," she said. "She's talking to Andrew first. Gotta admit, though, I was looking forward to this lesson a whole lot more before you got yours."

"You'll be fine. Just don't get mad at her."

She smiled, and I could see nervousness there, but excitement, too. She wanted to learn how to use her powers properly. We knew we were a danger and we didn't want to be. Why didn't anyone else see that? Why did they keep treating us like thoughtless, careless kids?

"You okay?" she asked.

"Sure."

She reached into her back pocket and pulled out folded sheets of paper.

"This might make you feel better."

I opened it. Blank paper, left over from the cemetery, after I'd taken down the ghost's message.

"I'm sure there's a pencil around someplace," she said.

"A pencil?"

"Uh, yeah, movie buff. What do they do in films when someone writes a note on a pad of paper and takes the top sheet?"

I smiled. "Use a pencil to bring up the impression of what was written."

"I doubt they'll be taking us to a post office anytime soon, but you can send a letter when we get a chance."

"Thanks."

She left. When I heard footsteps in the hall a little later, I thought it was Derek coming back, but Tori pushed open the door, walked to her bed, and thudded onto it.

"No lessons for me," she said.

"What happened?"

"Andrew's version? The group has decided to postpone training until they better understand our abilities. In other words, we've totally freaked them all out." She shook her head. "Andrew's a nice guy, but . . . too nice, you know?"

"Like me?"

"You're a different kind of nice. I know Andrew's trying

to help, but I really wish he had more . . ." She struggled for a word.

"Backbone?" I blurted, then felt my cheeks heat. "I—I don't mean—"

"See, there's your version of 'too nice.' You don't want to hurt anyone's feelings, even behind his back. *Backbone* is exactly right." She reclined on her bed. "Anyway, enough of that. Simon's looking for you, as usual. Go play, Chloe. I'll keep your brooding spot warm."

Sure enough, Simon was looking for me. Apparently, the guys had been unable to try getting into the basement that morning—Andrew had insisted on hanging out with them, kicking a ball around outside.

Now Andrew was locked up with his laptop in the study, so Derek had slipped into the basement. Simon was keeping watch, which was easier to do unobtrusively if he had someone to hang out with. We were in one of the unused rooms, checking out a wall of photos, when Andrew passed by. He saw us looking at the pictures.

"They're from the previous owner," he said, coming in. "None of us, as you see."

"Gotta fly under the radar," Simon said.

Andrew nodded. "Supernaturals always need to be thinking of that, Chloe—all the ways we can accidentally expose ourselves or call attention to ourselves. Even publicly associating with other supernaturals can be a danger. That's not to say you won't have supernaturals as friends. You will, and that helps. But we're always careful."

I said I understood.

"Now these are family photos of the man who owned the house. Todd Banks. The founder of the Genesis project. Dr. Lyle had the original idea, but he died before genetic modification was a possibility. It was Todd—Dr. Banks—who took his ideas and began the experiment. He was also the first to sound the alarm about the potential pitfalls. He warned the Edison Group, but they were too enamored with the possibilities to admit they'd made mistakes. Dr. Banks left and founded our group of concerned ex-employees. He bequeathed the house to us on his death a few years ago."

As Andrew talked, I noticed a photo of Dr. Banks . . . with a dark-haired boy off to the side. He looked about thirteen in the shot, but I still recognized his face. It was the Volo half-demon ghost.

"Is that Dr. Banks's son?" I asked as casually as I could.

"His nephew. That would be . . ." Andrew's brow wrinkled. "I can't remember his name. I never met him. I know he lived here for a while, with his cousin and his uncle. That's the older boy, which I only know because the younger one was blond."

I remembered the body in the bed. The horribly beaten body . . . of a light-haired boy a few years younger than the half-demon I'd met.

"You said Dr. Banks left this house to your group. What happened to the kids?"

"They went to live with another relative. A grandparent, I think."

Both boys were dead, and I knew it. The question was, did Andrew? Or was this a story he'd been told?

Were the boys part of the Genesis project? It seemed like it. Yet the kid I'd seen had been older than me. Even if he'd survived his uncle, he had to have died a couple of years ago, given his age in the photo. That meant if he was alive today, he'd be a few years older than Derek, who was supposed to be one of the first subjects.

"Was there a woman living here with them?" Simon asked.

"Hmm?" Andrew said as he waved us from the room.

"Chloe heard a woman's voice last night, and we thought it might be a ghost. Was there a woman living with them?"

"Not as far as I know. I could be mistaken, though. Now, I should get dinner going. I know you're supposed to eat at regular times, Simon. And I know you two have something special planned afterward." He winked at me and I'm sure I blushed.

As Andrew headed for the kitchen, Derek snuck up from the basement. The three of us went upstairs, ducked into the guys' bedroom, and closed the door.

"It's storage," Derek said. "Two big rooms full of stuff and one locked room."

"Locked?" Simon perked up.

"I busted it open. It's a workshop. Nothing but tools."

"So why would it be locked?" I asked.

"I'd love to say it's suspicious," Simon said. "But if this Banks guy had kids around, then I'm not surprised. My dad isn't exactly Mr. Handyman, but he kept a lock on his tool-box. You know parents. Paranoid."

"Yeah," Derek said. "Especially after their son flattens his finger trying to nail a drawing to the wall."

"Hey, I'm not the genius who suggested it." Simon glanced at me. "Tape wouldn't hold it, and Science Guy explained that the paper was too heavy for the adhesive. So I got some nails."

Derek rolled his eyes.

"So that's it?" I said. "Storage and a tool room? No clues at all?"

"Didn't say that. There are labeled boxes of clothes and stuff. Three names: Todd, Austin, and Royce. Todd's stuff is adult."

"Dr. Banks," Simon said. "The guy who owned this place. And let me guess, the other boxes were for teenage boys."

When I explained what Andrew said, Derek nodded. "Royce is your half-demon's name, then. His clothes are bigger. So Andrew said he moved away after Banks died? Maybe he was killed later and came back."

"I don't think so. I'm pretty sure it was Austin's body I saw last night."

A family, dead. Including two teenagers. All with connections to the Edison Group, maybe to the Genesis project. And we were taking refuge in the same house.

"We can't go anywhere," Derek said.

That's what we were all thinking, of course. Run. But where? None of us thought Andrew was secretly aligned with the Edison Group, holding us here while going through this elaborate ruse of plotting an attack on them. But what had happened to Dr. Banks and Royce and Austin? Did it have anything to do with us?

"I'll keep looking," Derek said. "Maybe ask Andrew a few things. You guys—"

"We'll be gone for a while after dinner," Simon said.

"Oh. Yeah. That's right." Derek's gaze flicked my way, but before I could meet it, he'd turned to Simon. "So, uh, Andrew was good with that?"

"Yep. You lose that bet, bro. Sure, he gave me a whole bunch of warnings—gotta walk through the woods, not on the road, Chloe can't go into the store, blah-blah. But we can go."

"Huh." Derek looked over his shoulder, like he'd been hoping Andrew would say it wasn't safe. After a moment, he nodded and said, "Okay, then."

"We've got some time to kill before dinner," Simon said. "How about picking up those self-defense lessons?"

"Sure," I said. "I'll get Tori . . . and don't make that face. I'm getting her. Derek, you joining us?"

"Nah." He turned and headed down the hall. "You guys go on."

Simon gave us a self-defense lesson in the backyard, teaching some basic holds, which Tori, with her binding spell, thought was kind of useless. But she only whispered that to me and didn't rub it in with Simon.

There was a moment during that lesson, when Simon was trying to show Tori a hold and they were standing side by side, me sitting on a patio chair watching them, and . . . For a second, I thought *Maybe they could be related.* I don't know what it was, the angle of their faces, I think, something about the cheekbones, the mouth. Dark eyes, same height, same slender build.

Then Simon stepped away and whatever I'd seen disappeared. I decided I was taking a few superficial similarities and letting my imagination fill in the rest.

Dinner came. Dinner went. I headed upstairs to get ready.

I always thought I wasn't the kind of girl who gave a lot of thought to stuff like this—first date, first kiss. Don't get me wrong. I wanted those things. But I didn't fantasize about the big day and what I'd wear and how I'd act. Or so I thought.

But I guess I still always had this image of my first date. I'd buy a new outfit and maybe get a haircut. I'd definitely wear makeup and I'd probably paint my nails. In short, I'd look better than I ever had, and when I opened my door to that first guy, I'd see it in his eyes, in his smile.

When Simon knocked at my bedroom door, I'd brushed my hair and found Vaseline for lip gloss. I couldn't even shower because Tori was running the washing machine. As for clothes, I wore the same jeans and shirt I had been in since escaping the laboratory, though I had managed to get the pizza sauce stain off the shirtsleeve . . . most of it, anyway.

Still, when I did open the door and he smiled at me, it was just like I'd always imagined, and I knew everything was going to be okay.

sixteen

ABOUT FIFTY FEET INTO the forest, Simon stopped dead and swore.

"What?" I said.

He waved at the woods. "I should have checked with you. Is it okay? Being out here?"

I assured him it was fine.

"Derek warned me the woods made you nervous, that you were worried about raising dead animals." He glanced at me. "And you weren't even thinking about that until I brought it up, were you?" He cursed again, more imaginatively now.

"It's okay," I said. "As long as I don't summon or fall asleep, I'll be fine."

"And if you *do* fall asleep, I need some serious work on my conversation skills."

We walked a little farther.

"Speaking of conversation, how, umm . . ." He made a face. "Sorry, I'm a bit nervous."

"Did you have a lesson with Andrew today?"

A dramatic whoosh of relief. "Thank you. Yes, I did. Boring, boring, boring. No sudden surge of power for me. I'm just a regular—" He paused. "Okay, that was incredibly insensitive. Did I mention I'm nervous? I should be happy to have normal powers. And I am."

"But still, it must be annoying, seeing Tori casting new spells right away when you've been training for years."

"Yeah. It wouldn't be so bad if it wasn't Tori."

"So what spells *can* you do?"

"Nothing useful. You need to master the basics first. I get that, but right now, all I care about are spells that will help us, and perfecting my fog spell isn't going to do that."

"That knock-back one is good."

He shrugged.

"Maybe Andrew can teach you the binding spell Tori casts."

He shook his head. "It's witch magic."

"That's different?"

"Do you want the quick answer or a lesson on the spellcaster races?"

"Option two please."

He smiled, hand tightening around mine. "There are

two major spell-casting races. Sorcerers are male and have sons, all of them sorcerers. Witches are female—same deal, but with daughters. Sorcerer magic uses hand gestures along with incantations, mostly in Greek, Latin, and Hebrew. And, no, I don't speak Greek, Latin, *or* Hebrew—I can just recite the spells. Knowing the languages would help, but memorizing spells is tough enough right now. Sorcerer magic is offensive—used to attack. Witches use the same languages for incantations, but they get to skip the hand gestures. Their magic is defensive."

"Used to stop an attack."

"Or escape one, which would be useful these days."

"You can't learn witch magic?"

"We can, with a whole lotta effort, because it's not our natural kind. Right now, I need to stick to my own, though I'd like to learn a few witch spells someday. Just not from Tori."

When we reached the service station, Simon bought the ice cream, then we went back out to a log and sat down.

"I would have been fine with a single scoop," I said.

"Too bad."

"But—"

"I've been diabetic as long as I can remember, Chloe. I've never had double scoop ice creams so I don't miss them. If it bothered me, I'd never eat with Derek, would I? And since I'll be done first, I can give you a spell demonstration as snack-time entertainment."

He did that, goofing around and making me laugh. Then we walked back, holding hands and talking some more. It was getting dark. When we could see the lights of the house through the trees, he stopped and tugged me in front of him. My heart hammered in what I told myself was anticipation, but felt more like terror.

"Was it okay?" he asked.

I smiled. "Better than okay."

"So I won my pass to date two?"

"You did."

"Good."

His face lowered toward mine and I knew what was coming. I knew it. But when his lips touched mine, I still jumped.

"S-sorry, I—I—"

"Skittish as a cat," he murmured. His hand slid to the back of my neck and he tilted my face up. "If I'm moving too fast—"

"N-no."

"Good."

This time, I didn't jump. I didn't flinch. I didn't gasp. I didn't do anything. Simon kissed me and I just stood there, like someone had cut the cord between my brain and my muscles.

Finally, the connection caught and I did kiss him, but awkwardly, some part of me still holding back, my gut twisting, like I was doing something wrong, making a huge mistake, and—

Simon stopped. For a moment, he hovered there, face above mine, until I had to look away.

"Wrong guy, huh?" he said, his voice so soft I barely caught it.

"Wh-what?"

He eased back, and his eyes went blank, unreadable.

"There's someone else," he said. Not a question. A statement.

"S-someone . . . ? A boyfriend, you mean? From before? No. Never. I wouldn't—"

"Go out with me if there was. I know." He took another step back, the heat of his body fading, the chill of night air moving in. "I don't mean a guy from before, Chloe. I mean one from now."

I stared at him. *Now? Who else . . . ? There was only one other guy—*

"D-Derek? Y-you think—"

I couldn't finish. I wanted to laugh. *You think I like Derek? Are you kidding?* But the laugh wouldn't come, just this thundering in my ears, breath catching like I'd been smacked in the chest.

"Derek and I aren't—"

"No, not yet. I know."

"I—I don't—"

Just say it. Please let me say it. "I don't like Derek."

But I didn't. Couldn't.

Simon jammed his hands into his pockets and we stood there in that awful silence until I managed to say, "It isn't like that."

"It wasn't. Not at first." He stared out at the woods. "It started to change after the crawl space. You guys hanging out together, the . . . vibe changing. I told myself I was just imagining it. When you and Tori escaped from the lab, it seemed like I was right. But then, after the truck stop, when you guys came back . . ." He went quiet, then looked over at me. "I'm right, aren't I?"

There was a note of pleading in his voice. *Tell me I'm wrong, Chloe. Please.* And everything in me wanted to say it. This was Simon. Everything I'd ever dreamed of in a boyfriend and here he was, mine for the taking. I only had to say the words, and I tried. I *tried*. But all I could manage was another weak, "It's not like that."

"Yeah, it is."

He started to walk away, back in the direction we'd come. Then he stopped and, without turning, he reached into his jacket and held out a rolled-up paper, murmuring, "This is for you."

I took it, and he continued walking.

Fingers shaking, I unrolled the paper. It was the picture he'd drawn of me, now colored. It looked even better than it had in the sketch. *I* looked better. Confident and strong and beautiful.

The picture blurred as my eyes filled with tears. I quickly rerolled it before I ruined it. I took a few steps after him and called out. I could see his figure in the distance, still walking, and I knew he heard me, but he didn't stop.

seventeen

I WATCHED SIMON WALK away, then wiped my eyes with my sleeve and headed for the lights of the house. I'd just passed the edge of the woods when the rear door opened, light spilling into the nearly dark yard. Then a hulking figure blocked the light.

"No," I whispered. "Not now. Just go back inside—"

The door slapped shut, sound echoing as Derek marched across the yard, dead on target.

I looked around, desperate for an escape route, but there was none. Go forward and deal with Derek, or run back toward Simon and have to deal with both of them. I kept walking.

"Where's Simon?" he snapped.

Relief washed through me. I didn't trust myself to speak, so I just pointed back to the woods.

"He *left* you? Out here? At night?"

"He dropped something," I mumbled, trying to get past him. "He isn't far."

Without a sound, he was right in front of me, blocking my path.

"You're crying?" he said.

"No, I—" I tore my gaze away. "Just dust. From the path. Simon's that way."

I tried to pass him, but he stooped, trying to get a look at my face. When I wouldn't let him, he caught my chin. I jerked back, flinching at his touch, heart thudding at it, too.

I told myself Simon was wrong. I'd never be dumb enough to fall for Derek. But I had. With him so close, my stomach kept doing weird little flips. It wasn't fear. It hadn't been fear for a while.

"You *have* been crying," he said, voice softer. Then his breath caught, the growl coming back as he snapped, "What did Simon—?" He bit off the words, cheeks reddening like he was embarrassed even to think Simon might be responsible.

"What happened?" he said.

"Nothing. It just didn't work out."

"Didn't work out?" He spoke slowly, like he was processing a foreign language. "Why?"

"Talk to Simon."

"I'm talking to *you*. What'd you do to him?"

I stiffened. Only he was right. I *had* done something to Simon. I'd hurt him. And for what? Some stupid crush on a guy who barely tolerated me most of the time? Was *that* the kind of girl I was? Pick the jerk over the nice guy?

"I screwed up. Again. You're shocked, I'm sure. Now, let me go inside—"

He blocked me. "What'd you do, Chloe?"

I sidestepped. He sidestepped.

"You like him, don't you?" he said.

"Yes, I like him. Just not . . ."

"Not what?"

"Talk to Simon. He's the one who thinks . . ."

"Thinks what?"

Step. Block.

"Thinks what?"

"That there's someone else," I blurted before I could stop myself. I took a deep, shuddering breath. "He thinks there's someone else."

"Who?"

I was going to say "I don't know. Some guy from school, I guess." But Derek's expression said he already knew the answer. The look on his face . . . It'd been humiliating before, having Simon accuse me of liking Derek, but that was nothing compared to how I felt when I saw Derek's look. Not just surprise, but shock. Shock and horror.

"Me?" he said. "Simon said he thinks you and I are—"

"No, not that. He knows we aren't—"

"Good. So what *does* he think?"

"That I like you." Again, the words flew out before I could

stop them. This time, I didn't care. I'd completely humiliated myself, and now I was just empty and ashamed. All I wanted was to get him out of my way, and if telling him that made him run in terror, then good.

But he didn't run. He just stared at me, and that was worse. I felt like the biggest loser at school, admitting to the coolest guy that she liked him. He stood there gaping like he must have heard me wrong.

"I don't," I said quickly. Those words came easily now, because at that moment, they were true. "I *don't*," I said again, when he just kept staring.

"You'd better not." His voice was a low rumble, the scowl settling into place as he finally eased back. "You'd better not, Chloe, because Simon likes you."

"I know."

"Simon's had girls calling him every day since he was twelve. They follow him at school. They even talk to me, trying to get to him. Cute girls. Popular girls."

"So I should be thrilled that a guy like him even *looked* my way, right?"

"Course not. I didn't mean—"

"Oh, I know what you meant. I should count my blessings that I happened to be around when his choices were, well, none, really, because otherwise I'd never have stood a chance."

"That's not— I never said—"

"Whatever."

I wheeled and headed the other way. He cut me off.

"Simon likes you, Chloe. Yeah, he's dated a lot of girls. But he *really* likes you, and I thought you liked him back."

"I do. Just not . . . not like that, I guess."

"Then you shouldn't have let him think it *was* like that."

"You think I led him on? For what? Kicks? I don't have enough excitement in my life, so maybe I'll tease a nice guy, get his hopes up, then laugh and skip away? How could I know how I felt until we went out and—?" I stopped. I couldn't win this fight. No matter what I said, I'd still be the evil bitch who'd hurt his brother.

I turned and started walking along the edge of the woods.

"Where are you going?" he called.

"You won't let me go into the house. I'm sure Simon doesn't want me around him either. So it seems like I'm going to take a moonlight stroll in the forest."

"Oh, no, you're not." He jumped in front of me. "You can't go wandering around alone at night. It's not safe."

I looked up at him. His green eyes glittered in the dark, reflecting the moonlight like a cat's. His scowl had vanished. The defiance was gone, too, replaced by a tightness around the mouth, a worry that clouded his eyes; and seeing that quicksilver change, I wanted to . . .

I didn't know what I wanted to do. Kick him in the shins seemed like a good option. Unfortunately, bursting into tears seemed more likely, because here lay the root of the problem, the contradiction in Derek that I couldn't seem to work out, no matter how hard I tried.

One second he was in my face, making me feel stupid and useless. The next he was like this: hovering, concerned, worried. I told myself it was just his wolf instinct, that he had to protect me whether he wanted to or not, but when he looked like this, like he'd pushed me too far and regretted it . . . That look said he genuinely cared.

I turned toward the woods and resumed walking. "I'll be careful. No dead will rise tonight. Go back inside, Derek."

"You think that's all I'm worried about? The Edison Group—"

"Could be camped out there right now, waiting for us to venture into the deep, dark woods. If you believed that, you'd never have let Simon go out."

"I didn't like it. But he promised you'd be back before dark, which is why I was at the door, getting ready to come find you two." He caught my arm, quickly releasing it and grabbing my sleeve instead. "Just—"

He stopped. I turned to see him staring into the forest, chin lifted, nostrils flared, face tense.

"Don't pull that," I said.

"Pull what?"

"Pretending you smell something out there. Someone."

"No, I thought—" He inhaled again, then shook his head sharply. "Nothing, I guess. Just—" He rubbed the back of his neck, wincing slightly, and I noticed the sheen of sweat on his face, shimmering in the moonlight. His eyes glowed brighter than usual. Fever bright. The Change was coming.

Not now. Please not now. That's the last thing I need to deal with.

He released my sleeve. "Fine, take a walk."

I set out, staying in the yard. I wasn't foolish enough to march into the woods to spite him. I'd gone about twenty feet when I glanced around to see where he'd gone. He was five paces behind, following soundlessly.

"Derek . . ." I sighed.

"I need some fresh air. Go on."

Another twenty feet. He kept following me. I turned and glowered up at him. He stopped and stood there, face impassive.

"Fine," I said. "I'll go in the house. You can track down Simon before the Edison Group snatches him."

He followed me to the door, then waited as I went in before heading out to round up his brother.

eighteen

TORI WAS IN OUR room, reading an old leather-bound book from the library downstairs.

"So, how was the big ice cream date?" she asked, without looking up.

"Okay."

She lowered the book. I quickly looked away and opened a bag that was sitting on my bed.

"Oh, that's your new clothes," she said. "Margaret bought them. Apparently Gwen wanted to, but the old bat insisted. Payback for this morning, I think."

It was bargain store stuff. From the children's department. At least it was for *girls*, unlike the ugly boys' sweatshirts Derek had bought me. Still . . . I unwrapped the pajamas. Pink flannel covered in rainbows and unicorns.

"Hey, you think that's bad?" Tori said. "She shopped in

ladies wear for me, and got a granny nightgown with lace. *Lace.* I'd trade you if those would fit me." A thump, as she tossed the book onto the floor. "So how'd the date go?"

"It didn't."

She hesitated. "Well, love to say I'm surprised, but don't forget, I'm the girl who was crazy about Simon until she was forced to spend twenty-four hours alone with him. That cured me, fast."

"Simon's fine."

"Sure, he is. Or he will be when he grows up a little."

"He's *fine*. It was me. I screwed up. I—"

I didn't continue. I could only imagine Tori's reaction if I said I might have a crush on Derek. I'd lose every ounce of her respect I'd earned.

I wished I could talk to someone, though. A girl with more dating experience, preferably one who wouldn't think I was a complete loser for liking Derek. Rae would be good. She didn't care for either of the guys, but she'd listen and give advice. Liz would be even better—always helpful, never judging. As for my school friends, it was like they belonged to another life, friends of another Chloe.

"Were you crying?" Tori peered at my face. "You were."

"I–it's nothing. I—"

"Simon pulled something, didn't he? Got you out on that walk, and the next thing you know, it's not your hand he's holding." Her eyes blazed. "Guys. They can be such—"

"It wasn't like that."

"If he pulled that crap, you can tell me. I've had a few surprise first dates myself. Wish I'd had my spells then. Especially the binding one."

"It wasn't like that." I met her gaze. "Really. Simon was fine."

She eyed me. "You sure?"

"The only thing he did was kiss me, and he asked first. He was fine. I—I froze up."

"Ah." She settled onto my bed. "First kiss?"

"N-no. Of c-course not."

"You know, it's hard to lie convincingly when you stutter, Chloe. So it was your first kiss. Big deal. My first one was last year, and I made him wait until the third date. I don't let a guy push me into anything I'm not ready for. They think because I'm popular I must put out. I don't, and by the end of the first date, they know it." She reclined on the bed. "So he kissed you and you froze up, and he thought that meant you weren't into him. It happens. He should have expected that— everyone knows how jumpy you are."

I glared at her.

"Well, it's true. Just tell him he surprised you, and ask *him* out. Try again."

And what if I didn't want to try again?

I finished gathering up my stuff. "You're getting the room to yourself tonight."

She sat up. "What?"

"I'm going to sleep in the next one. I just— I'm not really good company."

I could see that hurt her feelings. I was getting good at that. At the door I paused. "Thanks. For . . . everything today. I appreciate it."

She nodded and I left.

I should have stayed with Tori.

Being alone meant I had nothing to do except curl up under the covers and cry about how horribly wrong my life had gone, then despise myself for wallowing in self-pity.

I'd screwed up everything. I couldn't control my powers, even when our future depended on it. No one was talking about freeing Rae and Aunt Lauren and finding the guys' dad anymore. We'd be lucky if my cemetery summoning didn't turn *us* into prisoners.

The only people I could count on were Derek, Simon, and Tori. After they'd all apparently forgiven me for my cemetery screwup, now I'd hurt Simon, pissed off Derek, and rebuffed Tori.

I wanted to go home. If I had real guts, I'd pack my bag and leave before I made things worse. I couldn't even manage that, though. I hated, hated, *hated* myself for being so weak. I couldn't seem to do anything but cry until at last I fell into an exhausted sleep.

A rap on the door woke me. I squinted at the nightstand,

looking for the clock, only to remember that I'd changed rooms.

"Chloe? It's me." After a pause, he added, "Derek," like I could mistake that deep rumble for anyone else, like I could mistake that little part of me that perked up like an eager puppy saying, "It's *him*. Quick! Go see what he wants."

God, how had I been so blind? It seemed so obvious now.

Sad and pathetic.

Par for the course these days.

I pulled the covers up and closed my eyes.

"Chloe?" The floorboards creaked. "I need to talk to you."

I didn't answer.

Another creak, this time the door itself, and I shot up in bed as he slipped in.

"*Hey!*" I said. "You can't—"

"Sorry," he mumbled. "It's just . . ."

He moved into the moonlight. That was no accident. He wanted me to see his eyes burning with fever, his skin flushed, hair sweat soaked. He wanted me to say, "Oh, you're Changing," leap out of bed, and insist on going outside with him, help him through it, as I had the last two times.

I looked at him and I lay back down.

He stepped forward. "Chloe . . ."

"What?"

"It's . . . It's starting again."

"I see that."

I sat up, swung my legs out of bed, and stood. He breathed a sigh of relief. I walked to the window.

"Head down that path about thirty feet, and you'll find a clearing to the left. That should be a good place."

A spark of panic ignited in his eyes. After how he'd treated me today, I should have said "good." But I didn't. Couldn't. It took everything I had just to crawl back into bed.

"Chloe . . ."

"What?"

He scratched his arm. Scratched hard as the skin bubbled, his muscles writhing. He glanced at me, and the look in his eyes was so miserable that I had to clamp my jaw shut against the impulse to say, "Fine, I'll come with you."

"*What*?" I said instead.

"I—" He swallowed. Licked his lips. Tried again. "I—"

Even asking me to come with him was too much. He'd never had to before.

"I . . . I need—" He swallowed again. "I want . . . Will you come with me?"

I lifted my gaze to his. "How can you even ask me that? How many times did you chew me out today? Make me feel like everything's going wrong and it's all my fault?"

His eyes widened in genuine surprise. "That's not what I meant." He brushed his sweaty bangs back. "If I hurt you—"

"How could you not hurt me? This morning, after the cemetery, I needed your help. Your advice. All you could do was make me feel worse than I already did, which, believe me, wasn't easy. Then tonight, with Simon, you acted like that was all my fault, too, even when you could see how upset I was, how bad I felt." I took a deep breath. "After the truck stop, after our trip back . . . I thought we were friends."

"We are."

"No." I met his gaze. "Obviously we're not."

The look on his face, confused and miserable, made me feel awful, which only made me madder. He had no right to come in here and expect help, then make me feel guilty for refusing.

"Chloe, please." He rubbed his hand over his throat. The veins and tendons pulsed. Sweat beaded on his forehead. "It's coming faster this time."

"Then you should go."

"I c— I ca—" He swallowed hard and looked at me, fever making his eyes so bright they seemed to glow. "Please."

It wasn't the "please" that did it. It was the absolute panic in his eyes. He was terrified of the Change, of not knowing whether he could complete it, if the genetic modification had done something to him and that's why he kept suffering through this, only to fail before he reached the end.

He'd never actually said that, and maybe I'm a pushover, but I couldn't send him off to do it alone. So I grabbed my jacket and sneakers.

"Thank y—" he began.

I brushed past him to the door. "Let's go."

nineteen

W E KEPT TO THE shadows in the yard in case anyone looked out and saw us heading for the forest.
Once we reached the path, Derek stayed beside
me, sneaking glances my way, giving me that dejected look
that only made me madder, because I didn't want to feel
guilty, yet I did.

I wanted to set this aside and get back to normal. But when
he looked at me, I had only to think of that other look—the
horrified one when I said Simon thought I liked Derek—and
that shut down any impulse to make up.

"You wanted to talk about what happened at the cemetery," he said finally.

I didn't answer.

"We *should* talk," he said.

I shook my head.

We picked our way along the path. I tried to hang back, letting him take the lead with his better night vision, but he stayed at my side.

"About the other day, when I yelled at you for summoning without your necklace . . ." he said.

"It's fine."

"Yeah, but . . . I just wanted to say that testing without it is a good idea. We should try—"

I turned to him. "Don't do this, Derek."

"Do what?"

"I'm coming along for your Change, so you feel obligated to help me in return."

He scratched hard at his arm. "I don't—"

"Yes, you do. Now, let's find a place before you start Changing in the middle of the path."

He kept scratching, blood welling up in lines down his arm. "I just want to—"

I caught his hand. "You're making yourself bleed."

He stared down, struggling to focus. "Oh."

"Come on." I turned off the path, heading for the clearing I'd spotted earlier.

"I heard what Andrew said this morning," he said. "About me."

"I figured you did," I said, softer than I meant to, then cleared my throat, trying to find the anger again.

"He's got a point. I'm not—"

"You're fine. Andrew's an idiot," I snapped. Great. I'd found the anger and sent it in the wrong direction. "He's wrong, okay? You know that. Let's just drop it."

"When I blew up at you about the cemetery, I . . . I didn't mean to. I'm frustrated and I—"

"Please," I said, wheeling on him. "Just stop, okay?"

He did, for about five paces. "I was frustrated with the situation. Being stuck here. The Change coming on makes it worse. I know that's not an excuse."

I glanced up at him. He watched me, expectant. He wanted me to say maybe it did explain things. Cut him some slack. The problem was that *I* wanted to. And if I did, then the next time he felt like venting on me, he would.

"Chloe?"

I stopped at the edge of a small clearing. "Is this okay?"

He said nothing and I thought he was checking it out, but when I turned, he'd gone still, his chin up, staring into the forest. "Did you hear that?"

"What?"

He shook his head. "Nothing, I guess."

He stepped into the clearing and looked around, murmuring, "Good, good." Then he stripped off his sweatshirt and set it on the ground. "You can sit here." He glanced over at me. "Remember the other night at Andrew's? When you came out to keep me company, and we tried doing some training with you? We should do that again."

I sighed. "You aren't going to quit, are you? You think if you can just say the right thing, it'll all be okay."

His lips twitched in something like a smile. "I can hope, can't I?"

"Sure. And if it works, what does that make me? You get to treat me any way you want and as soon as you decide to play nice, all is forgiven."

"I *am* sorry, Chloe."

"For now." I turned away. "Forget it, okay? Let's just—"

He caught my elbow. His skin burned even through my jacket. "I mean it. I'm really sorry. When I get mad like that, it's not— it's not—" He released my arm and rubbed the back of his neck. Rivulets of sweat ran down his face. The skin on his bare arms rippled.

"You need to get ready."

"No. I need to say something. Just give me a sec."

He took a second. Then another. Then another, just standing there, rubbing his arm furiously, gaze fixed on that.

"Derek, you need—"

"I'm fine. Just give me—" He took a deep breath.

"Derek . . ."

"Just one sec."

He started scratching again. When I moved forward to grab his hand, he stopped.

"Right, right," he murmured. He flexed his hand, then

made a fist, as if to keep himself from scratching. "I tell you not to be scared of me. I snap at you when you back away. But sometimes . . ."

He reached around to scratch his shoulders, wincing as his nails dug in.

"Derek, you have to—"

"Sometimes that's exactly what I want," he said. "That's what I'm trying to do—scare you off."

"So you don't accidentally hurt me." I sighed. "You aren't going to—"

"No, it's not that. It's—"

His hand went to his forearm, then he stopped short as dark stubble sprouted.

"You're Changing, Derek. We'll talk later."

"Right. Yeah. Later. Good." The words rushed out in a whoosh of relief.

He looked around, blinking as sweat streamed into his eyes.

"You need to get down," I said gently.

When he still didn't budge, I caught his hand and tugged. He lowered himself with some difficulty, then got up on all fours, in position to begin the Change.

"Unless Margaret brought you a lot of new shirts, you might want to take that one off," I said.

"Right."

He pulled at the hem, tugging it up, but his arm wouldn't twist the right way to get the shirt up over his head, like his joints were already repositioning, fusing. So I helped. I drew the line at removing his pants, though. Luckily, he'd pulled on sweats to sleep in, and he was able to fumble them down to his knees, and I was okay with taking it from there. His shorts were staying on. If they ripped during the Change, I just hoped the transformation was far enough along that . . . well, whatever.

He barely had his clothes off before the full body spasms hit, his back shooting up, his spine bending at a seemingly impossible angle, wrenching a gurgling whimper from him as his face contorted in agony, the cry cut short as he spewed dinner into the bushes.

It went on like that for a while. The spasms, the convulsions, his skin and muscles rippling like something out of a horror movie. The gasps and moans and stifled cries of pain between retching and dry heaves. The stink of vomit and sweat.

You'd really think this would cure any romantic notions I had about the guy. But I'd seen it three times now, and I watched every time, knowing if I looked away, moved away, let him think I was horrified and disgusted, I'd only make it worse.

I wasn't horrified and disgusted. What I saw wasn't some guy puking and grotesquely contorting. I saw Derek, in unbelievable agony and scared out of his mind.

It took only that first awful spasm to chase away the last of my anger. There would be time for that later. Instead, I knelt beside him, rubbing his shoulders, telling him he'd be okay, he was doing fine, just keep going.

Finally, the retching stopped and he crouched there, head down, hair hanging, hiding his face, his body covered in short, black hair, his shoulder muscles hunched, arms and legs straight, clawlike fingers half buried in the earth. He panted, drawing deep, ragged breaths.

"You're getting there," I said. "It's coming faster this time." True or not, it didn't matter, only that he accepted it, nodding and relaxing a little.

Another spasm hit. His body convulsed in wave after wave. His legs and arms kept changing, thinning and shortening, his hands and feet doing the same. The hair on his head retracted as the hair on his body lengthened from stubble to thick fur. As for his face, I knew that was Changing too, but he'd averted it.

His body continued spasming until he had to stop again, heaving as he struggled for breath. I rubbed his back and he leaned against me. I could feel his muscles trembling, like he could barely hold himself up on all fours. I moved closer, letting him rest against me, my head on his shoulder, feeling his heart beating hard and fast as his shudders gradually slowed.

"You're almost there. Keep going. You're going to finish this time. Just—"

He tensed. Then his back flew up, knocking me aside. His body went rigid, head still down, back lifting higher and higher, like someone was pulling it up, head sinking lower still, black fur gleaming in the moonlight.

Bones crackled. Derek gave a deep moan that made me move closer again, rubbing his back, telling him it would be okay. Then, with a final shudder, it was. He lifted his head, turned to look at me, and he was a wolf.

TWENTY

THE LAST TIME DEREK had tried to Change, he'd made me promise to go someplace safe as soon as he seemed close to finishing. When I saw that wolf in front of me, a lead weight dropped in my gut telling me I should have taken his advice. But as soon as his eyes met mine, the dread evaporated. I might be looking at a massive black wolf, but in those green eyes, I still saw Derek.

He tried to take a step, but his legs slid out and he hit the ground with an earthshaking thud. I scrambled over to him as he lay there, eyes closed, flank heaving, tongue lolling.

"Are you okay?"

His eyes opened and he gave an awkward jerk of his muzzle, as if he was trying to nod, then his pupils rolled up and his eyes closed again.

He was fine, just exhausted, like the last time when he'd been too tired even to dress before he fell asleep. I stood and started for the path, wanting to leave him in peace. I made it two steps before he snorted. I turned to see him lying on his belly, ready to jump up. He jerked his muzzle, telling me to come back.

"I thought you'd want to be—"

He cut me off with a snort. It was hard for a wolf to scowl, but he managed a good glower.

I took the switchblade from my jacket pocket. "I'll be fine. I'm armed."

A snort. *I don't care.* A head jerk. *Get back here.*

When I hesitated, he growled.

"Well, you've got the growling part down pat already. Must be all those years of practice."

He began to rise, legs wobbly.

"All right, I'm coming back. I just didn't want to be in your way."

A grunt. *You're not.* Or that's what I hoped he meant.

"You can understand me, can't you?" I said as I returned to sit on his discarded sweatshirt. "You know what I'm saying."

He tried to nod, then snarled at the awkwardness of it.

"Not easy when you can't talk, is it?" I grinned. "Well, not easy for you. I could get used to it."

He grumbled, but I could see relief in his eyes, like he was glad to see me smile.

"So I was right, wasn't I? It's still you, even in wolf form."

He grunted.

"No sudden uncontrollable urges to go kill something?"

He rolled his eyes.

"Hey, you're the one who was worried." I paused. "And I don't smell like dinner, right?"

I got a real look for that one.

"Just covering all the bases."

He gave a rumbling growl, like a chuckle, and settled in, lowering his head to his front paws, gaze on me. I tried to get comfortable, but the ground was ice-cold through his sweatshirt, and I was wearing only my new pajamas, a light jacket, and sneakers.

Seeing me shivering, he stretched a front leg toward the sweatshirt, pawing the edge and snarling when he realized he couldn't grab it.

"The lack of opposable thumbs is going to take some getting used to, huh?"

He motioned me closer with his muzzle. When I pretended not to understand, he twisted and gingerly took the hem of the sweatshirt between his teeth, lips curled in disgust as he tugged it.

"Okay, okay, I'm just trying not to crowd you."

That wasn't the only reason I was uncomfortable getting too cozy with him now, but he just grunted, again seeming to say it was fine. I moved over beside him. He shifted, his torso making a partial wind block, the body heat from the Change still blasting like a furnace.

He grunted.

"Yes, that's better. Thanks. Now get some rest."

I had no idea what would happen now. I doubted Derek did either. He'd been focused on getting *through* the Change. What I did know was that this was only half the process. He had to Change back, and he'd need time and rest for that.

And how would it happen? Did he have to wait until his body was ready, like he did with the Change to wolf? How long would that be? Hours? Days?

Feeling his gaze on me, I forced a smile and pushed back my worries. It would be okay. He *could* Change. That was the important thing.

When I relaxed, he shifted closer, fur brushing my hand. I tentatively touched it, feeling the coarse top layer and soft undercoat. He leaned against my hand, as if to say it was okay, and I buried my fingers in his fur, his skin so hot from the Change it was like putting my numb hands on a radiator. My cool fingers must have felt just as good, because he closed his eyes and shifted until I was leaning on him. Within minutes, he was asleep.

I closed my eyes, meaning to rest for just a moment, but the next thing I knew, I was waking up, curled on my side, using Derek as a pillow. I jumped. He looked over at me.

"S-sorry, I didn't mean—"

He cut me short with a growl, telling me off for apologizing, then bumped my leg, knocking me back onto his side. I lay there a moment, enjoying the warmth. He snarled a yawn, flashing canines as long as my thumb.

Finally, I sat up. "So, I suppose you should do something wolfie. Hunt, maybe?"

A grunt, the tone saying *no*.

"Run? Get some exercise?"

Another grunt, less decisive, more like a *maybe*.

He pushed to his feet, wobbly, still adjusting to his new center of gravity. He gingerly moved one forepaw, then the next, one rear paw, then the other. He picked up the pace, but still slow as he circled the clearing. A snort, like he'd figured it out, and he broke into a lope, stumbled and plowed muzzle-first into the undergrowth.

I stifled a laugh, but not very well, and he glowered at me.

"Forget running. A nice, leisurely stroll might be more your speed."

He snorted and turned fast. When I fell back, he gave a growling chuckle.

"Still can't resist throwing your weight around, can you?"

He lunged again. This time I stood my ground and he checked his leap at the last second . . . and toppled sideways. I didn't hide my laugh that time. He twisted fast, grabbed my pajama leg and wrenched, and down I went.

"Bully."

He growled a chuckle. I fingered an imaginary tear in my pant leg.

"Great. I finally get some pj's and you rip them."

He walked over for a better look. I tried to grab his foreleg, but he darted out of my reach and tore across the clearing. Then he stopped, looking over his shoulder as if to say *how'd I do that?* He turned and tried racing across it again, but his legs tangled and he fell in a heap beside me.

"You're thinking too much, as usual," I said.

A dismissive snort as he got to his feet. He tried running again, and didn't fall, but did more lurching than loping, his legs threatening to tangle at every step.

"Apparently this could take a while, so how about you practice and I'll head back to the house—"

He darted past me and veered to block my path.

I smiled. "I knew that'd work. So am I right? It's better when you act, not think?"

A sigh whistled out of his nostrils, condensation hanging in the frigid air.

"You hate that, don't you? We should keep a scorecard, see who's right more often: me or you."

He rolled his eyes.

"Not a chance, huh? You'd never live it down if I beat you. But I am right this time. Your body knows how to move as a wolf. You just need to shut your brain off and let your muscles do their thing."

He dashed at me. When I didn't move, he tore around

me, circling wide, head lowered, picking up speed until he was a blur of black fur. And I laughed. I couldn't help it. It looked so . . . amazing. To be in another form. To experience the world that way. I was happy for him. Finally, he threw on the brakes, skidding to a halt, each leg shooting out in a different direction.

"You're going to need to work on that part," I said.

He growled and gave a head shake that I couldn't interpret until he got to his feet, muzzle lifting to catch the wind, ears swiveling forward.

"Someone's coming?" I whispered.

He grunted. *Shhh, I'm listening.*

I listened with him, straining to hear what he did. Then came a sound I didn't need werewolf hearing to pick up—a long, eerie howl. The fur on Derek's back rose, adding inches to his already huge frame.

"Dog?" I whispered. But I'd heard enough dogs in my life to know that wasn't what this was.

Derek dashed behind me and bumped the back of my legs. *Run.*

I raced to the path. Derek stayed behind, the thumping of his paws barely even betraying him, and I finally understood why he always moved so quietly. Predatory instinct. An instinct—and a skill—I lacked, and as we ran that became painfully obvious.

I might be half Derek's size, but I was the one who sounded like a two-hundred-pound beast plowing through the woods.

My breath chugged like a locomotive. My feet found every stick on the path, each snap as loud as gunfire. I tried to be quieter, but that meant slower. When my pace dropped, Derek bumped me from behind, telling me not to bother, to keep moving.

I could see the lights of the house ahead. Then, from somewhere between it and us came an earsplitting whistle. I stopped. Derek did, too, in a skid that knocked me to my knees.

He grunted an apology. As I rose, he'd already recovered and was in front of me now, muzzle raised to sample the wind. The breeze was coming from the side, though, and he paced, trying to catch a whiff of whoever had whistled. When he did, his body went rigid, ears back, growl bubbling up. Then he wheeled, almost slamming into me.

"Who—?"

He answered with a snap of his jaws, catching the hem of my jacket. *Just run.* I did.

twenty-one

Who were we running from? I'd seen enough horror flicks to know that howl had come from a wolf, and there were no wild ones left in New York State. That meant werewolf.

Liam and Ramon, the two who'd tried to grab Derek the other day, had said all of the state was the territory of the Pack, who'd hunt and kill any trespassing werewolves. Obviously they weren't that thorough—Derek had lived here all his life. But had they finally found him?

If it wasn't the Pack, then who had whistled? Andrew said the Edison Group didn't hire werewolves. Was he wrong? If they wanted someone to track their missing subjects, a werewolf would be the best supernatural bloodhound around.

Right now, it didn't matter. Derek knew who'd whistled; and even if he couldn't tell me, his actions said we were in trouble, and all we could do was hope to outrun it.

"There's a creek over there," I said, pointing. "If it's a werewolf that we're trying to lose, water will hide our trail, right?"

He answered by veering that way.

The creek wasn't much more than a trickle, but it was enough to swallow our trail. As we ran, it cut deeper into the earth, banks rising to small cliffs on either side. If we kept going, we might find ourselves trapped.

Derek took the lead, scrambling up the creek bank with me following, soaked sneakers sliding in the dirt as I grabbed roots to pull myself up. I moved as quietly as I could, knowing any werewolf would share Derek's keen hearing.

We ran along the embankment until we reached a thick patch of woods. Derek herded me into a clearing in the middle of it. He crouched in the center, his front legs stretched out, his head and tail down. Trying to Change back to human form. After a few minutes of straining and snarling, he gave up.

"We can't stay here," I said. "If it's a werewolf—"

He grunted, confirming that.

"Then he's eventually going to find our trail. These woods aren't that big."

Another grunt. *I know.*

"I think the house is that way."

He shook his head and pointed his muzzle a little more to the left.

"Okay, good," I said. "So we just need to—"

He went still again, nose rising, ears turning. I crouched beside him. He kept sniffing, grumbling deep in his throat, like he'd caught a scent he couldn't seem to find again. Finally, he prodded me toward the mouth of the clearing with a noise that I thought meant *run*, but when I shot forward, he caught the back of my jacket between his teeth.

"Go slow?" I whispered. "Quietly?"

A grunt. *Yes.*

He slid in front of me and took a step. Then another. A cloud rolled over the moon and the forest went black. We stopped. A twig cracked to our right. Derek spun so fast he crashed into me, pushing me back as I stumbled, snapping at me when I didn't move fast enough.

As I retreated into the clearing, I could make out a dark shape at the edge. At another twig crack, Derek slammed into the back of my legs, pushing and jostling me until I was at the far side of the clearing, then prodding me into the thick brush.

"I can't—" I whispered.

He snapped and growled. *Yes, you can.*

I got down on all fours and pushed into the brush, hands in front of my face to clear the way. I'd gone only a few feet when I hit a tree. Thick bushes blocked either side. I twisted to tell Derek that I couldn't continue, but he'd stopped at the edge of my hole, his backside blocking the entrance.

The cloud cover thinned, and a figure materialized in the

path. It was another wolf, as black as Derek. It seemed to roll toward us, silent as fog, slowly and steadily drifting our way.

The clouds finally passed by the moon, but the wolf was still black as night from his nose to his eyes. I noticed pale stripes along one flank. When I squinted, I saw that they were strips of missing fur, the uncovered skin pink and puckered with recent scar tissue. I'd seen those scars just a few days before.

"Ramon," I whispered.

Derek snarled, fur rising, tail puffing, fangs flashing. But the other wolf kept coming at us, steady and relentless. Finally, with a roar, Derek rushed at him.

Ramon stopped. He didn't back up. Didn't even growl. He just stood his ground until Derek was almost on him, then feinted to the side and ran straight at me.

Derek tried to stop, but he'd put too much momentum into the charge and he skidded into the brush.

As Ramon barreled toward me, I scrambled to get away, but the brush was too thick. Fortunately, it was too thick for him, too, and he couldn't get any farther than Derek had, just close enough for me to smell the stink of his breath as he tried to shoulder his way deeper into the undergrowth.

Then he yelped and flew back with Derek's teeth embedded in his haunch. Ramon yanked free and lunged at him. Derek ducked and tore past Ramon to block the mouth of my hiding place.

For a moment, all I could see was Derek's tail. Then I

glimpsed Ramon off to the side, backing up, peering around Derek, like he was assessing the situation.

He lunged to the left. Derek sprang that way, snapping and snarling. Ramon feinted right. Derek blocked. Left again. Blocked again. It was like that evening in the playground when Liam kept pretending to grab for me, taunting Derek, laughing as he reacted every time.

"He's teasing you," I whispered. "Trying to wear you down. Don't fall for it."

Derek grunted. He tensed, like he was locking his legs. But it didn't help. Every time Ramon made a move my way, Derek jumped, snapping and growling.

Finally Ramon tired of the game and ran full out at Derek. They hit with a bone-cracking thud and went down, biting and growling, grunting and yelping when fangs sank in.

My hand tightened around my switchblade. I knew I should do something. Leap into the fray. Protect Derek. But I couldn't. The other day, seeing Derek and Liam fighting in human form, they'd moved too fast for me to interfere. That was slow-motion compared to this, a frenzied ball of fur and fury rolling across the clearing, one indistinguishable mass of black fur and flashing fangs and spattering blood.

I *had* to do something, because Derek had a serious handicap: me. He couldn't seem to forget I was there, and every time Ramon rolled my way, Derek stopped fighting to get between us again.

I wanted to tell him to forget about me. I was fine,

burrowed deep in the undergrowth and armed, and there was no sign of Ramon's partner, Liam. But I knew it wouldn't do any good. That protective instinct overrode reason.

I stood, reached as high as I could, and grabbed the bottom branch of the tree behind me. My stitched arm complained, but I ignored it. I clambered up. Climbing was easy. The tough part was not looking down every time I heard a grunt or a yelp.

Finally I was too high for Ramon to reach. I called to Derek, telling him I was safe. He still had to check, of course, glancing up and getting a hunk of fur ripped out of his neck. But once he saw where I was, he threw himself fully into the fight.

Still, as big as Derek was, he was no match for an experienced adult werewolf. When faced with Liam, Derek had run the other way, admitting he was outclassed. There might be a streak of arrogance in Derek, but there wasn't any bravado. If he couldn't win a fight, he had no problem running.

This time, though, he couldn't run.

I clutched the knife and wiggled out along the branch until I was over the fighters.

Speaking of bravado . . .

I stopped, feeling a prick of guilt at even thinking of something so stupid. If I dropped onto them, I'd be lucky if I didn't get Derek killed trying to protect me.

I hated cowering there like a helpless heroine. Yet I *was* helpless against Ramon. I didn't have superhuman strength or superhuman senses or fangs or claws or magical powers.

Stop whining about what you don't have. Your brain still works, doesn't it?

Under the circumstances, I wasn't too sure.

Just use it. Think.

I stared down at the fight, racking my brain for a plan. As I watched, I realized I could tell which one was Ramon by the scars. If I could—

The scars.

I leaned down as far as I dared.

"Derek! His side! Where he's scarred . . ."

I struggled for a way to explain without giving away the plan to Ramon, but I didn't need to say another word. Derek twisted and clamped down on Ramon's flank. Without fur for protection, Derek's teeth sank in easily. Ramon yowled. Derek wrenched his head back, ripping out a big chunk of Ramon's flank.

Blood gushed. Derek pranced back out of the way and dropped the hunk of flesh. Ramon charged, but his rear leg faltered. Derek dodged around Ramon and bit his flank again.

Ramon roared in pain and fury, and wheeled, tearing himself from Derek's grip. Blood spattered as he tore around fast and grabbed Derek by the scruff of the neck. They went down, Derek struggling and clawing until one of those claws scraped across Ramon's opened flank. A yelp from Ramon, and Derek was free. Derek backpedaled toward the stream bank. It was at least a fifteen-foot drop and I called to warn him, but he kept backing up.

Ramon lunged at him, bristling and snarling. Then a whistle cut him short. Liam. Ramon checked his charge, threw back his head, and began to howl. Derek leaped on him. Ramon cut the howl short and threw Derek off, then kept advancing on him, driving him back toward—

"Derek! The cliff!"

This time, his gaze swung up, meeting mine. But he didn't stop, just kept going, gaze once again locked with Ramon's.

At the last second, Derek veered left, circling and hitting Ramon square in his wounded flank. Ramon sailed off his feet. Derek pounced on him. His fangs sank into that mass of shredded flash. Ramon let out an unearthly howl of agony.

Ramon managed to scramble up, his back to the cliff. Derek lunged at him. Ramon backpedaled. At the last second, he saw the looming drop and started to twist out of the way, but Derek head butted him in that wounded flank, sending him flying over the edge of the embankment.

I climbed down and ran over to Derek, poised on the bank, looking at Ramon, who was still conscious, struggling to get up, one foreleg twisted at an ugly angle.

The whistle came again. Derek turned sharply, banging my legs, then prodding me with his nose, telling me to get moving.

"Is it Liam?" I asked.

He dipped his muzzle in a nod.

As for why Liam would be in human form, I wasn't stopping to wonder. He was still a formidable threat. The only advantage was that if he wasn't a wolf, tracking us would be slower.

"It came from near the house," I whispered as we ran. "We should head for the road. Do you know where—?"

He answered by barreling past me. We ran for a few minutes, but I kept falling behind. He raced back to take up the rear.

"I'm sorry," I whispered. "I can't see and I keep tripping—"

He cut me off with a grunt. *I know. Just go.*

I took the lead, letting Derek tap the back of my legs whenever I started heading off course. Finally, I could see lights through the trees. Derek prodded me toward them and—

"Making a helluva racket, ain't ya, pup." Liam's Texas drawl echoed through the forest.

Derek knocked me flying. I hit the ground hard, chin scraping the earth, dirt spraying into my mouth. I tried to rise, but Derek was standing over me. I ran my tongue over my teeth, making sure I hadn't lost any.

Derek chuffed and prodded the back of my neck. I was going to interpret that as an apology, whether it was or not.

"Come out, come out, wherever you are," Liam sang.

Derek nudged me into a thicket so small we had to crowd in together and I got a mouthful of fur. When I tried to give him more room, he growled at me to be still. I sat down and he pressed against me, getting the rest of his bulk into the thicket, until he was practically on my lap.

He lifted his head to sample the wind. It was coming from the same direction as Liam's voice, meaning he couldn't smell us.

I closed my eyes to listen better. I could feel the pounding of Derek's racing heart. Mine must have been beating just as hard, because he nudged my arm until I opened my eyes and met his, dark with concern.

"I'm okay," I whispered.

He shifted, trying to take more weight off my legs. As he moved, my hand brushed a patch of wet fur. I drew back to see my fingers sticky with blood.

"You're—"

He cut me off with a grunt. *I'm okay. Now, shhh.*

I tried to see how badly he was hurt, but he shifted again, this time keeping me down.

We sat there, silently listening. His ears swiveled, and every now and then they'd twitch, like he'd caught a noise. But instead of tensing, he began to relax.

"He's moving away?" I whispered.

He nodded.

I settled in. It was hard to be afraid for your life when there was a two-hundred-pound wolf on your lap. It was oddly comforting. Between the heat of his body, the softness of his fur, and the beat of his heart I found myself blinking to stay awake.

"Is he gone?" I whispered.

Derek shook his head.

"How long should we stay—?"

Derek stiffened. I peered into the night, but when I glanced at Derek, he didn't have that pointer-on-a-scent look. His head was still down. His eyes were wide, and he held himself completely still.

Then I felt it. His muscles were twitching.

"You're ready to Change back," I whispered.

He grunted, tense, worry seeping into his eyes.

"No problem. It always takes a while after the first sign, right? We'll have time to get you back to the house. You can Change there—"

He convulsed, his front legs shooting out. He collapsed on his side, all four legs going rigid, head jerking back, eyes rolling wildly.

"It's all right. This is better anyway. Just let it happen."

Not like he had a choice. I crawled over him, getting out of the way of those flailing claws. Crouching behind him, I rubbed his shoulders and told him he was doing fine, everything was okay.

His head lowered, then flew back with a bone-cracking snap. He let out a yelp, ending in a snarl as he tried to be quiet, but the convulsions kept coming faster and a whimper escaped with each fresh spasm. When he finally stopped, everything around us stayed silent. But I knew Liam had heard.

I leaned over Derek, whispering encouragement, hoping to block any sound of Liam, keep him from panicking. Soon, though, Derek's head shot up and I knew Liam was coming.

Derek was well into his Change now, his muzzle shortening, ears moving to the sides, hair growing as his fur retracted. I leaned down to his ear.

"Just keep going, okay? I'll look after it."

He stiffened and made a noise that I knew was a *no*. I rose. He tried to do the same, only to be hit with another convulsion.

"I'll be okay," I said, pulling out my knife. "I won't do anything stupid. You're almost finished. I'll distract him until you are."

"*No*," his voice was garbled, guttural.

I turned to go. He grabbed for my leg, but his fingers were still knobby stubs and I easily pulled away. Without looking back, I ran from the thicket.

twenty-two

I RAN, GETTING AS far from Derek as I could. Finally I saw the figure of a tall, lean man with light hair, limping through the forest, cane in one hand. Liam. The limp explained why he wasn't in wolf form. If Changing was as painful as it seemed, I could only imagine how bad it would be if you were injured. That injury also meant he had a grudge to settle. With me.

I took a deep breath, trying to calm my galloping heart. It didn't work. Too bad. I couldn't let him get close enough to see or hear Derek Changing.

I ran as close as I dared, then pulled up short in his path. He stopped and smiled.

"Hello there, cutie," he drawled. "I thought I smelled you."

"How's the leg?"

His grin turned a little less friendly, more bared teeth than smile. "Hurts like a son of a bitch."

"Sorry about that."

"I bet you are."

He stepped closer. I stepped back.

"Don't worry," he said. "I forgive you for the leg. I like a little spirit in my fillies." His look sent a shiver through me. "Makes them more fun to break. Now where's that big ox of a boyfriend?" He raised his voice. "This is a coward's ploy, pup, sending the girl out to distract me. About what I'd expect, though, considering how fast you ran away last time."

He listened, seeing if the taunt would bring Derek out.

"He's busy," I said. "With Ramon. He figured I could handle you."

Liam threw back his head and laughed. "You *do* have spunk. We're gonna have fun, just as soon as I take care of your boyfriend."

He moved toward me. I sidestepped, leading him away.

"You wanna play chase, cutie? I'm real good at it. How about we let your boyfriend and Ramon have their fun while we have ours and—?"

Something buzzed. Liam sighed, reached into his pocket, and flipped open a cell phone.

"Kinda busy," he said. He paused, listening. I could hear a man's voice on the other end and thought I caught Derek's name. "Yeah, yeah. You keep calling, we're never going to catch him for you."

If Liam said "we," then it wasn't Ramon phoning. Someone from the Pack? Had Liam already promised them Derek and now had to deliver?

"Quit your moaning," Liam said. "I told you we'll have him by sunrise. We just hit a minor complication. There's a reason he came out into the woods tonight—messing around with his girlfriend."

Liam looked at me. "Cute little thing. Dyed black hair. Big blue eyes." He paused. "Chloe? Yeah, she looks like a Chloe."

The Edison Group? Had to be. Right now, though, all I cared about was that whoever it was, he was keeping Liam occupied, giving Derek time to Change.

"Well, see, that's the problem," Liam continued. "We can't seem to separate the two. So, taking him in might mean taking her, too." He paused, listening. "Of course, we'll try to leave her alone, but . . ." Another pause. "I understand. Getting rid of the pup—one way or another—is your main concern. So you accept the risk of collateral damage?" As he listened to the answer, he smiled at me. "Absolutely. If we can't separate them, you won't need to worry about the girl again. I'll make sure of that. Now, if you have anything else to say, how about texting me? I'm kinda busy."

He hung up. "Seems some people consider you expendable, Chloe."

"Who?"

He lowered his voice to a mock whisper. "Bad people. It's a hard lesson, but the world is full of—"

A distant cry stopped him short. He turned in the direction of the thicket.

"Speaking of bad people, seems someone's been telling me fibs. Your boyfriend's not playing with Ramon, is he?"

I stepped in front of him.

He started to brush past me. "I know you're eager to have some fun, but I need to get your boyfriend out of the way first. Don't you worry, though. It sounds like he's Changing, and, if so, this is going to be quick."

I jumped in his way again.

His smile turned brittle. "Save that spunk for later. Right now, it's only going to piss me off, and you don't want to do that."

I let him pass but stayed on his heels, struggling to think up a plan. I could hear Derek moaning. The Change might have come on fast, but it was taking time to finish.

Derek's defenseless. If Liam finds him like that, he'll kill him.

I know, I know.

Then do something.

I took out my switchblade, opened it, and crept forward, closing the gap between us, gaze fixed on Liam's back. He glanced over his shoulder. I hid the knife. He stopped.

"How about you walk in front of me?" he said.

"I'm okay."

His face hardened. "Get in front of me, where I can see you."

As I passed him, my gaze went to his cane. Like Ramon, he was wounded.

Use that.

"Y-you said you'd take Derek to the P-Pack," I fake-stammered. "That's still the plan, right?"

He just waved me on, gaze locked on the distant spot where Derek was.

"P-please d-don't—"

I lunged and grabbed for the cane, but he whisked it out of reach, then swung it around, hitting me in the back so hard it knocked the air from my lungs and the ground from under my feet.

I hit the dirt, gasping, injured arm burning. I lifted my head, struggling to focus as Liam continued bearing down on Derek's thicket. Every breath felt like a white-hot knife stabbing my lungs.

Do something.

Like what? I was powerless. I—

No. I wasn't powerless. There was something I could do. The thought of it made bile rise in my throat, but it was nothing compared to what I felt at the thought of Liam finding Derek before he finished his Change.

I had to buy him more time.

I closed my eyes and concentrated, pushing past the warning alarms. I poured everything I had into the summons . . . and nothing happened. All those genetically enhanced powers and, when I needed them, they failed.

Then you're going to have to do this the old-fashioned way.

I tried to rise. Pain ripped through me and the forest seem to tilt, my gorge rising again. I gritted my teeth and crawled to a nearby fallen branch. I wrapped my fingers around it, steeled myself against the pain, then pushed myself up. Once I was standing, I ran at Liam. He wheeled out of my path, but I managed to swing and hit his thigh in the same place I'd stabbed him three nights ago.

He howled and staggered. I hit him again. He went down. As he fell, he grabbed for me, but I danced back, stick raised. When he tried to get up, I swung again. This time, he caught the stick and whipped me off my feet. I let go of the branch, but I was already sailing through the air. I crashed down a few feet from him, then scrambled out of the way as he twisted to grab me.

I managed to get to my feet. He started pushing up, then stopped, staring at something behind me.

Please let it be Derek.

I turned to see a partially decomposed rabbit pulling its mangled body toward me. Its ears were shredded strips of leathery skin. Its nose was a crater, lips gone, big front teeth protruding. Its eyes were shriveled raisins. The back half of its body was flattened and twisted, hind legs to one side as it dragged itself forward.

"Stop," I said, my voice eerily calm.

The rabbit stopped. I turned to Liam. He looked at me, face screwed up. Slowly, he rose, still staring at me.

"Forward," I said.

The rabbit lurched toward Liam. He stumbled back.

I got to my feet. The rabbit stood beside me, gnashing its teeth.

I mentally commanded it to advance on Liam. It hesitated, then it swung its head in his direction and started toward him.

He let out a string of curses, backing away slowly. Then a growl sounded behind him.

Liam turned. A dark shape moved between the trees, hidden in their shadows. I could see only the outline—the pointed ears, bushy tail, and long muzzle. Had Derek reverted to wolf? As the beast crept forward, though, I realized it was barely half Derek's size.

It stopped under a tree, almost hidden there, only its teeth visible, lips pulled back, growl vibrating. When it stepped into the moonlight, I braced myself for a hideous undead beast. But it was only an ordinary, living dog, probably from a nearby home.

The dog advanced on Liam, still growling. Werewolves and dogs didn't mix—I knew that from Derek.

Liam locked gazes with it and gave a growl of his own. The dog kept coming at him.

"Shoo, pooch."

Liam drew back his foot to kick it. Then he caught sight of the rabbit drawing alongside him. He backed away. The undergrowth behind him erupted in a flurry of breaking twigs and squeals. I couldn't see what it was, but Liam let out an oath, almost backing into the snarling dog.

The dog lunged. Liam kicked it. As it flew back, moonlight caught the dog's flank, and I saw a hole the size of my fist, squirming with maggots.

Liam saw it, too, and he cursed and backed away. The dog threw itself at him. Liam swerved out of its path.

"Stop," I said.

The dog did. It stood there, teeth bared, eyes blazing, every hair on end, growling at Liam.

The rabbit lurched toward him. He kicked it, and it flew into the undergrowth, only to come back out again. Something else came out with it, some kind of rodent, mostly skeleton, rattling and gnashing its tiny teeth.

"Stop," I said.

They did. Liam looked at me.

"Yes, they're dead," I said. "Yes, I control them. And you can't kill them. You can try, but you can't."

"Well, then, I guess I'm going to have to fight the one I *can* kill."

He charged at me.

I commanded the dog to attack, but my brain stuttered, seeing Liam bearing down on me. I dove to the side. He grabbed my pajama leg and yanked. I fell onto my stomach, scrabbling to get up, fingers digging into the ground, nails tearing. I wrenched and his grip slid to my foot. I gave a tremendous heave and flung myself forward, leaving him with my sneaker.

As I scrambled to my feet, I heard a smack. I spun to see Derek—in human form—on Liam's back. Liam bucked and threw him off. Derek grabbed him, and they went down fighting.

The dog raced toward the two. I commanded it to be still, and it slid to a stop, snarling and straining like a rabid dog on a chain. I closed my eyes and gave it another order—to leave its body.

I kept releasing it and the other spirits, desperately trying to ignore the grunts and gasps of the fight. When I opened my eyes, the animals had collapsed, their souls freed.

Liam and Derek rolled on the ground, locked in combat, Liam's hands in Derek's hair, trying to yank his head back, Derek's hands around Liam's neck, neither one able to get the grip they needed to throw the other off.

I yanked out my switchblade as I raced forward. I hit the button . . . and felt the blade sink into my palm. I let go. The knife fell into the undergrowth. I dropped to my knees, digging for it.

A crack like the snap of a tree branch. I shot up. Derek

lay on his back, Liam over him, Derek's hands still around his neck. Both had gone still. Derek stared up, wide-eyed. Liam's eyes were just as wide, but they saw nothing, fixed in an empty look of final shock.

twenty-three

"I—I DIDN'T . . ." DEREK BEGAN.

He scrambled out from under Liam. The werewolf's body fell, limp, to the side, his head twisted, neck broken.

Derek swallowed. The sound echoed in the silence.

"I didn't— I just— I was trying to stop him."

"You didn't mean it," I said softly. "But he did."

He looked at me, eyes refusing to focus.

"He would have killed you," I said. "Killed both of us, if it came down to it. You might not have meant to do it, but . . ."

I didn't finish. I could have said the world was better off without Liam, but we both knew the point wasn't whether Liam deserved to die, but whether Derek deserved the guilt of killing someone. He didn't.

"It wasn't a fight to the death for you. But it was for him."

Derek nodded and rubbed the back of his neck, wincing as his fingers hit a scrape.

"Are you okay?" I asked.

"Yeah. Just a few cuts and bruises. I heal fast. Might need a stitch or two here—"

He glanced down at the blood-smeared cut on his side . . . and realized he wasn't wearing any clothing. I'd be lying if I said *I* hadn't realized it already. Kind of obvious. It wasn't like he'd been going to take time out to find his clothing before stopping Liam.

Fortunately, under the circumstances, I hadn't had time to dwell on the lack of clothing. With the fighting and, now, as he crouched, I hadn't seen any more than I had when he was in his shorts. That didn't keep him from turning bright red.

I peeled off my jacket and wordlessly handed it to him, and he tied it around his waist with a mumbled, "Thanks." Then, "We should get going."

Only we didn't get going. We lapsed into silence, with Derek still crouched beside Liam's body, his head down, hair hanging around his face, his back and arms covered in a sheen of sweat. He shivered.

"I'll go get your clothes," I said, pushing to my feet.

He caught my elbow. "Ramon."

"Right."

I blinked hard, feeling fuzzy—from shock, I guess. One of us had to kick-start their brain, and Derek seem stalled, unable to stop staring at the man he'd killed.

"We need to move him," I said. "At least into the brush for now, to cover the body. Then we'll have to come back tomorrow and bury him."

I couldn't believe what I was saying. Hiding a body? A *body*?

And what's the alternative? Leave him lying in the path and hope none of the neighbors ever walks through here?

Body disposal might be something I never expected to do outside a screenplay, but this was my life now. Adjust or give up.

I stood and took Liam's arm, giving it a tentative tug.

"I've got it." Derek rose. "I'll carry him. We can't leave drag marks or anything, and we'll need to bury him right away, so no dogs find him."

"Bury who?" said a voice beside me.

I jumped so high, my heart rammed into my throat.

"Chloe?" Derek said.

I turned to see Liam walking toward us.

"Chloe?" Derek said again.

"It's L-Liam. His ghost."

Liam stopped. "Ghost?" He looked at me, then at his body, on the ground. He swore.

"You're dead," I said.

"So I see. That must make you one of those people who

can talk to the dead and"—he glanced at the bodies of the dog and rabbit, lips curling—"raise the dead."

His gaze returned to his own corpse, and he swore again.

I cleared my throat. "As long as you're here, I have some questions."

He looked at me, brows lifting. "You're kidding, right?"

"No." I knelt beside his body and reached into his pocket.

"Chloe?" Derek moved closer, frowning.

I took out Liam's cell phone. "Someone called him. Someone who seems to have set the whole thing up, someone who knew me, my name." I looked at Liam's ghost. "Who is it?"

He choked on a laugh. "Seriously? I just *died*. Your boyfriend there killed me. You really expect me to stick around and chat? Love to, but I'm a little traumatized right now. Maybe later."

He turned to leave. I raced into his path.

"You're about to go to the afterlife," I said. "This is your last chance to do something good."

"Huh, well, since you put it that way . . ." He rolled his eyes. "I'm not interested in second chances. I didn't do a thing that I regret. If you want answers . . ."

He stepped up, towering over me. I resisted the urge to back away, but I must have stiffened, because Derek moved closer and whispered, "Don't let him harass you."

"Harass her?" Liam said. "She's the one who can't get

enough of my company." He looked down at me again. "As I was saying, if you want answers, find them yourself. And try to have some fun while you're at it, because I have a feeling I'm going to be seeing you again real soon . . . over on this side."

Derek's hand tightened on my arm. When I tried to pull away, he leaned down and whispered, "Let him go. It's not worth it."

"Listen to your boyfriend, cutie," Liam called as he strode away.

I pulled myself up straight. "What did you think of my zombies?"

Liam stopped, turned slowly.

I waved at the dead dog. "Do you know how I did it?"

"Do I care?"

"You should. Necromancers raise the dead by sending a spirit—a ghost, like you—back into a corpse, where it's under my control, as you saw. It works the same for animals and people. So either you answer my questions, or I'm shoving you back in there." I pointed at his dead body.

He laughed. "I'd say you've got balls, but that'd be kinda inappropriate."

"Do you think I'm kidding?"

He answered by turning his back and walking away. I closed my eyes and imagined tugging him toward his corpse, just a little pull.

"Hey," he said. "*Hey*!"

I opened my eyes to see him straining against an unseen force.

"Did you think I was bluffing?"

I ramped it up a notch and he stumbled. I gave another tug. His ghost shot a few feet toward his body.

"Okay, fine," he spat at me. "What do you want to know?"

"Who hired you?"

"You've got the phone. Figure it out."

I told Derek what Liam said, then asked, "Was it the Edison Group?"

His face screwed up. "The electric company?"

"Was it a man named Marcel Davidoff?"

"Who?"

"Diane Enright?"

"He's right," Derek whispered. "You've got the phone. Ask something else."

"When you found us the first time, in the playground, you said you'd pulled off the road and picked up Derek's scent. That was a lie, wasn't it?"

"Everyone lies, sweetheart. Get used to it."

"Someone hired you to get rid of Derek."

"You've figured it out. So you don't need me—"

"Why?"

"Why what?"

"Why do they want him gone?" I asked.

"Because I'm a werewolf," Derek said. "Like Andrew said, no one wants us around."

"Bingo, pup. It's a lesson best learned early. They're all afraid of us." He strolled over to Derek. "You're trying to be a good kid, aren't you? You think that'll show them they're wrong. So, how's that working out for you? Guess what? They don't care. To them, you're a monster, and nothing you do—or don't do—will change their minds. My advice? Give 'em what they want. It's a short, brutal life." He smiled. "Live it up."

Derek stared straight ahead, patiently waiting.

"He can't hear a word I'm saying, can he?" Liam said.

"Nope."

He swore. "Here I try to impart some final pearls of wisdom to the next gener—"

Liam disappeared. I jumped, startled, then looked around.

"Chloe?"

"He's gone."

"Left?"

"No, he just—" I kept looking, but couldn't see any ghostly shimmer. "He was talking and then he vanished, like someone yanked him over to the other side."

"What did he say?" Derek asked.

"Nothing we didn't already—"

Derek wheeled. A man appeared twenty feet down the path. Ramon. Derek stepped in front of me.

Ramon raised his hand, palm out, showing he wasn't armed. His broken arm hung at his side. As he walked toward us, I could see bruises on his jaw and blood soaking the side of his shirt. With every step, he winced.

"I'm not here to fight you, kid," he said. "If you insist, I'll give it my best, but I'd really rather call it a draw."

Noticing Liam's body, he stopped and shook his head.

"It was an accident," I said.

"Yeah, well, I'm sure he had it coming." Another head shake, but there was genuine grief in his eyes. After a moment, he tore his gaze from the body and looked up at Derek.

"So now what?" Ramon said.

"We call it a draw, like you said. But if you ever come after either of us again . . ."

Ramon gave a tight laugh. "Do I look like I'm in any shape to hunt you? Nah, this was Liam's scheme. Crazy son of a—"

"Someone hired you two. Who was it?"

"Ask him." He hooked his thumb at Liam. "He's the man with the plan. Always was. I just go along for the ride."

"So you have no idea who hired him?"

"Some supernatural. A healer guy."

"Sorcerer?" I said. "Shaman?"

"No clue. I'm not into that stuff. Anyway, someone put Liam in touch with this guy who wanted a werewolf to track you down"—he nodded at Derek—"and hand you over to the Pack. Just so happened we were already in trouble with the Pack—on account of Liam, as usual."

"And this was the perfect solution," I said. "Give Derek to the Pack, blame him for the man-eating, and get paid for your trouble. If you couldn't take him in alive, that was okay, too."

"Not at first. The guy wanted you handed over to the Pack, seemed to think that would be okay. Or pretended to, anyway."

"And if the Pack turned out to be killers, that wasn't his fault," Derek said.

"You got it. After we lost you the first time, he started getting antsy. Just wanted you gone one way or another. You want my advice?" He looked at Derek. "Take your girlfriend and start running. Whatever you're trying to do here—live with other supernaturals, pretend you're one of them—it won't work. They'll always be watching you, expecting you to lose control." Ramon shook his head. "You know much about wolves, boy?"

"A bit."

"There's a reason they live as far from humans as they can. Centuries of experience. People don't like other predators around. Makes them nervous. When they get nervous, they try to eliminate the threat. Now, I'm going to say good night and take my buddy there."

"And give him a proper burial?" I said.

A sharp laugh. "We don't get luxuries like that. I'm going to take the down payment on the job, then I'm going to take his body to the Pack, settle up with them. And, yes, it's a helluva thing to do to a friend, but out here, it's survival of the fittest." He met Derek's gaze. "For us, it's always survival of the fittest."

With Derek's help, Ramon managed to get Liam's body over his shoulder, teeth gritted against the pain of the extra weight. Then he hobbled off into the night.

twenty-four

W E RETURNED TO WHERE Derek left his clothes before his first Change. As he dressed, I checked Liam's cell phone. Derek walked up behind me and looked over my shoulder.

"He used initials for the name. RRB. But it's a 212 area code. That's New York City, so it could still be the Edison Group, using a local contact for the job."

"Yeah."

"You don't sound so sure."

He looked in the direction of the house.

"You think it's one of them?" I said. "But we met Liam on the way *to* Andrew's place."

"They could have known I was on my way, sent Liam to stake out the bus route."

"How? At the time, Andrew was being held by the Edison

Group. He didn't know we were coming, meaning no one in his group did either."

"They could have been watching his house, seen Simon and Tori, figured out we were on our way, made a few calls to the bus companies, found out two kids got off in Albany the night before. It's a stretch. But . . ." He shrugged.

"It's a possibility." I checked the initials again. "Did you catch Russell's last name? Ramon said the contact was a healer. Russell's a shaman. Unless Ramon meant a sorcerer."

"Sorcerers aren't healers. Witches are, kind of, but if it's a guy, he's a shaman."

"We need proof. And I know how to get it." I raised the cell phone.

Derek shook his head. "Too risky. I'm no good at imitating voices."

"You won't have to. Liam said if the guy wanted anything else, he should text him. So, presumably Liam might also text *him*."

"Good idea." Derek reached for the cell phone. "I'll tell him—"

I pulled the phone out of his reach, and I looked at him. He got the message, rubbing his chin and nodding.

"Go ahead."

As I typed, he stepped back and tried not to watch over my shoulder. It wasn't easy—he kept rocking forward to peek. But he managed to resist the urge to take over, and I appreciated that. Afterward I let him read what I'd typed and he approved.

According to the message, Liam had Derek and the girl cornered. He might be able to take them alive, but if he tried, he could lose them again. What did the boss want Liam and Ramon to do?

Whoever was on the other end must have been poised over his cell phone, waiting, because the reply came back in seconds. Five words. *Just take care of them.*

I sent back another, to be absolutely clear, saying if he wanted us to dispose of the bodies, that'd cost an extra 10 percent. Again, a quick response, one word this time. *Fine.*

I looked over to see Derek staring at the message. Just staring, like he still believed Liam and Ramon had only been trying to scare us and their orders were to leave me alone and deliver him to the Pack.

"Are you okay?" I asked.

He nodded. But he didn't look okay, face pale, eyes fixed on the screen.

"Derek?"

The phone vibrated. Another message, from the same sender, wanting to clarify that the extra 10 percent covered disposal of *both* bodies. And if they did take Derek alive, I had to disappear.

"Because if I go back, I can tell Andrew what happened," I said. "It's better if we both vanish, and it looks like we ran off together."

I glanced at Derek. He'd gone an odd greenish shade, like he was going to be sick.

"I'm so sorry," he said finally, the words little more than a whisper. "They were going to kill you because you came out here with me. To help me. I asked you to come."

"And how's that your fault?" I didn't mean to snap, but I was mad. Not at Derek, but at *them*—everyone who made him feel like this. Before I could apologize, he blinked hard, the shock falling away, and I knew my anger had worked better than any words of reassurance.

"They targeted you because you're a werewolf," I said. "That's it. It's nothing you did, and nothing you can change. It's their problem."

"But if I know it's a problem, I shouldn't endanger anyone else."

"So you should have come out here alone? That's—"

"Not just that. I put you and Simon in danger just by . . ."

"By being here? And what's the alternative? Take off? Give up on finding your dad? Leave Simon behind?"

He blinked. "No, I wouldn't leave . . . but I feel like . . ."

"Feel like what?"

He shook his head, looking away. I walked around in front of him.

"Feel like *what*, Derek? Like you should leave? Like we'd be better off if you did?"

He rolled his shoulders in a half shrug, then looked away

again. I was right. He just didn't like hearing the thought voiced; it sounded too close to self-pity.

"No one is better off if you leave," I said.

"Yeah." He mumbled the word, unconvinced.

"Simon needs you."

He nodded and stared into the forest.

I need you. I didn't say that, of course. How could I, without it sounding weird? But I felt it, heart hammering against my ribs, and it wasn't some romantic *I can't bear to be without you* nonsense. It was something deeper, more desperate.

When I thought of Derek leaving, the ground seemed to slide under my feet. I needed something to hold on to, something solid and real when everything around me was changing so fast. Even if there were times I thought it would be easier without Derek there, ready to tear a strip off me at my every misstep, in some ways I relied on that—someone to keep me thinking, keep me striving to do better, keep me from burying my head and praying it all worked out.

When he turned my way, he must have seen it on my face. As fast as I tried to cover it up, it wasn't fast enough, and when he looked at me, the *way* he looked at me . . .

Panic. I felt panic, like I suddenly wanted to be anywhere but here, and nowhere but here, and I wanted, I wanted . . .

I tore my gaze away and opened my mouth to say something, anything, but he beat me to it.

"I'm not going anywhere, Chloe." He rubbed the back of one shoulder, scowling, like he was working out a knot.

"I don't mean to get all . . ."

"Angsty?"

A short, sharp laugh. "Yeah, I guess. Way too much call for angst lately. I'm really better with action."

"I hear you." I lifted the cell phone. "And maybe with this, we can kick-start that action. Ready to go talk to Andrew?"

He nodded and we headed for the house.

It wasn't until we got back that the full impact of the night hit. Someone wanted Derek dead. That same someone had been willing to let me die because . . . well, I guess just because it didn't matter. *I* didn't matter. I was just an obstacle to the goal.

How could someone look at kids who'd never done anything wrong and see only a threat best eliminated with murder? Whoever did this was no better than the Edison Group.

Someone wanted Derek dead because he was a monster. But when he'd accidentally killed Liam, Derek had suffered and he'd continue to suffer, however justifiable the act.

So who was the real monster?

The house was quiet. That was weird. It was like we'd woken from a nightmare and could just crawl back into bed as if nothing had happened.

I let Derek get Andrew.

They found me at the kitchen table. Derek said, "There's something we need to tell you," and from the look on Andrew's face, I think he expected Derek to say he'd gotten me pregnant. It seemed to come as something of a relief to discover we'd only been hunted by killer werewolves—or at least until he realized it wasn't the Edison Group that had sent them. Once he saw that text message and confirmed it was Russell's number, things changed, and Andrew finally became the kind of guy we needed him to be.

He was furious, pacing the kitchen, vowing if not vengeance, at least answers. And safety. He promised us that nothing like this would happen again, even if it meant he had to take us away from the others and handle the Edison Group alone.

He called Margaret and told her to get over to the house. He didn't care if it was four A.M., this wouldn't wait until morning. He couldn't get hold of Gwen, but he left the same message.

Next, we got Simon and Tori up, me talking to Tori, Derek to Simon. I was quite happy not to have to face Simon just yet.

I told Tori what happened. Or a version of it, balanced between conveying the seriousness of the threat and not freaking her out. Derek and I also hadn't told Andrew everything because we didn't want to freak *him* out. In our version, Derek hadn't completed his Change. Everyone was already worried enough about him without us admitting he was now a full-blown werewolf. We also hadn't admitted that Liam was dead, saying Derek had just knocked him out, then Ramon called it a draw and carted his friend away.

Derek wanted all of us to pack our bags and run. I knew that's what he wanted because it's what I wanted, too. It wasn't an option, though. Not yet.

If anything, tonight had only opened another window on the danger lurking beyond our castle walls. I suppose it's dramatic to say we were under siege, but that's how we felt.

In a movie, we'd set out, braving Ramon and Russell and the Edison Group assassins. Those who refused to leave the castle would be branded wimps and cowards. But there's a reason people do stupid things in movies—no one wants to watch a bunch of kids pace and bicker and angst as they wait for the adults to come up with a plan. We didn't much like it either, but for now, we were stuck with it.

twenty-five

ONLY MARGARET SHOWED UP. While Andrew said Gwen must be at her boyfriend's, cell phone off, I could tell he didn't like that. Had she been in on the scheme to get rid of Derek? I hoped not.

If we expected the same outrage from Margaret that we'd gotten from Andrew, we were disappointed. But she was upset and concerned. Good enough for now.

When I came out of the shower, I found a piece of paper shoved under the door. It was a pictogram message from Simon, like the one he'd left at the warehouse. It started with a ghost as the salutation—meaning me—and closed with a cloud of fog and lightning bolt—meaning him. As for the message itself, it was a little more complicated than the last one, and it took me a while to work out.

The first symbol was a piece of paper with "I bequeath ..."

across the top. The second was the letter U. Then the number 4. Then two hands, one putting something in the other's palm. Then the musical note "mi." *Will you for ___ me?*

I stared at the two hands, trying to figure out the missing word until a loud sigh came through the door.

"Either the answer is no or my drawing sucks."

"Hold on." I quickly dressed and opened the door. Simon was leaning against the wall.

"So?" he said.

"I'm having trouble with one part." I pointed to the hands.

"Give," he said.

"Ah." I read the note. "Will you for . . . *forgive* me?" I looked up at him. "I think that's supposed to be my question."

"No, you did the right thing. You realized it wasn't what you wanted, and you said so. I'm the jerk who stomped off and left you alone in the forest. I'm sorry. Really sorry." He paused. "So . . . are we okay?"

Relief made my knees wobble. "We're okay. But I *am* sor—"

He held up a hand to cut me off. "I can't get mad at you for confirming something I already suspected. I gave it a shot. It didn't work out. I'm not going to say I'm fine with that, but . . ." He shrugged. "I like you, Chloe. And it's not a girlfriend-or-nothing kind of like, so I'm hoping we can skip the we-tried-dating-and-it-blew stage and jump straight back to where we were, if you want that."

"I want that."

When we got downstairs, Andrew was gone. We figured he went to confront Russell, but Margaret, left behind on babysitting duty, wouldn't confirm that. Was this how it would be? Left on the sidelines while the grown-ups took action? I hoped not.

Simon and I found Derek in the kitchen. Simon wanted to grab an apple and head someplace so we could plan our next move, out of range of the adults, but Derek handed him his blood tester and insulin pouch, then got bacon and eggs out of the fridge. Simon sighed and Derek gave him a look.

"I hope you don't expect me to make that," I said.

Now it was my turn to get the look.

"I'm just saying . . ."

"Not all of us grew up with live-in housekeepers," Derek said.

"I don't need breakfast," Simon said. "We have to talk."

"About what?" Derek said.

"Um, getting out of here?" he said. "Someone tried to *kill* you. Both of you."

"And the only thing new about that is that it wasn't the Edison Group," Derek said, "who are probably also on our trail, waiting for us to do something stupid like run away again." He put bacon strips in the frying pan. "We're staying. At least until we know what they plan to do next."

"I want to summon Royce," I said.

Derek jerked his head around fast enough to cause whiplash. "*What?*"

"I want to contact Royce. If I'm lucky, I'll get his uncle or cousin instead, but it's more likely that it'd be Royce, and we'll have to deal with that. We need to know what happened here, and we need to know it fast."

"She's right." Simon met his brother's gaze. "You know she is."

Derek's jaw worked as he chewed that over. Finally he said, "On one condition. No Tori. The last thing we need is her whipping a fireball at Royce."

"All right."

I went upstairs to get Tori down for breakfast. I took her into our confidence and asked for her help by keeping Margaret busy and letting us know if Andrew showed up. She'd have rather come to the summoning, but she seemed okay with that.

After breakfast, we decided to do the summoning in the basement—far from Andrew, without the dangers of the roof. And, I'll admit, Simon and I were eager to get a look down there.

For the first time in my life, I walked into a basement and shivered only from an actual draft. It was exactly as Derek had described it—two big rooms full of stored stuff and a small workshop. Simon joked about secret passages, but

Derek squelched that idea.

I did my usual thing—closed my eyes and knelt. I could imagine Dr. Banks from his photo. Austin was tougher, because I kept seeing his bloodied body, and that didn't help me relax. So I mainly focused on Dr. Banks, concentrating to the point where I could sense that inner alarm ready to go off, saying it wasn't safe to go farther.

"Nothing," I said.

"Are you sure?" Simon said. "You twitched."

"Try it again," Derek said.

I did, and still nothing happened, but Simon said, "Yeah, that was a definite twitch. Your eyelids moved, like you saw something."

The next time I tried, I *did* feel it, a little spark that made me flinch. I sighed and shifted.

"Take your time," Simon murmured. "No one's going anywhere."

I summoned, fighting the urge to crank it up another notch. There *was* a spirit present. I felt that same hyper-awareness that I did with bodies, like I was straining to hear a voice too faint for my ears to detect. Goose bumps speckled my arms.

"I want to take off my necklace."

I braced for a fight, but Derek only nodded. "Lift it over your head slowly, and keep it in your hands for now. See if that makes a difference."

I closed my eyes and grasped the necklace.

"No!"

I jumped, then looked from Simon to Derek, but I knew it wasn't one of them.

"She's back," I said. "The woman."

When I summoned again, the sensation returned, stronger now, and it took all my willpower not to ramp it up and yank the spirit through.

"Careful," the voice whispered.

My goose bumps rose higher.

"C-can I see you, p-please?" My voice wavered. I cleared my throat and tried again, but still stammered through it.

"Chloe?" Derek said.

I followed his gaze to my hands. They were shaking. I clenched the necklace and took a deep breath.

"Is it your aunt?" Simon asked.

I shook my head. "No. I—" I was about to say I didn't know who it was, but I couldn't get the words out. I knew who this was. I just didn't dare believe it.

"Listen, baby . . . Have to listen . . ."

Listen, baby. I knew who called me that. I knew this voice.

"Mom?"

twenty-six

"WHAT?" SIMON SAID, SHIFTING forward. "Your mom's here?"

"No." I shook my head sharply. "She's not. I—I—I—" I took another breath and clenched my shaking hands. "I don't know why I said that."

"You're exhausted," Derek said.

"What if it is?" Simon said.

I caught the look Derek shot him, telling him to be quiet. Still, he asked me, "If there's a ghost there, do you want to keep trying?" He met my gaze. "It probably isn't her."

"I know."

I closed my eyes. I wanted this to be my mom. From the day I'd learned I could speak to the dead, I'd been pushing this possibility from my mind as hard as I could. Even thinking about talking to her made my chest tighten.

But I was terrified, too. My mom was a distant, cherished memory. She was hugs and laughter and everything good about my childhood. Thinking of her was like being three years old again, curled up on her lap, completely safe and loved. But I wasn't three anymore, and I knew she wasn't the perfect mom of my memory.

My mother had put me in this experiment. She'd wanted a child so badly that she'd enrolled in the Edison Group's study. Yes, they'd told her they would fix the side effects that led to her brother's death. But still, she'd had to have known she was taking a risk.

"Chloe?" Simon said.

"S-sorry. Let me try again."

I closed my eyes and forgot all of that. If it was my mother, I wanted to see her, no matter what she really was, no matter what she'd done.

So when I summoned, I allowed myself to picture my mother, to call her by name.

"—hear me?" Her voice came again, so soft I could catch it only while I was concentrating. I pulled a little harder.

"No! . . . enough . . . not safe."

"What's not safe? Summoning you?"

Her answer was too weak to make out. I opened my eyes and peered around, searching for any sign of a ghost. To my left, I caught a shimmer, like heat rising off the floor. I held my necklace out for Derek.

"No!" the voice said. ". . . put it . . . not safe."

"But I want to see you."

". . . can't . . . Sorry, baby."

My chest clenched. "P-please. I just want to see you."

". . . know . . . can't . . . necklace . . . safe."

Derek gave it back. I lowered it over my head, but resumed summoning, stronger now, pulling—

"Chloe!" Her voice was so harsh my eyes flew open. "Not so hard . . . bring him."

"Royce? I've dealt with him before. I want to talk to you." I summoned again.

"Chloe! . . . keep . . . I'll leave . . . shouldn't be here . . . not allowed."

"What's not allowed?"

"You aren't allowed to speak to her," Derek murmured. "Necromancers aren't supposed to be able to contact their dead relatives. I've heard that. I didn't want to say anything, because I wasn't sure. Obviously, you can contact her, just not very well. And she doesn't want you to try harder, in case you bring Royce."

"But I *need* to—"

I didn't even get the sentence out, and the air began to shimmer, a shape taking form. My mother's shape, so faint I could barely see it, but enough so I knew. I *knew*. The tears started. I blinked them back, and she disappeared again.

"It was you that night at Andrew's," I said. "In the woods. When they were chasing us. You tried to help. You've been following me."

"Not always . . . can't . . . tried to warn . . . oh, baby . . . run . . ."

"Run?"

" . . . not safe . . . no place safe . . . not for you . . . so many lies . . . get away . . ."

"We can't run," I said. "The Edison Group found us that night at—"

"No . . . that's . . . tried to tell . . ." Her voice started to fade. I strained to hear, but it kept moving away. I held out my necklace.

"Um, Chloe?" Simon said. "If your mom said to leave that on—"

"She was trying to tell me something, and she's disappearing."

"Summon her again," Derek said, taking the necklace, "but carefully."

I gently pulled as I called for her. Derek stayed poised beside me, necklace stretched between his hands, ready to drop it over my head at the first hint of trouble.

"She's gone," I said finally. Tears prickled again. I blinked them back and cleared my throat.

"What'd she say?" Simon asked.

"That it's not safe for us anywhere, which we already knew. But there was something else. Something she wanted to tell me about that night at Andrew's."

"If you want to keep trying, go on," Derek said. "If you pull through Royce, you can send him back, right?"

I nodded. Margaret said it wasn't safe, but I wouldn't feel bad about shoving that particular ghost into the wrong dimension. So, still kneeling, I cranked up the power, trying to summon—

"Looking for someone, little necro?"

I jumped, losing my balance. Simon and Derek both grabbed for me, Derek catching me with one hand while awkwardly dropping the amulet ribbon over my head. I pulled it down and looked around.

"Royce," I said. "Can I see you? Please?"

He chuckled and appeared partway, like he had before. "Liked what you saw, huh?"

They say you can't fake a blush, but I sure tried. That was the way to deal with this jerk. Flattery, as painful as it was.

"You were right," I said. "We need your help. Things are going wrong."

"Surprise, surprise."

"Were you . . . one of us? Part of the Genesis project?"

"I'm genetically modified, but I'm not one of you imitations."

"Imitations?" I said.

"Of the original model. Me. Well, Austin and me."

"I thought we were the first subjects."

"They called it Genesis *Two*," Derek murmured. "I thought they meant two as in second to the biblical one. They meant the second study. They must have done one before us."

Royce laughed. "You kids really are idiots. Do you really think this is their only experiment? Yeah, you're the second wave . . . of the Genesis project. Then there's the Icarus project, the Phoenix project . . ."

Dr. Davidoff had hinted that the Edison Group was involved in other experiments, but I acted like this was all new. "How do you know all this?"

"I'm smart."

And his uncle was one of the group leaders.

"What went wrong?" I asked.

"Wrong?"

"You're dead. Austin's dead. Dr. Banks is dead. . . . Did that have anything to do with you? You and Austin?"

Anger flickered across his face.

"Something went wrong," I pushed. "With you two. That's how he knew—"

He feigned a yawn. "Anyone else finding this conversation really boring? Let's liven things up with a game." He walked over to Simon. "You joked about a secret passage earlier."

"He can't hear you, remember?" I said.

"Do you want to make your boyfriend happy, little girl? I'll tell you where the secret passage is. You know there *is* one. In a house this big, the basement has to be just as large."

I told the guys what Royce had said.

"Not necessarily," Derek said. "It was common in that period not to build full basements—"

"Boring. There is a passage to another room—one they don't want you to find. Especially you, little necromancer. They wouldn't want you to bring those bodies back, get their stories."

I hesitated. Simon asked what he'd said and I told them.

"I think he's full of it," Derek said. "But I'll bite. Where's the passage?"

Royce pointed and I relayed it.

"The workshop?" Derek said. "There's nothing in there. I already checked."

"Why do you think the door's locked?" Royce said.

"Because you're a genetically altered half-demon with telekinetic powers," I said. "As a prototype, they wanted you under careful supervision, but in a normal environment. So instead of the laboratory, you lived here with your uncle Dr. Banks."

"Really bored . . ."

"And your power, being telekinesis, means you can move objects with your mind, right?"

"Um, yeah. Want another demo?"

"No, just making a point. You lived here. You can move objects with your mind. Over there"—I pointed at the workshop—"is a room filled with tools. Why is it locked? I think that's kind of obvious."

Simon laughed. The ghost spun on him, but the scare was lost on Simon.

"Open that door," Royce said.

"Why? So you can bring out some toys? I don't think so."

Simon snorted another laugh.

A broom flew from the wall, coming straight at me like a javelin. An unwieldy javelin, I might add. I easily ducked out of the way, and Derek just as easily caught it in midflight.

"Good reflexes, big guy," the ghost said.

He strolled over to a bunch of plastic bins stacked against the wall and flipped open the top one.

"Oh, look, Uncle Todd kept my old stuff. He's so sweet, packing my things away after he murdered me."

"M-murdered you?" I said in spite of myself.

He rummaged through the box.

"Get ready to send him back," Derek whispered, then to Simon, "Go upstairs."

Simon shook his head. "I—"

Royce spun like a shot-putter, whipping something at us. I dove out of the way. Derek caught it—a bowling ball—then snarled at Simon, "Upstairs!"

"Oooh, good reflexes, superhuman strength, and a very convincing snarl. I think we have ourselves a werewolf." He got right in Derek's face. "How about a little one-on-one, wolf-boy? Battle of the superpowers?"

I shut my eyes and pictured Royce sailing backward. But he just kept taunting Derek.

"Maybe we should all go upstairs," Simon said. "Get away from this creep."

"He'd follow us," Derek said.

"Oh, don't listen to him," Royce said. "Sure. Go on upstairs. There are lots of fun things to play with up there. Razors. Scissors. Knives." He smiled and whispered in my ear. "I really like knives. There's so much you can do with them."

I glanced at Derek. He looked anxious, shooting glances from me to Simon, like he couldn't decide between letting me finish banishing Royce and getting us out before we were hurt.

"I'm trying," I said. "I'm really—"

"I know. Take your time." He shot an arrogant look of his own in the ghost's direction. "He's not dangerous. Unless you can talk someone to death."

The ghost spun and whipped a barbell. It came at us, but awkwardly, like he'd fumbled the shot. Derek moved mockingly slow and caught it before it crashed to the floor. I continued banishing Royce.

Royce started rooting around the box again. "Where's that other dumbbell? . . . Oh, that's right. I used it already." He got in Derek's face again. "To bash my brother's brains in while he slept. Do you sleep, wolf-boy?"

My brain stuttered, flashing images of Austin's body, the blood, blood everywhere . . .

"Chloe?" Derek said.

"I-I've got it."

"She doesn't have anything," Royce said. "She pulled me through and I'm not going back."

"Simon?" Derek whispered. "Upstairs. Now."

I had to stay here to banish Royce and Derek had to stay to protect me, but Simon was a bystander, one Royce would eventually target.

Simon left. I heard him stop on the stairs, unwilling to go too far in case we needed him.

A crash. My eyes flew open to see Derek on his feet, Royce picking up a piece of a smashed plate from the concrete floor.

"Oh, look," Royce said, running his finger along the broken edge. "Sharp. I like sharp."

Derek moved in front of me. I stared at his back and emptied my mind of everything except the image of Royce, sailing backward through the dimensions, through *any* dimensions. I concentrated until my temples throbbed. Still nothing.

You can't do it. Stop trying and get someplace safe.

But there was no safe place. Not from this ghost. I had to get rid of him.

"How much do you know about werewolves?" Royce was saying, pacing as he turned the shard over in his hands. "We grew up on that crap, Austin and me. All part of our cultural training, my uncle said."

"What's he saying?" Derek asked.

"I'm trying not to listen."

"Go ahead," Derek said. "Tell me."

Royce lunged at Derek, swinging the shard like a blade. Derek sidestepped out of the way, then kept going, circling wide around Royce, luring him away from me, motioning for me to resume banishing.

Royce charged. The china shard came a little too close to Derek, giving my mental shove a little panicky oomph, and Royce's half-materialized form wavered.

Again, Royce swung too hard. This time the shard sailed from his hand. He scrabbled after it. Derek got there first, stomping the piece under his sneaker.

Royce raced for the rest of the plate. Derek managed to step on the biggest piece, but Royce snatched up another. I gave him another big push. Again he wobbled.

Royce walked backward, eyeing Derek. Derek's gaze stayed glued to the new shard—tracking Royce.

"You like science, don't you?" Royce said. "Well, I'm going to try an experiment of my own. Like I was asking before, how much do you know about werewolf legends?"

Again, I repeated his words. Derek still said nothing, only backing up, keeping Royce's focus on him, letting me work at banishing the ghost.

"I don't remember many of them," Royce went on. "It was pretty boring stuff, at least the ones Uncle Todd told us. But he had others—books he didn't want us to read. There was this one about werewolf trials. Seemed every medieval serial killer tried to get off with the werewolf defense. There was this one cool story about a guy who told the court he was a werewolf. Only problem was, they'd seen him kill someone— and he looked human. So do you know what he said?"

Derek motioned for me to relay the message. I did, as best I could.

"He said, my fur is on the inside," Derek replied.

Royce laughed. "Guess I'm not the only one who likes the gory old stories. All right then, tell the little necro how it ends. What did the court do?"

I hesitated to relay the question, but Derek insisted on getting the message, then said, "Cut off his arms and legs and dissected them to check for fur inside the skin."

Royce looked at me. "Sadly, there wasn't any. But they'd saved themselves the fuss and bother of a trial."

He wheeled and ran at Derek. Derek's hands flew up to shield himself. The shard sliced the back of his hand, blood spurting.

Royce danced back. "I don't see any fur, do you? Guess we'll just have to keep going, to conduct a thorough experiment."

I saw the blood dripping down Derek's hand, shut my eyes, and gave one rage-filled shove. The shard clattered to the floor. Royce was still there, faint though, teeth gritted, tendons popping, struggling to hold on.

I walked toward him, mentally pushing, watching him fade until he was only a glimmer, and then—

"What have you done?" roared a voice behind me.

twenty-seven

I SPUN, EXPECTING TO see Andrew, but no one was there.

A ghost popped out in front of me, so close I fell back. Derek grabbed my arm to steady me.

"I think he's gone," Derek said. "Did you hear something?"

I looked up into the bearded face of Todd Banks, contorted with fury, eyes wild and red rimmed.

"I-it's Dr. Banks."

"Do you think this is a game?" Dr. Banks shouted. "Who told you about Royce? Did you think it would be amusing? Call him forth and see if he's as crazy as they said?"

Derek leaned down to my ear.

"Release him. Whatever he can tell us, it's not worth it."

I shook my head. Derek didn't like that, but settled for scowling and keeping his grip on my arm, like he'd yank me out of the room by force if things went bad.

Some of the anger seeped from Dr. Banks's eyes as he studied me.

"Chloe Saunders," he whispered. "You must be Chloe Saunders." He looked at Derek. "The werewolf boy."

"Yes," I said. "Derek. That's Derek."

The rage surged again, his eyes going crazy wild. "You must not summon here, girl. Leave my nephew in peace. Remember him, though, because that is your destiny. The power will grow until it consumes you and leaves a monster in your place. It will make you do things you could never imagine, things so horrible that—"

He teetered, as if fighting the memories. Hands closed around both of my arms, and I realized Derek had moved behind me. I could feel him there, strong and solid, his warm hands rubbing the goose bumps on my arms.

"Let him go, Chloe," Derek murmured. "Whatever he's saying, you don't need to listen to it."

"Yes," Dr. Banks said. "Yes, you do. You don't understand. Everything went wrong. We made mistakes. An error in the calculations—"

"With the genetic modification?"

"Yes, yes." He waved aside my interruption. "I told them. I *told* them. But they ran the tests and everything seemed fine. Only it wasn't. They manipulated the data."

"Manipulated the data?" I said.

That got Derek's attention. "What data?"

"For the modifications," I said. "What does that mean?"

"They changed the data so it gave the proper results," Derek said.

"Yes," Dr. Banks said. "Correct. See? Even a child can understand. But they couldn't."

"So Dr. Davidoff manipulated the data—" I began.

"Davidoff?" Dr. Banks snorted. "A fawning puppy who does whatever he's told."

"So who manipulated the data?"

Dr. Banks continued like he hadn't heard. "The experiments. Oh God, the experiments. Testing this and testing that, pushing the boundaries to discover what he could create and what he could sell. Such dreams. Mad and grandiose dreams of knowledge, power, and the fantasy of a better life for our kind. Fools that we were, we believed, and gave him free rein. He didn't care about us. And he doesn't care about you. That's why it's critically important that you—" He started to fade. "The magic in this place. You need to pull me back."

I did, gently at first, but he kept disappearing.

"Harder. Chloe. I need to tell you—"

He faded before I could catch the rest. I summoned again. He flickered in and out, and I caught only words, none meaning anything out of context.

"He's being pulled away," I said.

"Let him go," Derek said. "We've got enough."

"He was trying to tell me something."

Derek snorted. "Aren't they all? Must be a rule in the ghost handbook—if in danger of evaporating, make sure you're in the middle of a dire pronouncement."

I tugged off my necklace. I handed it to Derek, but he tucked it into my pocket.

"Keep it on you, okay?"

Dr. Banks came through easier now, but he wouldn't stay. When I ramped up the power, he said, "No, Chloe. You'll bring Royce." He faded, his voice pulsing in and out. ". . . else . . . try . . . Clear your mind . . . focus on me . . . don't pull . . . just focus."

I did. He kept talking, telling me to relax, focus not on yanking him through, but welcoming him.

The back of my skull began to throb. I kept going until a sharp, sudden pain made me gasp. I waited for Derek to ask what was wrong, but he just sat there, watching me.

Another stab through the back of my skull. Then a flood of ice-cold water rushed through my veins and I tried to scream, but I couldn't. Couldn't move. Couldn't make a sound.

"Chloe?"

I heard Derek, but couldn't even move my eyes his way.

"Do you want my help?" Dr. Banks whispered. "You need to welcome me in."

Welcome him in? In where? I'd barely thought the question when I realized the answer.

He was trying to get inside me.

I fought, mentally trying to shove him out, shut my brain down, block him, but that ice kept spreading through me. Derek's hand closed on my shoulder as he reached to grab the necklace from my pocket. I toppled over backward like a statue.

I caught a blur of motion, like Derek had lunged for me, but everything was fuzzy. Even his voice was distant and muffled. The only words I could hear were Dr. Banks's, crooning inside my head.

"Just relax," he whispered. "I won't hurt you. I'm only going to borrow your body. I need to fix this. I took the easy way out, killing myself before I'd put an end to the horrors I began."

My mother had been warning me about Dr. Banks, that he'd been driven mad by what Royce had done, by his role in it. And now he was inside me.

I felt the floor scrape my back, saw the ceiling whoosh past, like Derek was dragging me by my ankles. The room flickered and went dark. When it popped back, I was staring at the ceiling.

"Wha-what happened?"

I felt my lips move and heard my voice, but no one answered. I got to my feet.

"Chloe, come on," Derek said behind me. "Say something."

"Say what?"

I turned. He was crouched across the room. A pair of legs stretched out, sneakers pointing to the ceiling. My sneakers. My legs.

I raced over. There I was, lying on the floor as Derek fumbled to get the necklace over my head. I lifted my hand. It was my hand—still covered in scratches from the forest last night.

"Derek?"

He didn't answer. I reached for his shoulder.

My fingers passed right through it.

I was a ghost.

My eyes opened then—the eyes on my body, lying on the floor. The lips curving in a small smile that wasn't like mine at all.

"Hey, there." The voice coming from those lips was mine, but the tone, the inflection, were wrong.

Derek frowned, and tried getting the necklace on me again.

The other me batted his hand away. "I don't need that."

"Yes, you do."

"No, I don't."

Derek smacked my hand away and yanked the necklace over my head. The pendant hit my skin and I *felt* the slap of it, hot as a burning brand, and I gasped—me and my body, gasping in unison. A flash of darkness. Then I was staring at the ceiling again.

Derek's face appeared, green eyes dark with worry.

"Chloe?"

I breathed. That was all I could do. Inhale. Exhale. I felt Derek's hands around mine, and I focused on that.

"What happened?" he asked.

"I—I—I—"

A voice behind Derek laughed. "Do you think I can't get back inside you? I will. Then I'll help your friends stop the Edison Group." Dr. Banks loomed over me, face in mine, eyes flashing with madness. "We'll hunt down the other subjects and I'll end their suffering, and then I'll end your friends'. Once they're gone, you'll follow, and you can all be together . . . in the afterlife. I *will* finish this."

"No, you won't," I said, getting up.

He smiled. "You might have the power, Chloe, but you have no idea how to use it."

"Oh, yes, I do."

I reached out and shoved him—with my mind and with my hands, pouring all my rage into it, and for a second, I swore I actually felt him. Then he flew off his feet, sailing backward, screaming as he disappeared.

"Chloe?"

Derek touched my shoulder and I wanted to turn around, collapse against him, and tell him everything. I steeled myself against the urge and took a deep breath.

"We need to get out of here," I said. "As soon as we can."

*   *   *

As it turned out, we'd be leaving sooner than any of us dared hope. Andrew had returned, alone. Russell was gone. He'd packed and left his apartment before Andrew had got there.

We could hear Margaret and Andrew on the speaker-phone with other group members. It was clear, Margaret said, that we were indeed more than they could handle, and the best way to relieve themselves of the burden was to hand us over to someone else—namely Aunt Lauren and, if they could find him, Simon's dad.

I didn't care that Margaret's motivation was purely selfish—I could have run in there and hugged her.

We were leaving tomorrow, heading to Buffalo. That meant it was time to start planning in earnest. Andrew asked me to provide details of the laboratory. I tried—this was the moment I'd dreamed of—but every word was a struggle. It was like someone cut my energy cord. I was completely drained and numb.

The guys helped. Simon drew the lab floorplan as I explained. Derek got me a glass of ice water. Even Tori murmured "Are you okay?" at a break in the conversation. Only Margaret seemed oblivious, grilling me until she finally had enough and dismissed us. I made it into the parlor, walking only until I found an armchair, then curling up in it. I was asleep the second my eyes closed.

When I woke up, I was still in the chair, a blanket tucked in around me, my glass of water waiting on the table. Derek sat a few feet away on the sofa, lost in thought as he stood watch. Stood watch for what, I didn't know. It didn't matter. Threat or no threat, it felt good to wake up and see him there.

And as I watched him, I realized *how* good it felt. All my denials were just that—denials—because it would be easier if we were just friends. But it wasn't like that, not for me.

I wanted to walk over there. I wanted to curl up beside him, lean against him, talk to him. I wanted to know what he was thinking. I wanted to tell him everything would be okay. And I wanted him to tell me the same thing. I didn't care if it was true or not—I just wanted to say it, to hear it, to feel his arms around me, hear the rumble of his words, that deep chuckle that made my pulse race.

He turned my way, and I was so engrossed in my thoughts that I didn't notice for a second. Then I realized I was staring at him, and looked away fast, cheeks flaming. I could feel him looking at me. Frowning slightly, like he was trying to figure something out. Before he could, I gulped my warm water and said, "Must be almost lunchtime," which was a stupid thing to say, but all I could think of. It took him a moment before he answered, shrugging and saying, "Maybe." Then, "You okay?"

I nodded.

"You want to talk about what happened downstairs? With Banks?"

I nodded again.

"I should get Simon," he said. "He'll want to know."

Another nod, but he didn't move, just watched me as I kept sipping the warm water.

"Chloe."

I took my time looking up, certain he'd figured out what I'd been thinking and was about to let me down gently. He wouldn't say "Sorry, I'm not interested," because that wouldn't be Derek—too presumptuous—but he'd find some way to convey the same message, as I had with Simon. *I like you. I just don't like you that way.*

"Chloe?"

I looked up then, and what I saw in his eyes— My hands fumbled the glass, and I dropped it, water splashing over me, soaking my jeans. I scrambled to catch the glass before it hit the floor, barely making it, on one knee, prize gripped firmly in my hand. And I was still there when I felt the glass being tugged from my fingers. I looked up to see Derek crouching in front of me, his face inches from mine. He leaned forward and—

"What'd you lose?"

Simon's voice came from the doorway, and we shot to our feet so fast we collided.

"What were you looking for?" Simon said, walking in. "Not your necklace, I hope."

"N-no. I—I just dropped my glass." I gestured at my wet jeans. Then I glanced at Derek, who stood there, hands stuffed in his pockets.

"I was just about to . . ." I was going to say I'd been

about to explain what happened with Dr. Banks. Only I didn't want to. Not now. I wanted to rewind the tape, go back to that moment on the floor, pray Simon didn't show up for another minute, just long enough to find out if what I thought was going to happen *would* happen. But it wouldn't. Not now. The moment had passed.

"I—I should change my pants."

"Sure." Simon thumped onto the sofa.

I made it to the door, then Derek said, "Chloe?" and I turned, and it looked like he was trying to think of something to say, maybe find some excuse to come with me, and I wanted to help, to offer him one, and I think if I could have, he'd have taken it, but I couldn't. God knows, I tried, but I couldn't, and he couldn't either, so he just mumbled, "You want an apple or something? I'll grab it while you're getting changed," and I said sure, and that was that.

twenty-eight

HOW LAME DOES IT sound if I admit I stayed upstairs
longer than necessary, combing my hair, washing
my face, using a blow dryer on my jeans when I
realized my new ones didn't fit well, then brushing my teeth.

Considering Derek had seen me in ugly pink pajamas,
dirt on my face, my hair full of twigs, having minty-fresh
breath wasn't going to make him go "Wow, she's really cute."
But it made me feel better.

When I left our room, I went looking for Tori. She'd taken
off after the planning meeting, saying something about clean-
ing, so we hadn't had time to update her on Royce and Dr.
Banks. On the main level, I followed the vacuum cord in the
hall and found her in the library, at the bookshelf, dusting off
the old, leather books.

"I don't think you need to do that anymore," I said.

"We're leaving tomorrow."

"I don't mind."

She pasted on a smile, and I don't know what tipped me off—that smile or Tori claiming to enjoy dusting. I stepped in and looked around. A light flickered as the kaleidoscope screensaver started up on the open laptop.

"That's Margaret's computer," I said, walking over to it. "Were you on it?"

"Just trying to email some friends and let them know I'm okay, but there's no internet."

"Uh-huh."

"You don't believe me? Check. No wireless and I can't find an outlet, not surprising when this place doesn't even have the phones hooked up."

"That's not what I meant." I turned to her. "Endangering us by emailing your friends? No way."

She settled on the edge of the desk. "See, now that's progress, because a week ago, you would have totally bought it."

I jiggled the mouse. It brought up a file system window. I looked at her.

"It's not what you think," she said.

"What do I think?"

"That I'm a spy for the Edison Group, gathering intelligence. Or trying to contact them, let them know where we are."

"You aren't a spy."

A wry smile. "I don't know if I should thank you for the

vote of confidence or blast you for being too nice to accuse me to my face. I know that's what the guys think. Especially Derek. And I bet I know why they think that, too."

"Why?"

"Because I got away too easily at Andrew's house. They're right. I *did*." She eased back on the desk. "I didn't think so at first. When I escaped, I was all, like, 'God, I'm good. Those idiots didn't know who they were dealing with.'" She laughed, but it wasn't an easy laugh. "Once things cooled down, I thought, 'Yeah, I'm good, but not that good.' They knew I had magical outbursts when I got mad. So they knew I wasn't some helpless teenage girl. If I got away that easily, maybe it was because they let me."

"Why?"

"That's the question, isn't it? At first, I thought they'd planted something on me. I was shaking out my clothes, washing them. I even ironed them, to be sure."

"That was a good idea."

"No, it's nuts. I've been hanging around you guys too long. But I also figured, if the Edison Group could catch only one of us that night, planting a GPS and releasing me *would* be a good idea. I wasn't about to be the one who led them to us. So I went overboard making sure there was no transmitter."

"And there wasn't."

"As far as I could tell. That leaves option two: they released me because I'm the small fish in the pond. I wasn't worth keeping."

"I can't imagine—"

"Think about it. They get word that werewolf boy is on the rampage. Then they hear that Andrew has escaped. Suddenly, I'm not double-guard worthy. They leave me with one and hope he can keep me. He couldn't."

"Okay, so"—I waved at the computer—"what are you doing?"

"Trying to prove I'm not a spy. By spying." She turned the computer toward her. "Doing some intelligence work of my own is the best way to show I'm not a complete waste of space. When Andrew said they couldn't get in touch with Gwen that got me thinking."

She typed as she talked, fingers flying over the keyboard. "Russell obviously didn't act alone. Maybe Gwen was in on it, but I don't think so. She didn't like him."

"No?"

"He thought she was a ditzy blonde. The only time he got near her was when he was trying to look down her shirt. He's not evil genius material, either. Someone else masterminded the scheme to capture Derek, and they're also behind the plan to get rid of the rest of us. I nominate Margaret. I've gone through her files and email. Now, I'm digging into the stuff she deleted—or thought she did. Even after you empty your deleted folder or recycle bin, it's still there, if you know how to find it."

She started typing, flipping through folders so fast I got dizzy watching.

"You really are a computer—" I began.

"Say 'geek' and I'll use you for spell practice. I'm a software designer. But, yes, I know a few things about hacking, courtesy of a loser ex-boyfriend who used his talent to change his grades so he could spend more time gaming. Like World of Warcraft is going to help you through college. I had him teach me the basics, though, before I dumped him. You never know when it might come in handy."

I'm sure it had come in handy before now. I remembered how Tori had blackmailed Dr. Davidoff into letting her leave the lab.

"Okay, I've got some deleted emails. I'm searching on all our names and Simon's dad's. Who were those werewolf guys Russell hired?"

"Liam and Ramon, but Liam was the contact. That's L-I—"

She gave me a look. I shut my mouth and let her type. Nothing came up.

"Are there any to or from Russell?"

"Yep, he's MedicGuy56. I found him in her contact list. I'll take a look."

She was flipping past one sent to Russell when I caught a word that made me tell her to stop. Syracuse. Home of the werewolf Pack. The note gave instructions for finding a house outside a town called Bear Valley, near Syracuse.

I read on.

Tomas says not to go to the house. Wait and approach them off the property, preferably in a public setting, and definitely when the children are not present. If possible, approach the Alpha or the woman. Tomas says he cannot stress these things enough. Do not go directly to the house. Do not approach when the children are there.

"Alpha?" Tori said.

"It's a wolf term. It means the pack leader. These were instructions for turning Derek over to the Pack."

"Well, then, we've got our evidence."

"Keep looking. The more we can find, the better. Search on Alpha, Pack, Bear Valley, Tomas . . ."

"Yes, ma'am."

At a sound in the hall, I scurried to the door. It was Margaret, but she was heading the other way. Behind me, Tori murmured, "No, that's . . ." She trailed off, then swore under her breath.

I hurried over. She was staring at an email with only a few terse lines from Margaret, assuring the sender that she'd conveyed Tomas's instructions to the "person Russell has hired to resolve the situation."

"Great, more proof," I said. "So what's the problem?"

She just pointed to the recipient's email address: acarson@gmail.com.

"A-Andrew? No, that can't be right. Is there another Carson?"

"That's Andrew, Chloe. I checked her contact list and other emails. And there's a response, too."

She flipped to a second email. Another short one, basically an "okay, thanks" from Andrew.

"Check the date," she said.

It'd been sent the day we'd first met Liam and Ramon. A day when Andrew had, supposedly, been in the Edison Group's custody.

twenty-nine

TORI KEPT SEARCHING. THERE wasn't much more—just enough to confirm what we'd already figured out. Andrew had been part of the plot to turn Derek over to the Pack. And he hadn't been anyone's hostage.

"So Andrew is part of the Edison Group?" Tori said. "That doesn't make sense."

"No, it doesn't." I pushed the laptop back and sat on the desk. "You were with me at the laboratory. Between the two of us, we saw a lot of staff members. Did you recognize any of them that night at Andrew's?"

"That was a security team. We never got a chance to see them before."

"Sure we did. Simon, Derek, and I did on the night we escaped Lyle House. You and I did after we escaped the Edison Group. What we saw, both times, was mainly staff with only a couple of guards. If they had some high-powered secu-rity team, wouldn't they have called them in for that?"

"Maybe it *was* the staff and the guards. How would we know? They were wearing . . ." She looked at me. "They were wearing things on their hats, covering their faces. They didn't do that at the warehouse when they were chasing us."

"Or the night Derek and I escaped Lyle House. Why hide their faces when we'd already seen them?" I thought back to that night. "You weren't the only one who got away too easily."

"Andrew, you mean."

"Not just him. I was hiding up in a tree. One of the women found me. I dropped on top of her. Stupid thing to do, but it worked—she was knocked out cold. Or so I thought."

"See, we're both just that good."

"Apparently not."

We tried to exchange a smile.

"The Edison Group didn't track us to Andrew's," I said. "That's what my mom was trying to tell me."

"If you guys are going to talk about that, you might want to go up on the roof," Derek rumbled from the doorway. "Or be a little quieter. I could hear you from down the hall."

"Because you've got bionic hearing," Tori said.

I started to say something, but Derek beat me to it.

"Simon had to go talk to Andrew. I thought maybe you . . ." He glanced at Tori, annoyed, like she was eavesdropping. "I thought there might be old files in the attic. You want to come up and see? Maybe get some more info on Dr. Banks?"

I had to stifle the urge to say "Sure!" So what if we'd just discovered that the people giving us refuge were the same ones who tried to kill us three nights ago? Finding out whether Derek liked me was *so* much more important.

"I can't," I said. "We—"

"That's okay," he cut in, starting to retreat.

I stepped forward to stop him. "I would. But—"

"But Chloe can't come out to play right now," Tori said. "She's in the middle of helping me unravel a conspiracy, a matter of life or death. *Our* life or death."

"The Edison Group didn't attack us at Andrew's place," I said. "He did. Andrew and the others."

I told Derek what we'd found. For once, I hoped he'd say I was wrong, that my logic was flawed and there was a perfectly reasonable alternate explanation.

But when I finished, he swore. Then he paced, swearing some more, until he stopped and shoved his hair back.

"We're wrong, aren't we?" I said. "We misinterpreted the data."

"No, you didn't."

It was my turn to swear then, making Tori arch her brows.

"I'm just mad at myself," Derek said. "I saw the possibility. I wondered whether we all got away too easily that night at Andrew's. I wondered why they shot at us when they used darts before. I wondered why they covered their faces. I just never thought it could have anything to do with Andrew. I *did* think he might be behind the kidnapping attempt last night, though."

"But you said—"

"That I trusted Andrew. I did. But he thinks I'd be better off with my own kind, so I wanted to see his reaction. That told me he wasn't involved. Or so I thought."

"He seemed genuinely surprised," I said. "Furious, even."

"Guess he's a good actor," Tori said. "Okay, so am I the only one who's wondering why they went through the trouble of that fake Edison Group attack when we were already going to Andrew's place?"

"Going doesn't mean staying," Derek said.

"Huh?"

"We might not stay with Andrew," I said. "If things didn't quite go our way. We've already run away twice."

"So if they convinced us the Edison Group had tracked us down and was lurking out there, prepared to shoot to kill . . ."

"That would trap us better than guard dogs and barbed wire."

I quickly looked at the door. "You said Simon was with—"

Derek swore. "Right. He's with Andrew. I'm sure whatever's going on here, hurting Simon isn't part of the plan, but I'll go get him. I'll remind him it's past his snack time. He needs to have morning and afternoon snacks for his blood sugar, so that won't sound suspicious."

I nodded. "We need to be careful."

"Screw caution," Tori said. "I'm outta here."

We looked at her.

"Well, I am. As long as someone comes with me."

We kept looking at her.

She sighed. "Fine, but when everything goes to hell, just remember, I get to blame you guys, because I wanted to leave right away."

"We are leaving right away," Derek said, "just as soon as we know as much as possible about their plans. You said that was Margaret's laptop, not Andrew's, right?"

I nodded. "But I know a way to get Andrew's, if you want Tori to search it."

"Good. Do that. I want to know exactly what they have in mind."

thirty

"ANDREW?" I PEEKED INTO the kitchen, where he was getting a snack with the guys.

"Hmm?"

"That book you were going to let me read . . ."

"Oh, right. My laptop is in the office. Should be all powered up."

"Is there a password?"

He smiled. "Nope. As valuable as I think unpublished manuscripts are, there's not really a black market for them. There's a link to the book right on the desktop for you."

He gave me the title.

"Tori wanted to take a look, too, if that's okay?"

"Absolutely. The more feedback I can get from the target audience, the better. If anything sticks out—problems with the characters, the plot, the language—let me know."

Tori rolled her eyes at the lack of security on Andrew's laptop. Like most people who weren't tech-savvy, he presumed if he deleted stuff, it was gone. Or maybe he knew traces remained, but figured we wouldn't know how to find them. And he'd have been right . . . if we didn't have Tori.

We started with an email search and found the ones he'd exchanged with Margaret, removing any doubt it'd been him. There were also a few between him and Tomas, where Andrew seemed determined to ensure a safe transfer of Derek to the Pack. Had he really been that concerned for Derek's safety? Liam clearly had orders to kill if necessary. Was that decision made behind Andrew's back? That would explain why he'd seemed so genuinely shocked when he'd found out what had happened to Derek and me.

Or maybe I just wasn't ready to see Andrew as one of the bad guys yet. I'd liked him. I really had. Yet it only took one more email for those feelings to evaporate, one that had nothing to do with Liam and Russell or the Edison Group. When Tori found it, we both read it and read it again, neither of us saying a word until I managed a shaky, "I-I'd better get the guys."

"I'll see if there's more," she said as I raced off.

I finally tracked down Derek. He was alone in the library, thumbing through a book.

"Found you," I said on a sigh of relief.

He turned. His lips curved in a quarter smile, gaze softening in a way that did something to my insides, made me pull up short, momentarily forgetting why I was there.

"I-Is Simon around?"

He blinked, then turned back to the shelf.

"He's upstairs. He's really pissed about Andrew so that's probably the safest place for him until we're ready to go, or he'll say something to him we don't want said. You need him?"

"Actually, m-maybe I should show you first."

He glanced over his shoulder, frowning.

"We found something."

"Oh." He paused, like he was mentally shifting gears, then nodded and followed me out.

Tori swiveled in her seat as we came in.

"There are more," she said. "He sent one every couple of weeks. The last one was only a few days ago."

"Good," I said. "Would you mind keeping an eye on Andrew?"

"Sure." She took off.

"Wait." I grabbed Derek's sleeve as he headed for the chair Tori had vacated. I wanted to say something. I didn't know what. But there was no way to tell him that wouldn't be just as much of a shock, so I ended up stupidly murmuring, "Never mind."

When he read what was on the screen, he went absolutely

still, like he wasn't even breathing. After a few seconds, he yanked the laptop closer, leaning in to read it again. And again. Finally, he pushed back the chair and exhaled.

"He's alive," I said. "Your dad's alive."

He looked up at me and, I couldn't help it—I threw my arms around his neck and hugged him. Then I realized what I was doing. I let go, backing away, tripping over my feet, stammering, "I-I'm sorry. I'm just— I'm happy for you."

"I know."

Still sitting, he reached out and pulled me toward him. We stayed there, looking at each other, his hand still wrapped in my shirt hem, my heart hammering so hard I was sure he could hear it.

"There's more," I said after a few seconds. "More emails, Tori said."

He nodded and swiveled back to the computer, making room for me. When I inched closer, not wanting to intrude, he tugged me in front of him and I stumbled, half falling onto his lap. I tried to scramble up, cheeks burning, but he pulled me down onto his knee, one arm going around my waist, tentative, as if to say *Is this okay?* It was, even if my blood pounded in my ears so hard I couldn't think. Thankfully, I had my back to him because I was sure my cheeks were scarlet.

I hadn't misunderstood his look earlier. This was something. Or it would become something, I hoped. God, I *hoped*. Right now, though, there was too much else going on. I hated that, but I was kind of glad of it, too, giving my brain time to stop spinning.

After a second—still perched on Derek's knee—I forced my attention back to the screen.

I read the first email again. Dated two months ago, it was a chain of three messages, the first, short and to the point.

It's Kit. Got myself in some trouble. Do you know where the boys are?

Andrew answered.

No, I don't. What kind of trouble? How can I help?

The reply was longer.

Nasts caught up with me. Saw an article on D. Tracked me down before I could run. Went with them to distract them from the boys. Kept me a few months until I finally gave them what they wanted. The boys are long gone. Thought EG, but no sign at the lab. Maybe Nasts? Child services? No idea. I need help, buddy. Anything you can do. Please.

He signed off giving a phone number and saying both it and the email address were temporary, but he'd be in touch again in a couple of weeks.

I flipped to the next email as Derek read over my

shoulder. There were three more of the same—Mr. Bae begging for news, Andrew saying he was looking for Simon and Derek, but his Edison Group contacts swore the boys weren't there.

The last one from Mr. Bae was dated three days ago, when Andrew had supposedly been held hostage by the Edison Group. That meant he'd gotten this *after* he knew where Simon and Derek were.

"There's one more on the list," Derek said. "It must be a reply."

It was, sent the night when Andrew and the others had been staking out his cottage, waiting to make their fake SWAT team swoop and gather us up.

Still nothing. I might have a lead, though. A guy who works for the Cortezes says there's a rumor they're holding a couple of teenage boys. I'll call as soon as I have more.

"Cortezes?" I said.

"A Cabal, like the Nasts. Corporations run by sorcerers. Rich and powerful. More Mafia than Wall Street, though."

"So Andrew was lying."

"Not just lying. Trying to send Dad on a wild-goose chase when he knew exactly where we were."

"This changes everything."

He nodded.

"We need to get out of here."

He nodded again, but didn't move. I leaned forward to grab a pen and paper from Andrew's desk, then jotted down the latest email address and phone number. When I handed it to Derek, he took a second to even notice my outstretched hand.

"You okay?" I said, twisting to face him.

"Yeah, just . . . Andrew. Getting rid of me, I could see. But keeping Dad away . . . Dad trusted him."

"And now we can't," I said. "Which sucks, but the main thing is that your dad's alive."

He smiled, hesitant at first, then a blazing grin broke through that made my heart stop. I recovered and grinned back and went to throw my arms around his neck, then stopped, blushing. Before I could pull back, he caught my elbows and put my arms around his neck and pulled me into a hug.

Then he jumped, chair swiveling so fast I nearly went flying. I heard footsteps in the hall and I scrambled off his lap just as Simon swung in, breathing heavily, like he'd come running.

"Tori said you wanted to see me? Something about Dad."

I moved aside so Derek could show him the emails, then stepped into the hall to watch for Andrew and to leave them alone. This was the news they'd been waiting for and they'd gone through hell thinking it might never come, so I tried not to eavesdrop.

"Chloe?"

Derek stood in the doorway. He motioned me back in. Simon was at the keyboard, control panel open.

"There's no Internet connection," I said, "if that's what you're looking for. No phone either."

"Andrew has a cell," Simon said.

"Too risky," Derek said. "There was a pay phone at the service station. We'll call on our way out, set up a place to meet him."

Simon's eyes lit up at the thought of finally talking to his dad. Then they clouded with anger, the thrill of seeing news from his dad warring with the pain of Andrew's betrayal.

"So we're going now, right?" I said.

"Yeah," Derek said. "We're going."

thirty-one

B Y NOW, WE WERE experts at this escaping thing. We filled Tori in, then split up to gather what we needed—clothes, money, food. We took turns, two packing while the other two hung out, talking so Andrew didn't wonder why he had a house with four teenagers in it and sudden silence. Thankfully Andrew spent the whole time in the kitchen. I don't think any of us could have faced him.

Tori and I were on make-our-presence-known duty when Derek slipped in with an armful of ski jackets.

"Found these in the basement," he said. "It got cold last time." He passed me a red one and gave Tori a blue one. "Simon's finding one that fits, then coming up. We'll head out the back door. You three will go on ahead. I'll stay inside and make sure Andrew doesn't come out until you're safe in the woods."

"And if he does?" I asked.

Derek rubbed his mouth, meaning he'd rather not plan for that possibility.

"Don't tell me you'll have any problem taking him out," Tori said. "After what he did to you? I say we handle him now, save us all this sneaking around. I'll use the binding spell. You guys tie him up."

"Works for me," Simon said, coming up behind us. "I still remember my knots from Scouts."

Derek hesitated. Then he looked at me, which surprised me a little, and I said, "I—I agree," not really sure he was looking for that, but he nodded, and I said, more firmly, "It's the best way. Otherwise, once he figures out we're gone, he'll—"

The doorbell rang. I wasn't the only one who jumped. Derek grabbed our bags, ready to bolt.

"Guys?" Andrew called. "Can someone get that? It's Margaret."

"That makes things a little tougher," Tori murmured. "But not much. She's old, and she's just a necromancer." A glance at me. "Sorry."

"Guys?" Andrew's footsteps tapped down the hall.

"Got it!" Simon called.

"We'll take out Margaret first," Derek murmured. "Tori can bind her. Simon can tie her. I'll go for Andrew. Chloe? Move the coats and bags into the closet, just in case."

Move the coat and bags? Sometimes I really wished my

powers were a little more, well, powerful. I hefted two back-packs as Derek headed for the kitchen and Tori and Simon went to the front door.

I was coming back for the second load when I heard Margaret's voice. Had Tori's binding spell failed?

"This is Gordon," Margaret was saying. "And this is Roxanne. With Russell and Gwen gone, we thought it was safe to bring a few more of our members in to meet you. Now, let's all go review our plans."

Tori wanted to take on all four, but suggested it only halfheart-edly. Four adults versus four kids meant bad odds, especially when we had no idea what supernatural types Gordon and Roxanne were. Our plan, then, was to sneak out as soon as they started their meeting. Except they wanted us in on that meeting. Simon opted out—he couldn't face Andrew—so Derek and I covered for him. I was the one they most wanted to talk to anyway, asking more questions about the Edison Group laboratory and staff.

I had to call on all my years of drama training to pull off that performance. That, and not look in Andrew's direction any more than absolutely necessary. I seethed the whole time, knowing they didn't care what I said, that they weren't planning on going back. I had no idea what they *were* plan-ning, only that we weren't sticking around long enough to find out.

Finally, they released us.

"Get Simon," Derek whispered to Tori as we hurried down the hall. "I'm going to move the bags out to the woods. Chloe? Cover me."

It would make more sense for Tori—the girl with the spells—to cover him, but I didn't suggest it. Derek still didn't trust her enough for that.

Tori didn't even make it as far as the stairs, when a voice called, "Kids? Are you back here?"

Derek swore. It was Gordon, the new guy.

"Over here," I said, walking to where he stood in the hall. Derek followed.

Gordon was about Andrew's age, average height, with a potbelly and graying beard, the kind of guy who'd be recruited to play the office Santa.

"Do they need us again?" I asked.

"No, they're busy making plans, so I thought I'd say hi. We didn't get much of a chance to chat in there." He walked over to Derek and beamed a wide smile, shaking his hand. "You don't remember me, do you? I'm not surprised. You were just a little guy the last time we met. I used to work with your dad. We played poker on Tuesdays." He clapped a hand on Derek's shoulder and steered him into the living room. "Andrew tells me you're quite the science whiz. I teach physics over at . . ."

Gordon kept talking, leading Derek into the next room. Derek shot me a look, annoyance mingled with frustration. When I opened my mouth, though, he shook his head. We were stuck. Again.

"Are we going?" Tori whispered, returning with Simon.

"Not yet."

Gordon eventually called us all in. He'd known my aunt and Tori's mom, so now he wanted to get to know us a little better, too. Yesterday, we'd all have been thrilled with the chance to make a good impression and prove we were normal kids. Now, it was just creepy, giving our life stories to a guy who might be ready to kill us if our powers proved as uncontrollable as he feared.

After the meeting, they all decided to stay for dinner, and there was no way for us to get out, not all four of us with our backpacks.

"Can we leave them behind?" I asked. "We've got money. What if—?"

"Tori?" Andrew called. "Could you give me a hand with dinner?"

"Um, actually . . ." she began.

Andrew popped his head around the corner. Seeing all four of us clustered in the hall, he frowned, then forced a smile.

"Am I interrupting something?"

"Just making plans for a breakout," Tori said.

My gut twisted, eyes widening.

"We were hoping to sneak off for ice cream after dinner," she explained.

"Ah." Andrew ran his hand through his hair, looking uncomfortable. "I know you kids are tired of being cooped up here—"

"Developing serious cabin fever," Tori said. "Plus, my housekeeping wages are burning a hole in my pocket. We'll be careful, and we'll be back before dark."

"I know, but . . . No, guys. Sorry. No more going out." He tried for a smile. "We'll be leaving for Buffalo tomorrow and I promise we'll stop for ice cream on the way. Now, if I can get your help, Tori . . ."

He led her away.

"He knows," Simon said as we sat in the games room, pretending to play Yahtzee.

"It sure feels that way," I said. "But maybe we're just paranoid?"

We both looked at Derek.

He shook the dice onto the table a few times, deep in thought, then said, "I think we're okay. We're just nervous."

"We want out so it feels like they're blocking us." Simon exhaled and tried to settle into his seat, fingers drumming his leg.

"We should wait until tonight," Derek said. "Head to bed, then go after Andrew when he's asleep. The others will be long gone by then, and that'll buy us more time—no one will realize he's in trouble until morning."

"Makes sense," Simon said. "Question is, are we going to

make it that long without going nuts—"

He stopped as Derek cocked his head, then pivoted toward the door.

"Trouble?" Simon whispered.

"Cell phone."

"Um, yeah, they've all got them. So—"

"They're that way." Derek pointed left. "I'm hearing a muffled ring from the front door, where they left their coats."

"Okay, still not—" Simon shot up straight. "Cell phone. Dad." He scrambled up. "Where's the number?"

Derek held the paper with the number just out of his reach. "Cool it."

"Okay, okay." Simon took another deep breath, forcing himself to relax. "Cooled?"

Derek handed it over.

I hung back, again reluctant to intrude, but Derek motioned me along. As we neared the front door, he waved Simon ahead, whispering that we'd stand guard while he called.

"So what'd you think of that book Andrew is editing?" Derek asked.

I gaped up at him. Very attractive, I'm sure.

"Talk to me," Derek whispered.

"Right. Sorry. It's . . . good so far. I—"

"No signal," Simon hissed, peeking around the corner.

"Move around," Derek whispered back. "Andrew's been using his."

While Simon did that, I pretended to talk about the book, which wasn't easy when I hadn't read so much as a single line. So I blathered on with general comments about pacing and style, until Simon peeked again, waving frantically, phone at his ear as he mouthed "It's ringing!"

Derek motioned him back behind the corner, then told me to keep talking. I did, though I couldn't help hearing Simon.

"Dad? It's me. Simon." His voice cracked and he cleared his throat. "Fine. Well, okay." Pause. "He's right here. With me. We're with Andrew." Pause. "I know. We're trying to—" Pause. "No. Not Andrew's. It's a safe house. Belonged to a guy named Todd Banks. Big old— Dad? Dad?"

Derek strode off, motioning for me to stand watch.

"Signal," Simon whispered.

Derek started to say something, then swung around the corner, gaze fixed down the hall. Sure enough, a second later, I heard footsteps.

"Guys?" Andrew. "Dinner."

"Coming!" I called.

"Let me try—" Simon began.

"No," Derek said. "I need to erase the outgoing call. Get in the kitchen with Chloe. We'll phone again from the service station tonight."

Everyone picked at dinner, forcing down only enough to make it look good. Derek kept whispering for us to eat, fill our stomachs, but he barely finished himself, too busy straining to hear the ring of the cell phone, worried his dad might call back and expose us.

He didn't. From what I'd heard of their dad, Derek got his cautious streak from him. Where a normal person would automatically call back after being disconnected, I suspected their dad would look up the number first and something about it—like Gordon's name attached to the listing—had stopped him.

He wouldn't try calling Andrew, either. The fact that Andrew hadn't told him we were with him spelled trouble. He wouldn't make contact. He'd just come looking for his boys.

Had he heard the part about us being in Dr. Banks's house? Did he know where that was? If so, would he come for us too late, get captured trying to save his sons after they'd left?

I reminded myself that the service station was only a fifteen-minute walk away. We could warn Mr. Bae before he tried anything. Unless he was close enough to the house to come for us *before* we left . . . A nice thought, but I knew we couldn't count on it and probably shouldn't even hope. We had a plan. We'd get out safely, find Mr. Bae, and with his help rescue Aunt Lauren and Rae.

Thirty-two

I RETREATED TO MY room at nine. Tori was there, engrossed in *The Count of Monte Cristo*. She didn't do more than wave until she finished her chapter. We talked for a while. Nothing important. Just talk, struggling to stay calm as we prayed for time to speed up. We were almost there, though. Just a few more hours . . .

Derek said Andrew never went to bed before midnight. If we wanted to get him after he was sound asleep, that meant waiting until two.

To my surprise, I fell asleep, so soundly that I didn't hear the alarm on the watch Derek had given me earlier. I woke to Tori shaking me with one hand, while trying to shut off the alarm with the other.

I yawned and blinked hard.

"Running away after you've barely slept in a week isn't a great idea," she said. "Luckily, I anticipated this."

She popped open a can of Coke and handed it to me.

"Not as good as coffee," she said. "But I bet you don't drink coffee, do you?"

I shook my head as I gulped it.

"Kids," she said, rolling her eyes.

The door flew open, Simon rushing in.

"Excuse me?" Tori said.

"It's Derek," he said to me. "I can't wake him up."

We ran from the room. Derek was still in his bed, sprawled, the sheets draped onto the floor. He lay on his stomach wearing only his boxers.

I shook his shoulder. My fingers were cool from the soda can, but he still didn't move.

"He's breathing," Simon whispered. "He just won't wake up."

Tori walked toward the bed. Out of the corner of my eye, I saw her give Derek a once-over.

"You know, from this angle, he doesn't look too bad," she said.

I glared at her.

"I'm just saying . . ."

I leaned over Derek, calling him as loudly as I dared.

"Personally, I'm more a running back girl myself," Tori said. "But if you like the linebacker type, he's—"

My glower shut her up.

"You're in my light," I said, waving her aside.

"Do you know first aid, Chloe?"

I shook my head.

"Then you're in *my* light. Scoot."

I let her through. She checked Derek's pulse and his breathing, saying both seemed okay, then leaned down to his face.

"Nothing weird on his breath. Smells . . . like toothpaste."

Derek's eyes opened, and the first thing he saw was Tori's face inches from his. He jumped and let out an oath. Simon cracked up. I madly motioned for him to be quiet.

"Are you okay?" I asked Derek.

"He is now," Simon said. "After Tori jump-started his heart."

"We couldn't wake you up," I said. "Tori was making sure you were okay."

He kept blinking, disoriented.

"I have a Coke in my—" I began.

"I'll grab it," Tori said.

I turned back to Derek. He was still blinking.

"Derek?"

"Yeah." He mumbled, like he was talking through marbles, then made a face and cleared his throat.

"How do you feel?" I asked.

"Tired. Must have been sleeping hard."

"Like a rock," Simon said.

"Do you feel groggy?" I asked.

"Yeah." He made a face again. "What'd I eat last night?"

A chill ran through me. "Does your mouth feel fuzzy?"

"Yeah." He swore and pushed himself up.

I grabbed the Coke from Tori as she came back. "He's been drugged."

"Drugged?" Simon paused only a second, then said, "Andrew."

"I'll grab our bags," Tori said. We'd taken them to our rooms last night, worrying they'd be found in the closet downstairs.

I got Derek's as he chugged the rest of the Coke.

"Andrew brought us sodas last night, before bed," Simon said as he took his bag.

"And he said which one was Derek's?"

"He didn't need to. Mine's always diet."

I looked at Derek as he wiped his hand over his mouth. "Are you going to be okay?"

"Yeah. Just let me get dressed."

Why would Andrew drug Derek? Were they coming for him tonight? Or had our paranoia been well placed and the group knew exactly what we were up to? Either way, our best fighter was out of commission.

"I'll stay with Derek," I said. "Simon, can you cover Tori and get to Andrew's room?"

He glanced at Derek for confirmation. Derek blinked

hard, focusing, then managed a slurred, "Yeah. Do that."

"But be careful," I said. "There's a good chance Andrew's not in his bed."

They came back ten minutes later.

"He's not here," Simon whispered.

"What?"

"There's no sign of him anywhere," Tori said. "The truck's outside, but there aren't any lights on in the house."

"And his shoes are gone," Simon said.

"Meeting someone," I whispered. "Someone must be here to take Derek, and Andrew's outside with him, trying to figure out how to do this."

"Or he's been taken," Tori said.

Derek rubbed his face, then gave his head a sharp shake. "Forget Andrew. Let's just go and be careful."

Simon threw Derek's arm over his shoulders, despite his brother's protests. I carried Derek's bag as well as my own; Tori had Simon's.

We peered down the dark hall. Derek sniffed. The last trace of Andrew was old, meaning he hadn't come upstairs since delivering the sodas. Derek stood at the top of the main staircase and listened, then shook his head. No sounds from below.

We headed for the stairs at the back of the house, the narrow ones we'd found earlier, probably for servants once upon a time. It was one area Tori hadn't cleaned—nor had anyone in years, apparently, and I had to cover my nose and mouth so dust didn't set me sneezing.

When we reached the bottom, I was in the lead, Tori right behind me, and Simon helping Derek at the rear. The stairs ended at a door. I turned the knob slowly, trying to be quiet. It twisted partway, then stopped. I pushed. The door didn't budge.

Tori shouldered past me and tried. "Locked," she whispered. "I thought you guys—"

"Checked all the doors last night," Simon said. "We did. It was open."

"Move," Derek mumbled, his voice still thick.

We squeezed aside. He wrenched the knob and the lock snapped, making me wince at the noise.

The stairs opened into a dark, low ceilinged room. An old pantry or something. Tori flicked on her flashlight. The room was filthy and empty—another reason no one used these stairs. This time, she was first to the door. I knew what she'd find even before she announced it.

"Locked."

"Seriously?" Simon whispered.

Derek strode past, awake now. He twisted the knob and, again, the lock snapped. He yanked the door. It didn't budge. He pulled harder, making the hinges groan.

"It's spell-locked," said a voice behind us.

We turned as Andrew stepped through the stairwell doorway. Simon's fingers flew up for a knock-back spell.

Derek wheeled to charge. Andrew swung his hand toward me. Sparks flew from his fingers. Simon and Derek both stopped.

Andrew gave a wry smile. "I thought that might work. Simon, you know how this goes. I've got a spell all set to launch. It only takes a word to finish it."

"Wh-what kind of spell?" I whispered, hypnotized by those sparks jumping at me.

"Lethal," Andrew said.

Derek growled. A real growl, so wolflike it made the hair stand up on my neck.

Off to the side, Tori mouthed something at me. I couldn't make it out, but guessed she was warning me she was going to cast.

"No," Derek said, the word still almost a growl. His gaze was fixed on Andrew, and I thought he was talking to him, but then his eyes slid Tori's way. "No."

"Listen to Derek," Andrew said. "If he thought there was any way of getting to me before I launched this spell, he'd do it himself. Tori, move in front of me, please, so I can see your lips. Simon, sit on your hands. Derek?"

I glanced over at Derek. His gaze was riveted on Andrew, eyes blazing, the muscles in his jaw taut. Andrew said his name again, but he didn't seem to hear, fists clenching and unclenching at his sides.

"*Derek*," Andrew said, sharper.

"What?" Another growl passing as a word.

Andrew flinched, then caught himself and squared his shoulders. "Turn around."

"No."

"*Derek.*"

Derek only glowered. Then he tilted his head and I couldn't see his expression, but something in it made Andrew draw back, just a little. His Adam's apple bobbed. He tried to straighten again, tried to meet Derek's gaze, but couldn't quite manage it. His fingers flexed, sparks jumping as they faced off.

"Derek?" I whispered. "Please. Don't do this."

He started at the sound of my voice, breaking eye contact with Andrew, and the second he did, his expression changed, the wolf drawing back, Derek returning.

"Do as he says," I said. "Please."

He nodded and slowly turned to face the wall.

"Thank you," Andrew said. "I'd hoped to avoid this, but I guess I underestimated the dose. I don't want to hurt you, Derek. That's why I knocked you out. I don't want to hurt any of you. I'm here to protect you. I always have been."

Simon snorted. "Yeah, sure you don't want to hurt Derek. You asked those werewolves to kill him painlessly, right?"

"I didn't try to kill Derek."

"No, you hired someone to do it. You're too big a coward to look him in the face and pull the trigger. Or maybe it was the mess you were worried about. I know how much you like your clothes. Bloodstains are such a bitch to get out."

"I didn't—"

"We found the emails!" Simon jumped to his feet, then at a look from Derek, stopped and lowered himself to the floor again. "We know you were in on it."

"Yes, I was in on the plan to hand Derek over to the Pack. That's what you found, isn't it? Nothing about me giving them permission to kill him. That was entirely Russell's doing. Our plan was to turn him over to the Pack. Tomas and I learned everything we could about them until we were satisfied they wouldn't kill a sixteen-year-old werewolf. They're like any other organized group of supernaturals—a place for their race to learn how to control their powers and live in the human world. A place where they can be with their own kind."

I looked over at Derek, bracing myself to see a glimmer that said that's what he wanted. But he only stared at the wall, his gaze empty, emotionless.

"That's what I think is best for you, Derek," Andrew said. "Werewolves belong with werewolves."

"And sons belong with fathers," I said quietly.

Andrew stiffened. His gaze shot to mine, wary.

"We found those emails, too," I said. "You kept their dad away from them."

A pause. Then, "Yes, I did. And there's a reason."

"Sure there is," Simon said, his voice dripping with sarcasm. "Let me guess. Our dad is really an evil Cabal sorcerer. Or an Edison Group double agent. Take your pick. He's a bad, bad guy who'd kill us if he got the chance."

"No, Simon," Andrew said, his voice softening. "Your dad is the best father I know. He gave up everything—his career, his friends, his life—to go on the run to protect you. He refused to join our group because it could endanger you. His priority is you two, not taking down the Edison Group. He would never let me take you back to that lab to help stop them. If I called, he'd take you—all four of you—and run. He'll tell me to stop the Edison Group without you."

"Not a bad idea," Tori said.

Andrew shook his head. "If Kit takes you kids, then you're safe. If you're safe, then my people have no motivation to disband the Edison Group. I've been trying to convince them to do this for years, and now they're ready to act, but only if there's an immediate threat. If you're gone, they'll return to monitoring. And that's if they decide to *let* you go with him."

"Why wouldn't they?" Simon said. "Takes us off their hands."

"For many of them, that's the least of their worries, falling far behind their concern over the threat you pose to the supernatural world at large. If your dad comes . . ." He shifted, hand flexing, the spell wavering for a split second before surging again. "I hope that Russell acted alone when he told those werewolves to kill Derek and Chloe, but honestly . . . I don't know."

"Nice friends you've got there."

"Yes, some of them are my friends, Simon, but most are

like other members of a club. We share one interest, nothing more. That interest is protecting our world. For me, that means shutting down the Edison Group. For some of them—"

"It means shutting down us," I murmured.

"Don't listen to him, Chloe," Simon said. "He's a liar and a traitor. If these people are so worried about us, why are they leaving us alone with just you to watch us?"

"They aren't. That's why I had to stop you before you set foot out that door."

Simon laughed. It wasn't a nice laugh. "Right, because they're lurking in the dark, waiting to slam us with energy-bolt spells. No, wait, that's you, isn't it?"

Andrew lowered his fingers just a fraction, like he wanted to retract the threat. "Yes, they're there, Simon. Not right outside the door, but close enough, guarding the escape routes. Because that's exactly what they fear most. That you'll escape. That you'll run to humans and expose us. Or you'll lose control and expose us. You ran from Lyle House and you ran from the Edison Group. What's the first thing you'll do if you get a whiff of trouble? You'll run and—"

Derek lunged. He hit me in the shoulder and knocked me to the floor, landing on top of me. His body jerked, like he'd been hit with the spell, and I let out a yelp, struggling to get up, but he held me down, whispering, "I'm okay. It's okay," until the words finally penetrated.

I lifted my head to see Andrew caught in a binding spell as Simon hurtled to his feet. Simon tackled him and wrenched his hands behind his back. Derek got up to help. He pinned Andrew.

"Y-you're okay? He didn't hit you with a spell?" I said, walking over, knees wobbly.

"Yeah, he did."

Andrew lifted his head. "And, as you can see, it was the *nonlethal* energy bolt. I said I don't want to hurt you, Derek. I wouldn't have hurt Chloe, either. I only needed you to listen to me."

"We listened," Derek said. "Simon? I think I saw rope in the workshop. Chloe? Stay here. Tori? Cover Simon, in case there's anyone else in the house."

Thirty-three

DEREK HAD MORE QUESTIONS for Andrew. He asked about that night at Andrew's cottage. Andrew admitted he'd been part of the plan to stage his kidnapping and impersonate the Edison Group. The whole thing had been a setup—even giving us the opportunity to snatch a radio so we could hear about his "escape." They'd set themselves up as our rescuers, so they could take us into protective custody.

Simon came racing in and threw down a length of rope. "His cell phone. We can call Dad. Check his pockets."

"It's in the nightstand by my bed," Andrew said. "And it's useless. Reception has been cutting in and out and it's been out all night. I think someone's using a blocker on the house."

"I'm not taking your word for it," Simon said.

"I don't expect you to."

Sure enough, we couldn't get reception. Even sneaking onto the roof didn't help.

So Andrew was telling the truth about that. But what about the rest of it? Were his people really out there, waiting and watching? Or was this just another lie to keep us from running?

We bound and gagged Andrew and put him in the basement. Then we talked.

Not surprisingly, Tori wanted to make a break for it. Simon agreed. Neither wanted to be stuck here a moment longer than necessary. We should run and, if caught, as Tori said, "What are they going to do? Shoot us?" Problem was, that might be exactly what they'd do.

We didn't think Russell had acted alone. Had it been him and Gwen? Or more? How many people in this group secretly would be happy to see us dead—a convenient solution to the dilemma of our inconvenient existence.

Even if they didn't want us dead, if all four of us were caught sneaking through the woods with our backpacks, there'd be no question of what we were doing. We'd lose our chance to get away.

So, one of us should go. But who? Derek was the most likely to be killed if caught. Tori might roll her eyes at the suggestion we were in mortal danger, but she wasn't volunteering either. And Derek wouldn't entertain the idea of either Simon or me going.

We argued. Then we split up, Derek and Simon going downstairs to try to get more information from Andrew, and Tori deciding to keep searching Andrew's laptop, to see if there was anything there that we'd missed, something that might support or refute his claims.

As she searched, I knelt and tried to summon Liz. She'd be the perfect solution to this problem—she could zip out unnoticed and see if anyone was guarding the house. I was careful to picture her clearly and call her name, so I wouldn't accidentally summon Royce or Dr. Banks. There was someone else I'd love to contact—my mom—but I couldn't think about that. Even if I got her, I doubted I could hold her here long enough to search for us.

So I called Liz. And called and called, and didn't feel so much as a twitch.

"Derek with you guys?"

I jumped. Simon walked in. I got to my feet.

"I thought he was with you," I said.

"Nah. He made me test my blood sugar, and I grabbed a snack, but when I came back, Andrew was alone."

"I'll help you look."

I found Derek on the roof, looking, listening, and sniffing for signs of anyone guarding the house.

"Oh, this is a great idea," I said. "The guy they're most likely to shoot is standing on the roof, giving them a perfect target."

"They won't see me up here."

When I gave him a look, he sighed, like I was making a huge deal out of nothing, then sat and said, "Okay?"

"I don't think it's safe for you to be up here."

"Just a few more minutes." He took off his coat and held it out beside him. "Sit down here, between me and the chimney. It's safe."

"It's not me I'm worried about."

"I'm fine."

"How do you know that? They could have night vision goggles, sniper rifles . . ."

The corners of his mouth twitched and I braced myself for "You watch too many movies." He didn't say it, but I knew he was thinking it.

"You're not coming inside, are you?"

"I will. Just sit down. I want to talk to you."

"And I want you to come in. We can talk there."

"I don't smell anyone out here. I think Andrew's lying."

"Please, Derek? Come inside?"

"In a minute."

I turned and walked away.

"Chloe . . ."

I hoped he'd follow. I knew he wouldn't. He didn't.

*　　*　　*

"Found him," I said, meeting Simon in the upstairs hall. "On the roof."

"The *roof*? I suppose you told him he's an idiot."

"I asked him to come down. He won't."

"Because he thinks it's the right thing to do. The right thing for everyone *else*, that is. One day he's going to get himself—" Simon ran his hands through his hair. "I can talk to him. I can yell at him. It just doesn't get through. He's not suicidal. It's not that he doesn't care if he lives or dies. It's just—"

"Not a priority."

"Not if it interferes with protecting us. He can argue that's the wolf, but those two werewolves you met weren't throwing themselves in the line of fire to save each other, were they?"

"No."

He exhaled. "I might know a way to get him down. But don't hold your breath."

"I won't."

After Simon left, I knew what had to be done. There were only a few hours until daylight and we were sitting around like headlight-stunned deer, waiting for the car to hit us. We needed to know if there was really someone guarding the property, and there was only one way to do that properly.

Thirty-four

I STEPPED OUT THE back door and edged along the house, where Derek couldn't see me from the roof. The wind blew at my back, meaning my scent wouldn't carry to him. Good. I slipped into the woods.

The best way to find out if there was anyone watching the house was to send out a decoy. Of the four of us, I was the best choice. I didn't have Derek's strength or Tori's and Simon's spells. I was the smallest and the least able to defend myself; and as much as I might hate that, right now it was an advantage because I posed the least threat.

There was only one problem. The property was huge. That meant there was a lot of perimeter to cover. So how were they doing it? When Derek had asked that, Andrew said they were using spells. Simon wasn't convinced that was possible, but admitted he didn't know for sure.

And what about last night? It made sense that they hadn't been guarding the property when I was out with Derek—they had Liam and Ramon to do that. But what about earlier, when Simon and I had gone for ice cream? Andrew said they'd been tracking us and hadn't been concerned, knowing Simon wouldn't leave Derek behind. Still . . .

Did I really think we were under guard? No. Andrew was setting up imaginary bogeymen to keep us in the house until his friends showed up in the morning and rescued him. So all I had to do was prove I could make it to the service station.

To reach it, I needed to cut through the woods. As I walked, the lights from the house faded, and it got dark— "can't see my hand in front of my face" dark. I'd brought a flashlight, but once I was in the woods, I'd realized that wasn't my cleverest idea ever. I might as well stick a neon arrow over my head.

Without the flashlight, I'd be just as likely to alert some- one by stumbling and crashing around in the dark. So I used it—with my hand over the light, letting only a faint glow seep through.

The forest was dark, but it was far from silent. Twigs and leaves crackled. A mouse shrieked, its cry cut short by a sickening crunch. The wind whispered and wailed overhead. Even my feet made noise with every step. I tried to concen- trate on that, but the more I did, the more it sounded like a heartbeat, *thump-thump, thump-thump, thump-thump.* I swallowed and clutched the flashlight, plastic slipping under my sweaty fingers.

Just keep walking. Stay on the path. One foot in front of the other.

An owl hooted. I jumped. A snort, like a stifled laugh, and I spun, fingers slipping from the lens, the beam spinning in an arc, revealing nothing.

Who did you think was there? One of Andrew's group? Laughing at you?

I released my death grip on the flashlight and switched it to my other hand, wiping my damp palm on my jeans, then covered the beam again. I took a deep breath, breathing in air that smelled of rain. Rain and damp earth and the faint stink of decay. Dead things. Rotting things.

Another deep breath, then I started walking again, trudging along, shoulders hunched, burrowing as far into the ski jacket as I could, the bitter wind freezing my nose and ears.

I peered up, hoping for moonlight, seeing only patches of gray sky through the thick trees, branches entwined over my head like long, crooked—

I looked down, but the view wasn't any better. Endless trees stretched out on all sides, dozens of thick trunks, any of which could be a ghost, standing there, watching me, waiting . . .

The ground was softer here, and each step made a creepy, sucking sound. Undergrowth rustled to my left and I caught a whiff of decomposing flesh. An image flashed—the zombie dog and zombie rabbit and whatever else I'd raised last night.

Had I really released them all? Or were they still out here, waiting for me?

I walked faster.

A wordless whisper sounded behind me. I wheeled, fingers tightening on the flashlight. The voice kept whispering, the sound rippling around me. I followed it with the wavering light beam, but saw nothing.

Something hit my bandaged arm. I yelped and jumped. The flashlight flew from my hand, hit the ground, and went out.

I dropped and fumbled around until I found it. I flicked the switch. Nothing.

I knocked the flashlight against my knee, but it stayed off. I blinked hard, and gradually I could make out the squatting lumps of bushes and the gnarled trunks of trees.

"Afraid of the dark?" a voice whispered.

I knocked the flashlight again. Harder. Still nothing.

"That's a pretty red coat you're wearing. Little Red Riding Hood, all alone in the woods at night. Where's your big, bad wolf?"

A chill crept through me.

"Royce."

"Smart girl. Too bad you aren't smart enough to know what happens to little girls all alone in the woods at night."

I remembered the residual of the girl I'd seen at the truck stop, bloodied and beaten, crawling through the undergrowth, trying desperately to escape her attacker, only to have her throat slashed, to bleed out in the forest, be buried there.

Royce laughed, a deep laugh, rich with pleasure. He enjoyed my fear. Fed off it. I sucked it in, shoved the flashlight in my pocket, and started walking again.

"Do you know whose coat you're wearing? That's Austin's. His ski jacket. The color of blood. Fitting, isn't it? He died in a coat of red. Blood and brain and little bits of bone."

I walked faster.

"When I saw you coming, for a second, I thought it was Austin. But you don't look like him. Not at all. You're a pretty little girl, you know that?"

I tried to block his voice, concentrate on the thump of my footsteps instead, but they were softer now, too soft, and there was nothing else, just this dark, silent forest and Royce's voice. He'd materialized now, walking beside me. My skin crawled, and I resisted the urge to rub my arms.

"I like pretty girls," he said. "And they like me. Just gotta know how to treat them." His grin flashed in the darkness. "Would you like to meet one of my girls? She's not far from here. Sound asleep under a bed of leaves and dirt. You can wake her up, have a nice girl-to-girl talk, ask her what I did." He leaned over, whispering in my ear. "Or do you want me to tell you?"

I stumbled a little, and he laughed. I looked around, getting my bearings, but all I could see was the endless black forest. Something scampered across my path. Royce laughed again.

"Jumpy, aren't you? That's not good for a necromancer.

Your nerves will be shot long before the madness gets you."

I kept walking.

"Did they warn you about the madness?"

"Yes, your uncle told me how we'll all go crazy like you." Hearing my voice calmed my racing heart.

"Me? I'm not crazy. I just like hurting things. Always have. Uncle Todd just wouldn't see it. Told himself Austin's puppy had an accident, the neighbors' cats were killed by coyotes . . . You know how grown-ups are."

I walked faster. He kept pace beside me.

"When I said madness, I meant the curse of necromancy. They did tell you about that, didn't they? Or maybe they're afraid to. You're such a delicate little thing."

I said nothing.

"See, after a lifetime of seeing ghosts, necromancers—"

"I'm not interested."

"Don't interrupt me." His voice chilled.

"I know all about the madness," I lied, "so you don't need to tell me."

"Okay, we'll talk about the girl, then. Do you want to hear what happened to her?"

I veered left.

"Are you walking away from me?"

That cold edge slid into his voice again. I made it three steps, then something hit the side of my head. I staggered. An egg-sized rock bounced on the ground and rolled into my path.

"Don't ignore me," Royce said. "Don't interrupt me. Don't walk away from me."

I stopped and turned. He smiled.

"That's better. Now, what do you want me to talk about? What I did to that girl? Or the curse of necromancy? Your choice."

I gave him a mental shove. He flickered, then shot back, face screwed up with fury.

"Are you trying to piss me off? Because that's really a bad idea."

He disappeared. I spun, trying to find him. A rock hit me in the back of the head, so hard I blacked out for a second, coming to on my knees, blood trickling down my neck.

I leaped up and ran. The next stone hit my shoulder. I kept going, trying to envision him flying into the next dimension, but I couldn't focus, didn't dare shut my eyes even for a second, the undergrowth grabbing at my feet, branches whipping my face, path long gone.

A rock hit the back of my knee and I stumbled. I managed to keep my balance, staggering forward, then breaking into a run again. A branch poked my eye. Then my foot snagged in a vine and down I went, sprawling face-first on the ground.

I pushed myself to my hands and knees. Something whacked me between the shoulder blades, and I was knocked flat again, face in the dirt. A half-buried stick jabbed my cheek hard enough to draw blood.

I didn't try to get up this time. I lay on my stomach, head

down, eyes closed, trying to send Royce back to the other side.

"I told you to stop . . ." His voice trailed off as the blow struck—a light, glancing blow. The stick fell beside me, as if he'd weakened too much to hold it.

I pushed harder. The stick rose. I counted to three, then rolled out of the way. He materialized then, face a mask of rage. I leaped to my feet. He swung again, wildly now, and I easily ducked it. He flew at me, wielding the stick. I mentally hit him with everything I had. He flew clear off his feet, landing flat on his back, stick falling.

He grabbed for the stick, but it rolled away. He tried to snatch it. It jumped off the ground, spinning into the air. He glowered at me, like I was doing it. I wasn't.

The stick dangled above his head. He jumped for it. It swung sideways, out of his reach. He jumped again. It dropped to the ground.

Royce glared at me, and when he did, a figure appeared beside him—a teenage girl with long blond hair, dressed in a Minnie Mouse nightshirt and orange giraffe socks.

"Liz!"

"What?" Royce followed my gaze, but she'd disappeared.

I backed away. Royce grabbed for the stick. It rolled away from his fingers. He snatched it up—and it snapped in two.

When he glared my way, Liz appeared, wildly gesturing for me to banish him.

I closed my eyes. It was a struggle to keep them shut and not brace against a blow, but I trusted that Liz had it under control. I pushed him as hard as I could, envisioning all kinds of helpful scenarios—Royce falling off a cliff, Royce falling off a skyscraper, Royce falling out an airlock. It wasn't hard to come up with ideas.

Royce raged. He cursed. He threatened. But if he threw anything, it never reached me. His words surged and faded, growing weaker each time, until finally there was silence and Liz said, "He's gone."

Thirty-five

LIZ STOOD THERE, GRINNING. "We did it."

I laughed, a shaky two-seconds-from-crying laugh, my knees weak with relief.

She walked over. "So, I'm going to guess that loser is a telekinetic half-demon like me. From the experiment?"

I nodded.

"That doesn't mean I'm related to him, does it?"

"I don't think so."

"Whew, 'cause I've got enough nuts in my family tree already. And speaking of nuts, you have some kind of radar for them, don't you?"

"Apparently."

"It worked on me, though my crazy quotient must not be high enough yet, because it took me forever to find you. I could hear you calling, but answering was another matter."

"Thank you."

My voice wobbled. Liz hurried over, arm going around my shoulders. I couldn't feel her hug, but I could imagine it.

"Your poltergeist bodyguard is back on duty. Between the two of us, we can handle all the big, scary ghosts. I trounce 'em and you bounce 'em." She grinned. "Hey, that's pretty good."

I smiled. "It is."

"And speaking of big and scary, I'm going to guess you're out here with Derek, helping him Change into a wolf. You'd better grab him, because there's more in these woods than losers throwing sticks and stones. There are losers with spells and guns." She studied me. "And why do I get the feeling that's not a surprise?"

I explained, as quickly and quietly as I could.

"That Andrew guy is telling the truth," she said. "There are four people out here, dressed in black, carrying radios and rifles. That's not a lot, but they've got some high-tech gadgetry on their side—normal and supernormal. They've set up trip wires and those infrared laser things, and I heard them talking about something called perimeter spells."

"We need to get back, then, and—"

"Shhh. Someone's coming."

I crouched.

Liz whispered in my ear. "I don't think it's our poltergeist pal, but wait here. I'll go check."

She took off. I huddled as close to the ground as I could

get. When a huge figure reared up in front of me, I let out a yelp. It sprang forward.

"It's me," whispered a familiar voice.

"Der—"

Thwack. He stumbled, Liz behind him, a sturdy branch raised.

"Liz, it's—"

She hit him again, a home-run swing between the shoulders, and he went down with an *oomph* and an oath. She recognized the voice—or the curse—and leaned over, getting a look at him.

"Whoops."

"I'd say he deserved that, always sneaking up on people." Simon appeared from the direction Derek had come. He glanced around. "Hi, Liz . . ." I pointed and he turned her way.

"Hey, Simon."

I relayed her greeting as Derek got up, muttering.

"Did someone say Liz is here?" Tori stumbled out of the forest.

When I pointed at Liz, Tori smiled the brightest smile I'd seen from her since . . . well, I don't know when. Liz had been Tori's friend at Lyle House, and they said hello, me playing go-between.

"What are you guys doing out here?" I asked.

"We're your official search party," Tori said. "Complete with bloodhound."

She waved at Derek, who was brushing off his jeans.

"I left you a note," I said to Derek. "I told you where I was going and what I was doing."

"He got it," Simon said. "Didn't matter."

Derek glowered. "You think leaving a note makes it okay to do something—"

"Don't say stupid," I warned.

"Why not? It *was* stupid."

Simon winced and murmured, "Ease off, bro."

"That's okay," I said. "I'm used to it."

I looked up at Derek. He wavered for a second, then crossed his arms, jaw setting.

"It was stupid," he said. "Risky and dangerous. Those guys could be out here with guns—"

"They are." I turned to Simon and Tori. "Liz saw them. Andrew was telling the truth. We need to get back inside before they hear us fighting."

It was a silent walk back. At the rear door, Liz stopped. She reached, palm out, and it was like pressing against a pane of glass.

"I think there's a spell to keep ghosts out, like at Lyle House," I said. "You might be able to get in the basement or the attic, like you did there. Other ghosts have. I'll go—"

"I'm fine out here, Chloe. You go do your thing."

I hesitated.

She smiled. "Seriously. I'm not going anywhere. When

you need me, I'll be here, okay?"

I barely got through the door before I was wishing I'd stayed outside with Liz.

"You were mad at me for staying on the roof," Derek said, bearing down on me.

"So I took off to spite you?"

"Course not. But you were mad at me for taking a risk. So you did the same, to prove your point."

"No fight with you is ever worth risking my life, Derek. And I wasn't mad at you. Upset, yes. Worried, definitely. But if I thought my opinion counted more with you now, it's a good thing you straightened me out fast."

He blanched at that. "I—"

"I went out there for the very reason I said in my note. Because we had to know and I was the best suited to get the answer."

"How? Do you have night vision? Superhuman strength? Superhuman senses?"

"No, but the guy who did wouldn't come off the roof, so the next best choice was the person *without* all that. The one they know isn't a threat."

"She's right," Simon murmured, coming up behind us. "You don't like what she did, but you know it needed to be done."

"Then we should have decided that together."

"Would you have listened?" I asked.

He didn't answer.

I continued. "I couldn't talk to you, because you'd have stopped me. I couldn't talk to Tori because you'd blame her for letting me leave. I couldn't talk to Simon because he'd *know* you'd blame him, so he'd stop me, too. I don't like sneaking around, but you didn't leave me a choice. It's black-and-white to you. If Simon or I take a risk, we're stupid and reckless. If you do, we're stupid for worrying."

"I never said that."

"Did you listen to me up on the roof?"

"I said I was coming in."

"When? I left twenty minutes later, and Simon was still up there, trying to talk you down." I shook my head. "Enough. We don't have time to bicker. We need to make plans."

thirty-six

W E CONSIDERED HAVING LIZ scout for safe passage, but we were dealing with spells and high-tech alarms—things a ghost wouldn't trigger. We had to presume the perimeter was locked tight.

We also had to presume it wouldn't be locked as tight during the day, when they had Andrew and Margaret and the two new people to keep an eye on us. That's when we had to escape.

Until then, we needed to play along with their plan. Andrew had used us; now we'd use him. That meant setting him free, though. We racked our brains to come up with another solution, but there wasn't one. To escape, we had to convince them everything was okay. To do that, Andrew had to be right where they expected him to be.

We weren't letting him in on our scheme, of course. We'd

leave him in the basement until morning, then announce that we'd decided the only way to take down the Edison Group was to follow his plan.

Come morning, when Margaret and any others arrived, they'd find us eager to get going. So, we hoped, they'd let their guard down and that's when I'd send Liz out to make sure the exit route was clear.

If that failed, we'd fight our way out. Then we'd call Mr. Bae.

It was almost six when we finished our plans, meaning we still had at least a couple of hours before Margaret showed up. Tori kept working on Andrew's computer. By this time, we didn't expect to get anything more from it, but it gave her a purpose. The guys watched Andrew. That gave them a purpose. And me? I was lost. Scared and lost and frustrated. And hurt. As much as I tried not to think about Derek, I couldn't help it.

I found a pad of paper and a pen, and went into the parlor to turn tonight's walk through the woods into a movie scene. I hadn't written a single line since first arriving at Lyle House. Right now I desperately needed that escape.

I was sketching out the scene when the door opened. I looked up to see Derek standing there.

I kept my expression neutral. "Hmm?"

"Got something for you." He held out an old eight millimeter video camera. "I found it downstairs. It's not working, but I think I can fix it."

A video camera? What would I use it for? Recording our great escape? I didn't say that, because I knew it wasn't the point. This was a gift, a way to say "I know I screwed up and I'm sorry."

His eyes begged me to take it. Just take it. Forgive him. Forget what happened. Start over. And that's what I wanted to do—accept his gift and smile and see that spark in his eyes and—

I took the camera and set it on the table.

"It's cold in here," Derek said. "Is the radiator working?" He walked over and put his hands on it. "Not very well. I'll grab a blanket."

"I don't need—"

"Just a sec."

He took off. A minute later, he came back and handed me a folded blanket. I laid it on my lap. He looked around, then crossed the room and sat on the couch.

After a few moments of silence, he said, "Why don't you come over here? More comfortable than that chair. Warmer, too, closer to the radiator."

"I'm fine."

"Hard to talk to you over there, across the room."

He moved down to the end of the couch, though there'd already been plenty of room. He put his arm along the back. He tried for a smile and didn't really manage it, but my heart still did a little flip.

He's sorry, Chloe. He really is a sweet guy. Don't be a bitch about this. And don't screw it up. Just go over there. Give him a chance and, in no time, you'll forget everything else.

And that's exactly why I stayed in my chair. I didn't want to forget everything else or the next thing I knew, he'd be back on that roof, putting his life in danger.

"You don't get to do this," I said finally.

"Do what?" He asked the question innocently enough, but his gaze dipped slightly. "I'm sorry. That's what I'm trying to say, Chloe. That I'm sorry."

"For what?"

He looked up, confused. "Making you mad."

I didn't answer, just got up to leave. I made it as far as the door. Then he was there, behind me, hand on my elbow. I didn't look back at him. I didn't dare. But I stopped and I listened.

"When I got mad about you leaving," he said, "it wasn't because I thought it was stupid or I didn't think you'd be careful."

"You were just worried about me."

An exhale, relieved that I understood. "Yeah."

I turned. "Because you think I'm worth it."

He put his fingers under my chin. "I absolutely think you're worth it."

"But you don't think you are."

His mouth opened. Shut.

"That's what this is about, Derek. You won't let us worry

about you because you don't think you're worth it. But I do. I absolutely do."

I lifted onto my toes, put my hands around his neck, and pulled him down. When our lips met, that first jolt . . . It was everything I hadn't felt with Simon, everything I'd wanted to feel.

His hands went around my waist, pulling me closer—

Simon's footsteps thudded through the hall. We jumped apart.

"And he says *I* have lousy timing," Derek grumbled. Then he called, "What's up?"

"Andrew says he needs to go to the bathroom," Simon said, walking in. "I'm all for saying too bad, but . . ."

"Fine. I'll handle it," Derek said. "Chloe? Wanna come—"

"I need to talk to Simon."

He gave me a weird look at that, but only for a second, like he wasn't jealous, just maybe a little hurt that I wasn't jumping to come with him.

"It's important," I said. "Grab Tori, though. She can help with Andrew."

He nodded and left.

thirty-seven

"So," Simon said. "Looks like you and Derek are getting along again. What happened? Did he give you the look?"

"Look?"

"You know. The one that makes him look like a whipped puppy, and makes you feel like a jerk for doing the whipping."

"Ah, that one. So it works on you, too?"

He snorted. "It even works on Dad. We give in, we tell him it's okay, and the next thing you know, he's chewing up slippers again."

I laughed.

Simon slumped into a chair. "The problem is, you know he's trying to do the right thing. So what if he doesn't think about himself enough? Would we rather he was a self-centered jerk?" He shook his head, then said, "You wanted to talk?"

"There's something I need to suggest, but . . . Derek's not going to like it."

"Spill."

I told him what I had in mind. When I finished, he swore.

"Bad idea?" I said.

"No, good idea. But you're right—he'll never go for it. If you even suggest it, he'll think it's a test and either get mad or do it to humor you, which won't help, because if he's just humoring us, he won't stay there."

"Stay where?" a voice asked.

We looked over as Tori walked in.

"I thought I heard Derek calling me," she said. "What's up?"

I told her my idea.

"We should have done that the minute we knew they were gunning for him," she said. "Why would he complain? It's not like you're telling him to get lost—just hide out for a few hours, make them think he's gone." She sat on the sofa. "You've got my vote, not that it counts for anything."

"It does," I said. "You're part of this. We need to start acting like you are."

I looked at Simon.

He shrugged. "I guess so."

"Gosh, I've never felt so wanted," Tori said.

"I trust you not to stab me in the back for fun," he said.

"But if it's in your best interests? I'm not turning around. Just in case."

"So I've gone from evil incarnate to ordinary bitch. I can live with that." She stretched out her legs. "So who's telling Derek?"

"No one," I said. "That's the problem. He won't do it and even by suggesting—"

"You want me to lie low?" The deep rumble from the doorway had us all look up. Derek stepped in. "Pretend I took off?" He turned to Simon. "Is that what you want?"

"It is," Simon said.

"Chloe?"

"It's not about what we *want*," I said. "Who was the one Andrew knocked out last night? Who's the one they're all watching? They want you gone, Derek, and I honestly don't think they'll make a move until you are."

He met my gaze, searching it, like he was looking for something there. He must have seen it, because he nodded. "Okay. You're right. We need them to relax, and they won't do that with me around."

Not exactly the rationale I hoped for, but I took it.

We decided the best place for Derek was the attic. There were windows that Derek could jump out of easily, so it was safer than the basement. Dirtier, but safer.

While Simon helped Derek gather food and blankets, I went outside and called Liz.

"I need to know if you can get in the attic," I said.

"I'm one step ahead of you. I can get on the roof, in the attic, and kind of in the basement, but not so well."

I told her about our plans for Derek.

"You want me to keep him company?" She grinned. "We can play tic-tac-toe in the dust." She saw my expression and stopped smiling. "That's not what you need, is it?"

"I'm worried about him. He's not very good at looking after himself."

"And he could use a poltergeist bodyguard?"

I nodded. "Take care of him for me. Please."

"I will."

Next we released Andrew. We told him that Derek had decided it was safer for everyone if he left. We'd tried to stop him, but he'd snuck off into the woods, where he was presumably going to hide until he found a way to get off the property.

We didn't tell Andrew that *we* planned to find a way off the property, too. As far as he knew, we were going along with his plans.

Margaret showed up while we were having breakfast, and we discovered another advantage to Derek's disappearance—it gave us an excuse for being anxious and quiet.

As we were finishing, the doorbell rang. All three of us jumped, Simon dropping his spoon into the bowl with a clatter.

"I guess Derek wouldn't be ringing the bell, huh?" I said.

"He might." Simon pushed back his chair. "I'll answer."

I knew what he was thinking—hoping. That it was his dad. The chances of Mr. Bae ringing a bell at a house where his sons might be captives seemed pretty remote, but I followed, if only as an excuse to get away from Andrew and Margaret.

I got to the door as Simon was swinging it open. There stood Gwen.

"Hey, guys," she said with a strained smile. She held up a box. "No donuts this time—I learned my lesson—but I brought some amazing muffins. You can eat those, right?"

"Uh, sure," Simon said.

Simon backed up to let her in. He shot a glance at me, a clear *What's she doing here?*

"Andrew's b-been trying to get in touch with you," I said.

"I know. Work. You know how it is." A forced laugh. "No, I guess you don't, lucky kids. Enjoy it while you can because the truth is"—she leaned over and whispered—"grown-up life sucks. But I'm here now and ready for action. Andrew's message said we're leaving for Buffalo today."

I nodded.

"Great. I'm just in time, then. Come on in and let's chow down on these muffins. They are amazing."

When we showed Gwen into the kitchen, I tried to gauge Andrew's and Margaret's reaction. Both seemed surprised. For Andrew, it was pleasant surprise. For Margaret, not so much. She didn't seem angry, just annoyed at the flighty girl zipping in and out at whim.

They adjourned to the living room. The three of us made excuses and took off.

"She's lying," Tori said. "I don't care how ditzy she is, no one ignores a half dozen urgent calls, then sails in with blueberry muffins."

"Russell sent her to spy," Simon said. "He's up to something."

"It doesn't matter," I said. "Whatever their scheme, we'll be gone soon enough. Just keep an eye on her until then. I'm going to send Liz out looking for escape routes."

Thirty-eight

I WAS NEARING THE stairs when Simon hailed me.

"Can you give something to Derek?" he whispered. "It's in my room."

We went up. He pulled his bag from its hiding place, took out his sketch pad, folded a page in quarters, and handed it to me.

"Give him that. And tell him it's okay."

"Okay?"

Simon's gaze dropped and he shrugged. "He'll understand." After a moment's pause, he looked up again and forced a smile. "Now let's do this and get out of here."

Simon walked me to the stairs leading to the attic and roof.

"Chloe? Simon?" It was Margaret, downstairs.

Simon swore. He glanced at me.

"Can you go?" I said. "I really need to send Liz out or we'll never get away."

He nodded. I slid into the nearest room and shut the door as he called, "Right here!"

"I need to speak to you two."

Margaret's pumps clicked up the stairs underscored by the thump of Simon's feet, running toward her. I leaned against the door to listen.

"Have you seen Chloe?" she asked.

"Mmm, no," Simon said. "She was trying to find a quiet place to do some writing. Did you check the sunroom, around back? She likes—"

"I'll look. I need you to go to the basement and help Tori bring up extra chairs for lunch."

"Lunch? We just had breakfast. And we have plenty of chairs—"

"No, we don't. The rest of the group is arriving to make final preparations. Andrew's gone to the airport to pick them up, so I need you kids to help with the chairs."

"Tori can handle—"

"I asked *you*, Simon."

"All right," Simon said, raising his voice to be sure I heard. "I'll get the chairs from the basement. I wouldn't bother Chloe with it, though. Those chairs are bigger than she is."

Margaret sent him on his way, saying she'd be right down to supervise. Simon's sneakers pounded down the steps. Then

Margaret called Gwen, who answered from downstairs.

"I need to speak to Chloe," Margaret said when Gwen got there. "I brought a necromancy book for her. Simon said she's up here. You look at the front of the house, and I'll take the back."

Simon had said I was probably in the sunroom . . . on the main level.

I looked down at the door handle. There was a lock, with an old-fashioned key on the inside. I turned it as slowly as I could.

I glanced around. I was in one of the unused bedrooms. There weren't any closets, but the wardrobe across the room looked big enough to hold me. As I stepped toward it, my sneakers squeaked. I considered pulling them off, but the floor was filthy, and it'd be just my luck to step on a rusty thumbtack and yelp loud enough to bring everyone running.

I picked my way across the room. I was halfway to the wardrobe when a thump stopped me midstride. I looked up. Derek?

I listened. Silence. I took another slow step. Then another.

"Chloe?"

It was Gwen's voice, a stage whisper from just outside the door. I froze.

"Chloe? Are you up here?" Then lower, under her breath. "Please, be up here. *Please*."

I looked at the wardrobe. It was too far for a silent dash.

"Chloe? I know you're here."

I looked around. There was a huge dresser beside me, draped in a sheet. I backed up alongside it and crouched.

The door is locked, silly. She can't get in.

I didn't care. If I was found hiding in a locked room, they'd be suspicious, and we couldn't afford that. I should have just gone with Simon.

"Please, Chloe." Her voice sounded like she was inside the room.

You're imagining things.

"Why did I come back?" Gwen whispered. "What was I thinking?" Then, louder, "There you are. Thank God."

My heart slammed into my ribs. I looked at the dresser, but I was completely concealed, the sheet right down to the floor, hiding even my feet.

She's bluffing. She can't see you. She can't possibly—

Gwen stepped in front of me, her short hair wild around her pale face, makeup streaked, eyes huge.

"Come on, Chloe. Quickly!"

I rose. "I—I was l-looking for—"

"It doesn't matter. You need to find Simon and Tori. Do you know where they are?"

"In the basement, but—"

"Hurry!" She reached for me, then stopped short, and pulled back. "You have to warn them."

"About what?"

She shook her head. "Just come on!"

She waved me to the door. I grabbed the knob and turned. It stopped.

Locked. The door was still locked.

"Open it, Chloe. Please."

I reached for Gwen. She backpedaled, but not fast enough. My fingers touched her arm . . . and passed through. I clamped my hand over my mouth.

"Don't scream, Chloe. Okay? Please, please, don't scream."

I nodded.

Oh God! She's a ghost. She's dead.

She couldn't be. I just heard her a minute ago, heard her footsteps when she headed down the hall to search. And that was the last time I'd heard them.

I remembered Margaret's words: *Simon said she's up here. You look down there, and I'll take this end.*

Then a thump. The sound of a body falling.

Margaret killed Gwen? That was crazy. Impossible.

Sure, she just happened to fall and break her neck while searching for you.

I swallowed. "Margaret," I whispered.

"Seems that old bag is a whole lot nastier than I ever gave her credit for," Gwen muttered. "I didn't like the way things were going. I . . . I'd heard things. Margaret and Russell. That's why I took off when Andrew called. I didn't want to get involved. But I couldn't do it. I had to come back, thought I should warn Andrew, help him watch out for you kids. Bad idea, obviously. Never even got to the warning part."

I wheeled toward the door. "Derek."

Gwen stepped in front of me. "Is he someplace safe?"

I walked through her.

"Chloe, is he someplace safe? Because if he is, then you have to leave him there. You need to warn Simon and Tori. You said Margaret sent them—"

"To the basement for chairs. For the others coming this afternoon."

"No others are coming, Chloe."

I raced to the door. As I unlocked it, Gwen slipped through the wall.

"Careful," I whispered. "Margaret—"

"Can see me. I know."

Gwen came back and waved me out, motioning for me to dash into the next room and wait again. That's how we did it—me darting from room to room, heading for the rear stairs as Gwen scouted the way.

I did as she said, but inside I was a panicked mess. All I could think was: *Gwen's dead, and now Simon and Tori are in the basement, and Derek's in the attic, and am I making the right choice, and will I get to them in time, and oh my God,* what *is going on?*

I was nearly at the back stairs, when Gwen motioned for me to hide. I scooted under a bed, covering my mouth to keep from breathing in dust.

Margaret's heels clicked in the hall. They seemed to be receding. *Please. Please, please— Yes!* She marched down the main stairs as she called a name—Russell. Russell was here?

Oh God, I had to warn Derek. I had to get up to the attic—

And if he finds out Simon's in danger, he'll barrel down there and get himself killed. He's better off where he is, thinking everything is okay.

I closed my eyes and breathed in and out until my heart slowed to a gallop. Gwen checked to make sure the coast was clear, then I hurried to the servants' stairs.

With Gwen watching, I made it to the bottom of the stairs. From there I could see the basement door, ajar. I listened for Simon and Tori—for once I'd have loved to hear the sound of their bickering—but instead I heard Margaret and Russell's muffled voices coming from behind a closed door . . . a door between me and the basement.

Gwen led me forward, step by careful step. I listened for a break in the conversation or the sound of footsteps, but they kept talking.

I was three steps from the basement when Margaret's pumps clicked against the hardwood.

I looked toward the basement, but it was too far. I wheeled and pushed open the nearest door.

"No!" Gwen whispered.

I turned. She madly waved me out. Then, in mid-gesture, she disappeared. I froze for a second—just long enough to hear Margaret turning the doorknob—then spun to find a hiding place. I stopped short. Andrew stood on the other side of a coffee table.

He was looking at me, frowning.

"Chloe?" he said, my name coming slowly, carefully, like he wasn't quite sure.

"Hold on," Margaret said as the door creaked open. "I thought I heard someone."

Andrew's eyes widened. He motioned me over, gesturing for me to hide behind the table—it was long and solid, so I wouldn't be seen. I hesitated only a second, then ran for it. My sneaker slid in something and I tried to keep my balance, but my other foot slid, too, the floor slick, and I crashed onto the coffee table, hands smacking the top of it, knees cracking against the edge.

"We've found Chloe," Margaret said from behind the doorway, her voice completely calm.

I looked up to see Russell coming at me, a syringe in his hand. I backed away, scrambling over the other side of the table.

"Andrew?" I said, looking up. "Help—"

Andrew was gone.

A needle jabbed into the back of my leg. I kicked Russell, hearing him grunt as my foot made contact. The room swayed. I blinked hard, fighting to stay conscious. I tried to get up, get off the table, but my arms gave way and I toppled over the other side.

I hit something soft and rolled off it, landing in a warm puddle. I struggled to focus and lifted my hands. Blood. I was lying in a pool of blood.

I tried getting up, but my muscles refused, and I slumped to the floor. The last thing I saw was Andrew's face, inches away, dead eyes staring into mine.

thirty-nine

COLD METAL VIBRATED AGAINST my cheek. A car roared past.

"How's his blood sugar?" A distant woman's voice. Margaret.

"Low." A man's voice, closer. Russell. "Very low. I can give him a glucose shot, but we really should—"

"Do that."

"Derek." Simon's voice now, the name coming out as a moan.

My eyes fluttered open. We were lying on the floor of a van. Simon was a few feet from me, still asleep, face screwed up, like he was in pain.

"And give him more sedative," Margaret called back from the driver's seat. "I don't want them waking up."

"He really shouldn't get too much—"

"Just do it."

I closed my eyes to slits, so they wouldn't realize I was awake. I tried to look around without moving my head, but all I could see was Simon and, over his head, Tori's sneaker.

Derek. Where is—?

My eyelids closed again.

The van stopped moving. Cold air rushed over me, exhaust fumes blasting in. The engine rumbled, then died. Another rumble, like a closing garage door. The wind disappeared and everything went dark. Then a light flicked on.

Simon retched beside me. The stink of vomit filled the van. I pried my eyes open to see him, sitting, supported by Russell, who held a plastic bag for him.

"Simon." My voice came out thick.

He turned. His eyes met mine and struggled to focus. His lips parted and he rasped, "You're okay," then he gagged and hunched back over the vomit bag.

"What did you give him?" a man's voice snapped.

I knew that voice. Cool fingers wrapped around my bare arm. I looked up. Dr. Davidoff's face hovered above mine.

"It's all right, Chloe." He smiled. "You're home."

A guard rolled me through the halls in a wheelchair, my arms and legs strapped down. Tori rode beside me, also restrained, pushed by another guard.

"It's a temporary measure," Dr. Davidoff had assured me

when the guard bound me to the chair. "We don't want to sedate you again, so this is our only alternative until you've had time to reacclimatize."

Dr. Davidoff walked between the guards. Behind them, Margaret and Russell walked as they talked to Tori's mom, who hadn't said a word to her daughter since we'd arrived.

"We decided this was the best place for them," Margaret was saying. "They need a level of control and supervision that we just can't provide."

"Your compassion and consideration are overwhelming," Diane Enright said. "And where did you want us to deposit your finder's fee again?"

I could feel the chill in Margaret's tone when she answered. "You have the account number."

"We aren't leaving until we've confirmed the deposit," Russell chimed in. "And if you get any ideas about not paying us—"

"I'm sure you've taken precautions against just such a possibility," Mrs. Enright said drily. "A letter to be opened in the event of your sudden disappearance, exposing us all?"

"No," Margaret said. "Just someone waiting for our call. A colleague with a direct line to the Nast Cabal and all the details of your operation. I'm sure Mr. St. Cloud wouldn't want that."

Dr. Davidoff only chuckled. "Threatening a Cabal with a Cabal? Clever. But that won't be necessary." The good humor drained from his voice. "Whatever Mr. St. Cloud's interest in our organization, we remain an independent operation, meaning we do not operate under the auspices of his Cabal. You made a deal with us—a sizable payment in return for our subjects and the disbanding of your little rebel group. You have earned that payment and you will get it without treachery or threat of violence."

He glanced back at them. "However, considering it is, ultimately, Mr. St. Cloud's money that is paying you, I would suggest that when you leave the safety of our walls, you get as far away as you can, as fast as you can."

When Tori's mom led Margaret and Russell away, I asked about Simon. I hated giving Dr. Davidoff the satisfaction of hearing the tremor in my voice, but I had to know.

"I'm taking you to see him now, Chloe," he said in that condescending fake-cheerful tone I knew too well. *Look how good we are to you*, it said. *And look how you treat us. We only want to help.* My fingernails dug into the arms of my wheelchair.

Dr. Davidoff strode ahead and opened a door. We went up a ramp and found ourselves in an observation room overlooking an operating room. I looked down at the shining metal operating table and the trays of gleaming metal instruments, and I gripped the chair tighter.

A woman was in the room, off to the side of the observation window, so I could only make out a slender arm in a lab coat.

The door to the operating room opened, and a gray-haired woman entered. It was Sue, the nurse I'd met last time I was here. She wheeled a gurney. Simon lay on it, strapped down.

"No!" I flung myself against the restraints.

Dr. Davidoff chuckled. "I don't even want to know what you think we have in mind, Chloe. We're bringing Simon in to hook him up to an IV. Being diabetic, he's easily dehydrated by vomiting. We don't want to take any chances, not while that sedative is still upsetting his stomach."

I said nothing, just stared down at Simon, my heart thumping.

"It's a precaution, Chloe. And what you're looking at is simply our medical room. Yes, it's equipped for surgery, but only because it's a multipurpose room." He bent and whispered. "If you look closely, I bet you'll see dust on those instruments."

He winked, the genial uncle humoring the silly little girl, and I wanted to— I don't know what I wanted to do, but something in my expression made him flinch and just for a second, that genial uncle vanished. I wasn't the docile little Chloe he remembered. It would be safer if I was, but I couldn't fake it anymore.

He straightened and cleared his throat. "Now, if you'll look down there again, Chloe, I believe you'll see someone else you recognize."

I turned toward Simon, still lying on the gurney, pale as the sheet pulled over him. He was listening to the woman in the lab coat, but I could only see her from the back. She was slender, below average height, with blond hair. And it was that hair, the way it swung as she leaned over Simon, that made my breath catch.

Dr. Davidoff rapped on the window. The doctor looked up. It was Aunt Lauren.

She shaded her eyes, like she couldn't see anyone through the tinted glass. Then she turned back to Simon, talking as he nodded.

"Your aunt made a mistake," Dr. Davidoff said. "You were so upset when we brought you here that she panicked. She was under a lot of stress and she made some bad decisions. She sees that now. We understand and we've forgiven her. She's a welcome member of the team once again. As you can see, she's back to work, happy and healthy, not chained in a dungeon or whatever horrible fate you'd imagined befalling her."

He looked down at me. "We aren't monsters, Chloe."

"So where's Rachelle?" Tori's voice made me jump. Her chair was next to mine, but I'd forgotten she was here. "She's up next on the happy-friends reunion tour, I suppose."

When Dr. Davidoff said nothing, the sneer fell from Tori's face.

"Wh-where's Rae?" I asked. "Sh-she is here, right?"

"She's been transferred," he said.

"T-transferred?"

He forced a jovial note into his voice. "Yes. This

laboratory is hardly the place for a sixteen-year-old girl to live. It was only temporary lodgings, which we would have explained if you'd stayed long enough to let us. Rachelle has been moved to—" He chuckled. "I won't call it a group home because, I assure you, it's a far cry from Lyle House. More like a boarding school. A very special boarding school, just for supernaturals."

"Let me guess," Tori said. "You can only get to it by a magical train. How stupid do you think we are?"

"We don't think you're stupid at all. We think you're special. There are people, as you've discovered, who think *special* means dangerous, which is why we've designed a school for your education and protection."

"Xavier's School for Gifted Youngsters," I said.

He smiled at me, completely missing the edge in my voice. "Exactly, Chloe."

Tori twisted to look at him. "And if we're all very, very good, we'll get to go there and live with Rae and Liz and Brady. Is Amber there, too?"

"As a matter of fact—"

"*Liar!*"

The venom in Tori's voice made him flinch. The empty chairs rattled and the guards glanced over at them, and fingered their sidearms. I barely noticed. All I could think was: *Rae. No, please, not Rae.*

"Liz is dead," Tori said. "We've met her ghost—seen her

throwing stuff, using her powers. Even my mother saw it. She knew it was Liz. Or didn't she mention that?"

Dr. Davidoff unclipped his pager and pressed a button, undoubtedly summoning Tori's mom, while using the delay to find the right expression—regret and sadness.

"I wasn't aware you knew the truth about Liz," he said carefully. "Yes, I admit it. There was an accident the night we brought her in from Lyle House. We didn't tell any of you because you're all in a very fragile state—"

"Do I look fragile?" Tori said.

"Yes, Victoria, you do. You look angry and distraught and very vulnerable, and that's completely understandable if you think we killed your friend. But we didn't."

"What about Brady?" I asked.

"Chloe saw his ghost, too," Tori said. "Here. At the lab. He said he was brought in to talk to you, saw her aunt Lauren, and then *poof*, game over."

His gaze flicked from me to Tori, assessing the chances that Tori somehow had proof of Brady's death as well.

"Chloe was still experiencing aftereffects from her sedatives," he said. "She had also been on a regime of drugs to keep her from seeing ghosts, either of which may have caused hallucinations."

"How did she hallucinate a boy she'd never met? Do you want her to describe him, because he sounded an awful lot like Brady to me."

"I'm sure Chloe saw a photo of him, whether she remembers it or not. Brady was close to Rachelle. She probably described him—"

"You have an explanation for everything, don't you?" Tori said. "Fine. Brady, Rae, and Amber are all living happily ever after in your superspecial boarding school. You want to calm us down? Get them on the phone. Better yet, set up a video conference. Don't tell me you can't do that, because I know Mom has the equipment."

"Yes, we do, and we will let you speak to them just as soon—"

"Now!" Tori roared.

Sparks fizzled at her fingertips. The empty chairs wobbled. One crashed over backward. Her guard pulled out his sidearm.

"I want to see them now! Rae and Brady and Amber—"

"You can *want* all you like, Miss Victoria." The door opened and Tori's mother walked in. "But your wants no longer matter. You lost that right when you ran away."

"So you still recognize me, Mom? Whew. I thought maybe I'd changed so much that you'd forgotten who I was."

"Oh, I recognize you, Victoria. You're still the same spoiled princess who ran away from her responsibilities last week."

"Responsibilities?"

Tori's fists clenched and her restraints snapped open. My

guard lunged forward, but Dr. Davidoff waved him back and motioned for the other to put away his gun.

Tori got to her feet. Her hair bristled, popping and sparking.

"Sedate her," Mrs. Enright snapped. "If she can't behave herself—"

"No, Diane," Dr. Davidoff said. "We need to learn how to handle Victoria's outbursts without resorting to medication. Now, Tori, I understand you're upset—"

"Do you?" She wheeled. "Do you really? You locked me up at Lyle House and told me I was mentally ill. You shoved pills down my throat. You murdered my friend. You made me into this genetically modified freak, and yet you tell me it's my fault!"

She slammed her fists against her sides. Tiny bolts sparked off them, making her guard step forward.

"Does that make you nervous?" she said. "That's nothing."

She lifted her hands. A ball of energy spun between them, barely bigger than a pea at first, then growing and growing. . . .

"That's enough, Victoria," Dr. Davidoff said. "We know you're very powerful—"

"You have no idea how powerful I am." She tossed the ball of energy in the air, where it spun, shooting sparks. "But I can show you."

Behind Tori, her mother moved out of everyone's sight as they all stared at Tori. Mrs. Enright's lips moved in a spell. As I opened my mouth to warn Tori, a bolt shot from her mother's fingertips, whipping past Tori and hitting the advancing guard in the chest.

The guard dropped. Dr. Davidoff, Mrs. Enright, and the other guard rushed to his side.

"He's not breathing," the guard said. He looked up at Dr. Davidoff, eyes wide. "He's not *breathing*."

"Oh my God." Mrs. Enright slowly turned to Tori. "What have you done?"

Tori jumped, startled. "I didn't—"

"Get Dr. Fellows," Dr. Davidoff snapped to the other guard. "Quickly."

"I didn't do that," Tori said. "I didn't."

"It was an accident," her mother murmured.

"No, I did not do it. I swear to God—"

"She's right." Everyone looked up sharply at the sound of my voice. I twisted to face Mrs. Enright. "Tori didn't cast that spell. You did. I saw you cast—"

A sudden smack against my cheek, like an invisible slap, so hard my wheelchair rolled back. Blood spurted from my nose.

"Tori!" Mrs. Enright said. "Stop that!"

"I didn't—"

Tori froze, caught in a binding spell.

Mrs. Enright turned to Dr. Davidoff. "Now do you see

what I mean? She's completely out of control. She lashes out at enemies and friends alike and she doesn't even realize she's doing it."

"Restrain her," he said. "I'll take Chloe to her room."

forty

AND SO, AFTER A week on the run, I ended up exactly where I began. In the same cell. Lying on the same bed. Alone.

Dr. Davidoff had hustled me out before Aunt Lauren came for the guard. I thought he might want her to check my bloodied nose, but he'd just brought me a wet cloth and a clean shirt from my closet at Lyle House, telling me I could see my aunt as soon as I was calm and ready to listen. As rewards went, spending quality time with my aunt who'd turned traitor—again—wasn't really the incentive he thought.

For the past week, I'd dreamed of the day I'd come back here and rescue Aunt Lauren and Rae. Now I was here and there was no one to save. Aunt Lauren had returned to the fold. Rae was dead.

I squeezed my eyes shut, but tears rolled down my cheeks anyway.

I should have tried harder to persuade Rae to come with me. I should have come back for her sooner.

Rae was dead. And Tori was next. Her mother had murdered that guard to frame her. I couldn't comprehend the evil of that, but I knew what it meant. Diane Enright wanted her daughter dead. She'd become a liability, a threat.

Tori would die and I wouldn't be far behind. And what about Simon? And Derek? I wiped away the tears and sat up. I had two choices: escape or accept my fate. I wasn't accepting it. Not now, not ever.

I took stock of my surroundings and what I could use. As for the room, nothing had changed. As for me, all I had were the clothes I wore—the new shirt and my jeans, still stained with Andrew's blood. I tried not to think about that.

I patted my pockets, hoping for my ever-present switchblade. Gone.

One pocket crackled, though. Paper. I tugged it out and unfolded it. When I remembered it was the picture Simon had made for Derek, I started to refold it, but I'd already seen what he'd drawn—a sketch of me, crouching beside a black wolf, my arm around its neck, and I remembered Simon saying "Give him that. And tell him it's okay."

My eyes stung. I shakily refolded the message, and tucked it back into my pocket. Then I straightened and gave my head a sharp shake. I still had one very big trick up my sleeve. I pulled my legs up onto the bed, closed my eyes, and called the demi-demon.

I'd barely finished summoning her when warm air tickled the top of my head.

"Well," whispered her tinkling voice, "this looks very familiar."

"I need your help."

"Now that's new. And quite welcome, I might add. The first thing you need to do is free me. Then we'll rain down hell on all who have wronged us."

"I'll free you *after* you help me. And we'll skip the raining-down-hell part."

"Oh, but it's so much fun. All that fire and brimstone and rivers of lava. Demons beating their ragged wings and fanning the flames." A pause, then a deep sigh. "Sarcasm is lost on the young and gullible, isn't it? I meant it figuratively. Wreak havoc, if you will. Smite our mutual enemies."

"No smiting."

"You're going to ruin all my fun, aren't you? Fine. Free me and—"

"*After* you help me."

"Details, details. I suppose you want to escape again. I'm not quite sure why, given that you seem rather fond of this place. You keep returning."

I glared in her direction. "Yes, I want your help escaping, but we're also going to free Simon and Tori and, if

Derek's here, he comes, too."

"Presuming you mean the werewolf boy, he hasn't passed through those doors since he left years ago. But if they do bring him in, I will include him in the plan. I am nothing if not fair in my dealings with mortals."

I'd seen enough demonic-pact-gone-wrong horror movies to know I needed an iron-clad agreement. The problem was that I didn't know exactly what I needed her to do. Get me out, sure. But how?

Not surprisingly, she had an idea. Also not surprisingly, I didn't like it.

"Isn't there another way?"

"There's always another way. Personally, I would prefer that witch Diane Enright. I'm quite fond of witches, as I believe I've mentioned. True, she's still alive, but that's an obstacle easily overcome. Tell the guard you wish to speak to her and I'll guide you through the rest. Breaking her neck is the simplest method, but you are rather small for that, so—"

"No."

"Then it's back to my original suggestion, isn't it?"

A minute later, I was kneeling on the carpet, doing something I'd sworn I'd never even consider. Return a human ghost to his corpse. Right now, though, it was the only way I could see to keep from becoming a corpse myself.

I focused on the memory of his face, commanding him back.

"A little more," the demi-demon murmured. "Yes,

that's it. Now call him to you."

I did. And I braced myself for screams.

"They're all in the meeting room," the demi-demon said, as if reading my mind. "Just bring him quickly."

A minute later, the card lock clicked. The door swung open. And there stood the guard Mrs. Enright had killed.

Earlier, he'd just been "the guard." I didn't know his name. Didn't want to. I'd had to struggle to recall his face for the summoning. He'd just been an anonymous minion of the Edison Group. And now, when I desperately wanted to depersonalize him again, instead I saw a man. Young. Short brown hair. Freckles. Traces of acne on his cheeks. Was he much older than me? I swallowed, and made the mistake of lifting my eyes to his. Brown eyes, dark with rage and hate. I dropped my gaze.

He still had the card key in his hand, raised, and I fixed on that. Another mistake. A wedding band sparkled on his finger.

Oh God, he had a wife. Kids? A baby maybe? One who'd never see—

I squeezed my eyes shut.

You had nothing to do with his death.

But I'd done something that felt just as bad. I'd brought him back to life. And when I glanced at his face, I saw how terrible that was—the hate, the fury, the disgust.

"Close the door," the demi-demon whispered.

I did.

The guard watched me, eyes narrowed, card still raised, like he'd love to shove it down my throat. Watch me choke on it.

When he spoke, his words were garbled. "Whatever you want me to do, I won't."

The demi-demon chuckled. "Then you don't know much about necromancers, particularly this one," she said, though he couldn't hear her.

"I don't want anything," I said. "I'm sorry—"

"Sorry?" He spat the word and stepped toward me. His coat swung open, showing a charred hole in his chest. The stink of burned meat wafted out. I gagged, and my mouth filled with bile. He stepped toward me again.

"Stop," I said, voice quavering.

He did, and stood there, skewering me with those burning eyes.

"I might suggest you take his gun," the demi-demon said. "To be safe."

I looked down. His fingers rested on the butt of his pistol.

"Don't move," I said.

I tugged out the gun.

"You're going to use me to escape, aren't you? You won't. You belong in here. They were right. You're monsters. I hope they kill you all." He sneered down at me. "No, actually, I hope they don't kill you. I hope they lock you up and experiment on you. Poke and prod and test until you wish you were dead."

A week ago, I'd have shivered at those words. Today, I wasn't going to cower under his threats and name-calling, and I wasn't going to shy away from what I had to do.

I told him to sit. He did. He had no choice. Then I freed his soul, envisioning not a release but an exchange. Eyes shut, I sat cross-legged, necklace on the floor, inches from my hand. I willed this to work. Please work. Just—

"Well, that's better," the guard said, his mumble replaced by a weirdly musical lilt. He cleared his throat. "No, *that's* better," he said, in his normal voice.

I snatched the necklace back. The guard gave a girlish laugh. His eyes glowed orange. He blinked and rolled his shoulders, then cleared his throat again and the laugh deepened. His eyes went black, then brown.

"Will I pass?" the demi-demon asked from inside the guard's body.

I picked up the gun from the floor.

The demi-demon laughed. "Do you really think I'd shoot you and doom myself to eternity in a rotting mortal shell? I am as much your slave as the mortal, and I promise, I shall obey with far less unseemly whining."

I rose, the gun still in my hand.

"I would suggest you keep that," she said. "But you'll need to find a place to hide it."

I tucked it into the back of my waistband. Whenever I'd seen that on the big screen, I'd rolled my eyes, thinking "one wrong move and you're going to shoot yourself in the butt."

But, right now, it was the only place I could think of.

As I adjusted my shirt over it, my fingers trembled. I took a deep breath.

"Yes, I know," the demi-demon said. "That experience was far from pleasant, but at least he was angry about it."

When I glanced over, her brows arched. "Would you rather he'd been grateful? Happy to be resurrected? Pleading for a few final minutes with his family?"

She had a point. I pulled the shirt down one last time, then finger-combed my hair.

"You look marvelous, my dear," she said, and fluttered her fingers at the door. "Shall we?" She paused. "Let's try that again." Her voice went gruff. "Ready to go, kid?"

I was.

forty-one

AS THE DEMI-DEMON HAD said, all the major players were in a meeting. Given how loath they were to admit to problems, we hoped they hadn't rushed to tell all the other guards about the death of their colleague, so anyone we encountered wouldn't find it odd to see him escorting the prisoners through the building.

As it turned out, the halls were empty. We made it to the security office without seeing or hearing anyone. The door was unlocked. The demi-demon opened it. A guard sat inside, his back to us as he monitored the screens. I stayed behind the demi-demon, but when the guard turned, I caught enough of a glimpse of him for my heart to sink. It was the one who'd been with us earlier.

I jerked back out of sight, and I plastered myself to the corridor wall.

"Hey, Rob," the demi-demon said.

"Nick?" the guard said. His chair scraped the floor, as he scrambled out of it. "I thought you were—"

"So did I," the demi-demon said. "Seems it takes more than a witch's spell to kill me. Whatever mojo that shaman Phelps uses, it's good stuff."

"They called in Phelps?" The guard exhaled. "I didn't think they would. Dr. Fellows is good, but . . ."

"She's no shaman healer. A lot easier on the eyes than old man Phelps, though."

They both laughed at that.

"Anyway, I'm back in action, and apparently, almost dying doesn't even earn me the rest of the shift off. They want you up front, manning the door. Trudy's nervous with those kids back."

"I don't blame her. Personally, I don't know why they keep trying to rehabilitate them. After what that brat did to you, I'm ready to lock them up and throw away the key. I'll go keep Trudy company, though." The squeak of shoes, then a sniff: "What's that smell?"

"Smell?"

"Like something burned."

"Yeah. I think Trudy burned popcorn in the microwave again."

"No, it's not popcorn." Another shoe squeak. "It's coming from—"

A gasp. Then the thump of a falling body. I raced into

the room. The demi-demon was tugging the guard into the corner.

"Do you see a ghost, child?" she asked without turning.

"N-no."

"Then he isn't dead, is he?" She arranged him, mostly hidden behind the chairs. Then she took my hands and pressed them to the guard's neck where his pulse beat strong. "You're giving me the first chance at freedom I've had. Do you think I'd spoil that?"

She looked at the guard, then slid a sly glance my way. "Still, this would be an excellent opportunity to obtain a far more suitable body for me, one that *no one* thinks is dead."

I glared at her.

She sighed. "All right then. Find your friends."

I scanned the monitors while she watched the door. There was no sign of Tori, but I'd expected that—it only meant she was in one of the camera-free cells. I found Simon, still in the surgery, still strapped down, an IV in his arm, no sign of a guard.

I checked the other screens. Dr. Davidoff was in a meeting room with Mrs. Enright, Sue, Mike the security guy, and the two others. They were deep in debate.

The rest of the rooms were dark, all except one that wasn't any bigger than my walk-in closet at home, crammed with a twin bed, small desk, and chair.

Someone sat at the desk, writing, chair pulled as far from camera range as possible. I could see only a shoulder and arm, but I recognized the dark purple silk blouse. I'd been with Aunt Lauren when she bought it this winter.

The woman stood, and there was no doubt. It was Aunt Lauren.

I brought the demi-demon in and pointed at the screen. "What room is that and why is my aunt in there?"

"Because she was naughty. Apparently, distaste for imprisonment runs in the family. She was scarcely confined to a regular cell for a day before she tried to escape. They decided she needed more direct supervision."

"So she's a captive?"

"She helped you escape. Did you think they'd throw a feast in her honor? Sacrifice a goat or two?"

"They said she'd changed her mind and admitted she made a mistake."

The demi-demon laughed. "And you believed them? Of course you did, because they've never been anything but perfectly honest with you."

My face heated.

"Yes, they tried to make her see the error of her ways," the demi-demon said. "They offered immunity and forgiveness and feather pillows. She's a very valuable member of the team. But she refused." She looked at me and sighed. "I suppose you want to rescue her, too."

I nodded.

"Then let's get on with it."

I grabbed her arm before she walked away. "Rae. The

fire half-demon girl. They said she was transferred. Is she here, too?"

The demi-demon hesitated, and when she spoke, there was a softness in her voice. "No, child. She's not here. And I don't know what became of her, so don't ask me. She was here one evening, and come morning, she was not."

"They killed—"

"There's no time for that. Your friends await and they"— she pointed at the Edison Group meeting—"will not be in there forever."

We freed Tori first.

I tried to prepare her for the shock of seeing a dead man walking by going in first, but she caught a glimpse of him, and after a split second of surprise, said "Good idea."

I was going to explain that I hadn't created a zombie guard slave, but the demi-demon was already at the next door, checking the third cell, Tori right behind her. I decided that if Tori was fine with me raising the dead for personal use, then there was really no reason to tell her I'd actually made a deal with a demon.

That didn't work so well with Simon, who knew I wouldn't be nonchalantly controlling dead people. And I couldn't use the no-time-to-explain excuse because we had time—undoing his restraints, getting out his IV, bandaging him, and looking for his shoes, while the demi-demon guarded the door.

So I told them the truth. Tori took it in stride. I was

beginning to think Tori would take anything in stride.

Simon said nothing for a moment, and I braced myself for *Are you nuts?* but this was Simon. He only slid off the bed, crouched beside me while I checked under a table for his shoes, and whispered, "Are you okay?" I knew he meant the part about raising the dead, and when I nodded, he searched my face and said, "All right." I assured him I'd been careful with the demi-demon and he said, "I know, and we'll keep being careful." And that was that.

forty-two

"NEXT STOP, DEAR AUNTIE Lauren," the demi-demon trilled. "Then straight to the nearest exit and"—she smiled—"freedom for all."

"Not all." Tori glanced at me as we walked. "We need to download the project files. There are other kids out there thinking they're mentally ill, like Peter and Mila. Plus others who might not have come into their powers yet."

Peter had been at Lyle House when I arrived, and he'd been released before we escaped. I hadn't known Mila, only that she'd been there before me, and had been "rehabilitated" and sent back into the world.

"I would love to get those files," I said. "But we don't have time to access and print—"

Tori pulled a thumb drive from her pocket. I wasn't even going to ask where that came from.

"You have Dr. Davidoff's password," she said. "We have access to his office. I can download the files while you're getting your aunt."

"And there's got to be a phone," Simon said. "I can try my dad again."

They were right. I'd regret it if we left without those names. And I'd regret it even more if we got locked up again and had passed up the chance to tell Mr. Bae where we were.

We got to the office. It needed an additional code, but the demi-demon knew it. Then I said the demi-demon and I would get my aunt and come back.

"So the sorcerer is staying with his sister?" the demi-demon asked.

"Sister?" Simon said. "She's not—"

"Sister spell-caster," I said to him quickly. "She talks like that."

When we were far enough away, I whispered, "So Simon's dad really is Tori's father?"

"The worst-kept secret in the building." Her singsong tone jarred with the guard's gruff voice. "And that, my child, is saying a lot."

"Guess that explains why her mom freaked out when Tori admitted she liked Simon."

"Oooh, that would be awkward. A lesson to you in keeping secrets. They will come back to haunt you in the most uncomfortable ways. Whether that one feels any guilt, though, is quite another matter. She has the morals of a succubus. I must admit, it was quite amusing, watching her attempt to seduce the sorcerer. Quite a blow to her ego when she failed."

"Failed?" I said as we turned the corner. "But if Tori is his daughter, then obviously—"

"Obviously nothing. What do they teach children in school these days? Sex is hardly the only way to reproduce. Arguably the most fun, but if that fails, and you have access to a complete laboratory, with every excuse to procure the necessary bodily fluids . . ."

"Eww. That's—"

An alarm bell clanged right over my head.

"Time's up, it seems," the demi-demon murmured.

She opened the nearest door with the card and propelled me inside, slipping through after me.

"My aunt—"

"Is fine. She's only a few doors down, safe for now. You're the pigeon who's not in her coop."

The demi-demon led me across the room to a second door, opening into a big closet. She ushered me inside.

"Simon and Tori—"

"Are, I presume, in possession of functioning ears and brains. They will hear the alarm and take cover, which is what we need to do."

As I stepped into the closet the guard's body collapsed. I fell to my knees beside it.

"I believe you'll find he's still quite dead." The demi-demon's voice came from above my head. "As useful as that mortal form was, this one is better equipped for sneaking about."

"I thought you said you couldn't get out of there without my help."

"*Implied*, never said. I'm a demon. We know all the loopholes. Now, I'm going to take a look around. You still have that gun, don't you?"

"Yes, but—"

"Take it out and hope you don't need to use it. I'll be right back."

A rush of warm air. Then I was alone with the guard's body.

The alarm continued to whoop.

Did I hear the pounding of running feet? A shout? A shot?

Relax. There's nothing you can do.

That was the problem. I was stuck cowering in my hidey-hole, shaking hands wrapped around a gun that I didn't know how to fire, knowing there was nothing I could do, nothing that wasn't so reckless Derek would have reason to yell at me if he were here, and God how I wished he were. I'd take the yelling just to know he was safe—

He is safe. Safer than if he was *with you.*

If he'd been left at the house then, yes, he'd be fine. He had Liz to watch out for him, and he had no idea where we'd gone and no way to come after us. He'd be furious, but safe.

I glanced over at the guard. He lay in a heap, dead eyes

staring up at me. I thought about him, wondered—

Don't think about him. Don't wonder anything. Or you'll get your wish and you won't be alone in this closet.

I looked away quickly and erased his image from my head. I checked out the gun instead. I'd written shoot-outs in screenplays but, to my embarrassment, had no idea whether the gun was loaded or if there was a safety on it. Stuff like that doesn't matter in a screenplay. You just say "Chloe fires the gun" and leave the rest to the actor and the props department.

It looked like a Glock, though, and from what I remembered, they didn't have safeties. Just point and shoot. I could manage that if I had to.

See, you're not helpless. You have a weapon. Two weapons.

Two? My gaze slid to the guard and I swallowed hard. No, I'd never—

Sure you would, if it came down to it.

No, I—I . . .

Can't even finish the denial, can you? You'd do it if it was the last resort. Controlling the dead. That's your power. Your greatest power.

I squeezed my eyes shut.

"You can't see anyone coming like that."

It took a moment to realize that the voice hadn't come from inside my head. The demi-demon was back.

"What set off the alarm?" I asked.

"I haven't a clue, but your friends are safe. They've

retreated to Davidoff's reading room. The group realizes you've escaped, but, shockingly, they presume you actually tried to get out of the building. Fortunately, you're nowhere near an exit. Unfortunately . . ."

"We're nowhere near an exit."

"I can get you out. I may even be able to rescue your aunt on the way. But your friends are in the opposite direction, and I can't possibly—"

"Then I don't go. Not until it's safe for all of us."

"A noble choice. However, there's only one alternative and I fear you'll like it even less than my last suggestion."

"Free you."

As I said it, my inner voice screamed that I'd been tricked. But I could hear the shouts of the Edison Group. They really *had* been alerted and there was no reason for the demi-demon to do it herself, not when she could have easily escorted us out the door and claimed her reward.

"Free me and you will cripple the magics cast on this place," she said.

"Great. That'll help end the experiments, but how does it get us out? It's not the magic I'm worried about. It's the alarms and guys with guns. What I need—"

"Is a distraction. And that's what I'm offering. My magic permeates this place. The disruption will affect far more than their spells. You will get the distraction you need."

Our plan had failed and she had every reason to lie now and convince me to free her, before I realized I was trapped.

"I made a bargain," she said. "A demon's bargain is binding. Free me and I am bound by my word as tightly as these bonds."

Did I trust her? Of course not. Did I have another option? Not one I could see.

"Tell me what to do."

forty-three

FREEING THE DEMI-DEMON WASN'T much different from freeing a ghost. I suppose that made sense, since she'd gotten here by a type of summoning.

"Almost there, child," she said, her warm breath swirling around me. "I can feel the shackles falling. A quarter century of servitude and finally I will be free. The very walls will tremble with my leaving, and they'll scurry like frightened mice. Just a little more. Can you feel it?"

I couldn't feel a thing, just wished she'd shut up and let me concentrate.

She let out a cry that made me jump, and the closet filled with whirling hot air. I braced myself. The wind whipped around me, then gradually subsided to a pleasant breeze before disappearing altogether.

Silence.

"Is that . . . it?" I said.

"Hmm. Do you feel anything else? A vibration, perhaps?"

"No." I glowered in the direction of her voice. "You promised a distract—"

The closet shook. A dull rumble sounded overhead, like a train chugging across the roof. As I looked up, a sudden tremor knocked me off my feet.

A ceiling tile hit my shoulder. Then another. The tiny room creaked and groaned and crackled, walls splitting, chunks of drywall raining down.

"Out, child!" The demi-demon shouted to be heard above the din. "You need to get out!"

I tried to stand, but fell back to all fours. The room kept shaking and creaking, walls groaning as they ripped open. Drywall dust filled my nose and stung my eyes. I crawled blindly, following the demi-demon's voice as she led me.

I made it out of the closet and into the main room. It was shaking just as much, the floor tiles buckling beneath me. A chunk of falling plaster hit my back. Another the size of a fist glanced off my injured arm, shattering as it hit the floor, bits flying into my mouth.

As I spat out the plaster, I smelled something other than drywall dust. A sweet scent, strangely familiar.

"*Faster,*" the demi-demon said. "Keep moving."

As I crawled, the shaking stopped. The groaning stopped. The room went completely silent and still.

I looked around. Dust still filled my eyes, making them water. The floor was carpeted in plaster. The walls were a patchwork of cracks and hanging chunks of drywall.

The room groaned again, softer now, like it was settling, and all that remained was the sweet smell.

The demi-demon kept urging me on. I got to my feet. Outside, I could hear the distant shouts and cries of the Edison Group. Overhead the light flickered like a strobe, throwing the windowless room into darkness.

"You have your distraction," the demi-demon said. "Now take advantage of it."

As I stepped toward the door, something brushed my leg. I jumped and looked down. Nothing was there. Another step. Warm fingers stroked my cheek. Hot breath whispered wordlessly in my ear, blowing strands of hair, tickling my neck.

"I-Is that you?" I asked.

"Of course," said the demi-demon . . . from across the room.

I looked around. I couldn't see anything except debris. The light continued to flicker. Distant voices shouted about finding the computer tech.

"Their systems are down," the demi-demon said. "Perfect. Now go."

I started forward. At a giggle to my left, I spun. A growl sounded behind me and I spun again.

"The *door*," the demi-demon said. "Get to the door."

A blast of hot air knocked me off my feet, flat onto my back.

A giggle erupted above me. Then a low voice, speaking in a foreign language. I pushed up. Another blast slapped me down. Hot air whirled around, drywall dust flying like a sandstorm, filling my eyes, my nose, my mouth.

I crawled toward the door. The wind buffeted me from all sides. That sweet smell—sickly sweet now—made my stomach churn. Invisible hands stroked my head, my back, my face. Fingers plucked my shirt, pulled my hair, pinched my arms. Voices whispered and growled and shrieked in my ears. But the only one that mattered was the demi-demon's, urging me on, guiding me to the door.

My head struck the wall. I patted around until I found the doorknob, pulled myself up, and turned it. Yanked. Turned. Yanked.

"No," I whispered. "Please, no."

Seems those electrical failures might not be so convenient after all.

Fingers ran through my hair. Warm breath caressed my cheek. Hot wind whipped around me. The light flickered.

"Sweet child," a voice whispered.

"What is she?" another asked.

"Necromancer."

A giggle. "Are you sure?"

"What have they done to her?"

"Something wonderful."

"Get away from her," the demi-demon said. "She's not yours. Shoo. All of you."

"Wh-what's going on?" I asked.

"Nothing to worry about, child. It's simply a bit of fall-out from the liberation ritual. There are usually precautions taken against such a thing, but we didn't have the time. Or the materials."

"Precautions against what?"

"Well, when you free a demon, you open a . . ."

"Portal into the demon world?"

"*Portal* is a strong word. More like a teeny tiny tear."

The voice continued as we talked. The unseen fingers touched me, poked me.

"These are demons?" I said.

"Hardly," she said with a sniff. "Minor demonic spirits. Little more than pests." She raised her voice. "Who are going to be in serious trouble if they don't heed my commands."

The spirits hissed and spat and chortled. And stayed where they were.

"Ignore them," she said. "They can't do more than touch you, and they can barely do that. Think of them as an infestation of otherworldly insects. Annoying and inconvenient, but hardly dangerous. They can't manifest in this world without a dead body—"

She stopped short. We both looked at the closet door.

"Quickly," she said. "Send me back to that guard. If his corpse is occupied, they can't—"

A thump sounded from the closet. Then a low hiss. I spun and yanked on the exit door. Growls erupted from the closet. As I whaled on the door, I heard a scratching, like nails scraping wood. The click of a knob. The squeak of the door hinges. I spun toward the closet. The lights went out.

forty-four

FINGERS BRUSHED MY FACE, making me jump back from the door. Across the room, nails scraped along the floor.

"He's coming," a voice whispered. "The master is coming."

"M-master?" I said.

"They lie," the demi-demon said. "It's just another—"

A wail at my ear drowned her out. I jumped back, knocking over a chair and falling hard. A blast of desert wind whipped my hair in my face, twisting my clothing, binding me. I heard the sounds of struggle, the curses of the demi-demon barely rising over the gibbering and shrieking of the spirits.

Then, as suddenly as it had begun, it ended. The wind died and the room went silent.

Completely dark and completely silent.

"A-are you there?" I called.

She didn't answer. Instead, I heard the scrape of nails, then the whisper of fabric as it slid across the floor. I leaped to my feet only to tangle in the fallen chair and topple over it, bashing into another piece of furniture. The back of my head cracked against something and the wound from earlier reopened, blood streaming down the back of my head.

The scratching stopped, and I heard sniffing. Sniffing and the smacking of lips.

I wiped the blood away and scuttled back, thumping into the wall. A chattering, then a hiss, and it went quiet again. I could pick up the distant voices of the Edison Group, and I clung to that, a reminder of where I was, in the lab, not locked away in a basement crawl space with dead bodies crawling toward me.

Umm, actually, yes, there is a dead body—

But it wasn't a rotting corpse.

True, it's a nice fresh one . . . possessed by a demonic spirit.

The scraping started again. I wrapped my arms around myself and squeezed my eyes shut.

Oh, that'll help.

No, but *this* would. I concentrated on freeing that spirit. I kept at it, as hard as I dared, but that whispering of fabric and scratching of nails kept coming closer, so close now I could hear the scrape of buttons against the floor. I scrambled to a new spot, hit another chair, and crashed down on top of it.

Just release it. Stop worrying about getting away. Release it.

I closed my eyes. Not that it mattered. The room was so dark I couldn't see a thing, couldn't see the guard's body slithering across the floor, couldn't see how close it was, couldn't see it—

Focus!

I released and released and released, but it still kept coming, the whispering and the scratching, the hissing and the chattering. I could hear more now—teeth clicking and grinding. And I could smell that sweet demon odor mixing with the stink of burned flesh, making my stomach heave.

Concentrate.

I did, but no matter how hard I tried, the thing didn't pause, didn't growl or hiss, gave no sign it felt anything.

Hot breath seared my ankles. I yanked my knees in and hugged them, blinking hard, desperately trying to see even a shape, but the room was completely dark. Then the scratching and whispering and chattering all stopped, and I knew it was right in front of me.

A sharp rip, like fabric tearing. Then another kind of rip, a dull, wet sound that made the whimper die in my throat, and I huddled there, knees drawn tight, listening to that awful wet tearing sound, punctuated by popping, like bones crackling and snapping.

I squeezed my eyes shut. Dismiss, dismiss—

Something wet and cold flicked across my ankle. I pulled my foot back, hands flying to my mouth, stifling my scream. I leaped to my feet, but icy fingers grabbed my legs and yanked me down. It held me tight, hands climbing up my legs as it pulled itself onto me.

I went wild, kicking and punching, but it held me down with superhuman strength and then it was on me, crouched over me, pinning me, hissing, sickly sweet breath blasting in my face. I felt something cold and wet on my neck. It was licking me, licking the blood.

I punched and kicked and imagined releasing it and for a second felt that iron grip loosen. I heaved and rolled, and managed to get free, scrabbling backward until I hit the wall.

I pushed to my feet and tried to run, but tripped over the chair I'd toppled earlier. I caught myself before I fell, then scurried back, expecting any moment the thing would pounce and knock me down. But it didn't, and when I listened I could hear a wet rasping noise where I'd left it. I backed away slowly.

With a click, the lights came on, and I saw the guard crouched on all fours, arms and legs bent . . . wrong, bent where arms and legs shouldn't bend. It looked like some kind of monstrous insect, limbs broken and twisted, bones sticking through fabric. Its head was down and it kept making those wet rasping noises.

I stepped to the side and saw what it was doing—licking

my blood from the floor. I backed up fast, and it turned its head—completely turned it, the flesh on its neck ripped through, the head swiveling freely. It curled its bloodied lips back, bared its teeth, and hissed. Then it skittered toward me, those broken and twisted limbs moving so fast they seemed to skim the floor, body held only inches above it.

I ran for the closet door. With lightning speed it raced into my path. Then it reared up, hissing and spitting.

"Release it, child," a familiar voice whispered at my ear.

"Y-you're back." I looked around, bracing against the pokes and pinches. "The others . . ."

"Gone, and staying gone. Only this one remains. Release it and you'll be done."

"I've tried."

"And now I'm here to distract it while you try again."

A gust of hot air whooshed between me and the thing, and it reared again, gaze following the wind as the demi-demon whipped past.

I closed my eyes.

"Your necklace," she said.

"R-right." I tugged it off and looked at it, reluctant to put it down.

The thing spun on me again. The demi-demon said something in another language, getting its attention. I set the necklace on a chair, within grabbing distance, then closed my eyes and worked at dismissing it.

I felt the spirit slipping away, snarling. At a click, my eyes shot open, gaze following the sound to the door.

"Yes, it's open," the demi-demon said. "And not a moment too soon. Now finish this."

Knowing the door was open gave me the extra boost I needed, and the next sound I heard was a thump as the guard's broken body fell to the floor.

"Excellent," the demi-demon said. "Now retrieve your trinket and—"

A furnace blast of hot air hit me, so strong it made the others seem like a gentle breeze.

"Wh-what's that?" I said.

"Nothing, child," she said quickly. "Now, *hurry*."

forty-five

I GRABBED MY NECKLACE and pulled it on as I raced for the door. I was about to veer around the guard's body when it rose, pushing to its feet as if its bones weren't broken in a dozen places. I started around it.

"Stop!" it thundered.

I did. I have no idea why. It was just that kind of voice.

I turned to see the guard's body standing straight, chin up, eyes blazing an unearthly green. I could feel the heat radiating off it even from a half-dozen feet away.

"Diriel!" it roared, peering about the room.

"Um, over here, my lord," the demi-demon said. "And may I say, it's a pleasure to see you—"

He spun in her direction, and when he spoke, his voice was weirdly melodic. Like the demi-demon's, only deeper, masculine, hypnotic even. I stood there, rooted to the floor, just listening.

"For over two decades you have not answered my summons. Where have you been?"

"Well, you know, it's a funny story. And I'll be happy to tell you just as soon as I—"

"Are you asking me to wait on your convenience?" His voice was low, but it made me shiver in spite of the heat.

"Certainly not, sir, but I've made a bargain with this—"

"Mortal?" He wheeled, as if seeing me for the first time. "You made a bargain with a mortal *child*?"

"Like I said, funny story, and you are going to love—"

"She's a necromancer." He stepped toward me. "That glow . . ."

"Isn't it pretty? There's such charming variation among these mortal supernaturals. Even the weakest among them gets something, like that lovely glow."

"A necromancer's glow is indicative of her power."

"Quite right, and it's a good thing, too, because being such a weak necromancer, she needs a very strong glow to attract any ghosts."

He gave a dismissive snort and walked over to me. I didn't flinch—but only because I was frozen with terror.

This was a demon. A full demon. I knew that with a certainty that made my legs quiver.

He stopped in front of me and tilted his head, sizing me up. Then he smiled.

"So," said the demi-demon—Diriel. "I'm just going to help this poor, defenseless necromancer child . . ."

"Out of the goodness of your heart, I suppose."

"Well, no, it seems the silly chit freed me. Completely accidental. You know children, always playing with the forces of darkness. So it seems she's done me a favor, and if you'll let me complete the contract, sir, I will be right with you—"

"How powerful does a child necromancer need to be to free a demi-demon?" he mused. "I can feel your power, little one. They've done something to you, haven't they? I have no idea what, but it is wondrous."

His eyes gleamed, and I felt them slicing through me as if he were peering into the heart of my power, and when he did, he smiled again, and it made me shiver.

"Perhaps, but she's a child, my lord. You know what the Berithian Treaty says about wooing youths. Quite unfair, I agree, but she will be an adult soon enough, and if you allow me to cultivate the child by completing my contract . . ."

He glanced in her direction. "Whatever deal you've made with the child can be completed another time. I'm not letting you slip away again so easily. You have a penchant for disappearing."

"But she—"

"Is powerful enough to summon you when she wishes." He turned back to me and before I could move away, his hand was under my chin, holding it, the guard's dead fingers oddly warm. He tilted my face up to his and murmured, "Grow up strong, little one. Strong and powerful."

A blast of hot air. Diriel whispered, "I'm sorry, child." And then they were gone.

I jumped over the guard's fallen body and raced to the door. The handle turned before I touched it. I looked around, ready to run, but there was no place to run *to*. I took out the gun and backed against the wall. The door opened. A figure peeked in.

"A-aunt Lauren," I whispered.

My knees wobbled. There'd been a time when I'd chafed under Aunt Lauren's constant mothering, but after two weeks of relying on myself and other kids who were as scared and lost as I was, her look of concern was like a warm blanket on a freezing night, and I wanted to throw myself into her arms and say, *Take care of me. Fix this.*

But I didn't. She was the one who ran over and hugged me and as wonderful as it was, that feeling of wanting to be rescued passed, and I felt myself pulling away and heard myself saying "Come on. I know the way."

As we hurried out, she glanced back in the room and saw the guard's body.

She gasped. "Isn't that—?"

Without missing a beat, I cut her off, stammering, "I—I don't know what happened. I g-got scared and he just walked in here and—"

She hugged me, whispering, "It's okay, hon."

She believed me, of course. I was still her little Chloe

who'd never *think* of raising the dead.

As we slipped into the hall, she saw the gun and took it from me before I realized what she was doing. When I protested she said, "If we need to use it, I'll be the one who pulls the trigger." I knew she was trying to protect me from having to shoot someone. I didn't *want* to shoot anyone, but there was something about giving up the gun that chafed, the feeling of being shoved back into a role I no longer fit.

"Simon and Tori are in Dr. Davidoff's office," I whispered.

"We'll go this way. It's longer, but we're less likely to bump into anyone."

We turned a corner and a balding guard stepped from a room. I tried to tug Aunt Lauren back, but he'd already seen us.

"Don't move, Alan," Aunt Lauren said, raising the gun. "Just step back into that room and close—"

"Alan," said a voice behind him.

He turned. A shot fired. The guard dropped. Mrs. Enright stood there, lowering a gun.

"I really do hate these things," she said, lifting the gun. "So primitive. But I thought it might come in handy."

I glanced at Aunt Lauren. She was frozen in a binding spell.

"Look what your aunt did, Chloe." Mrs. Enright waved at the guard, motionless on the ground. "Such a shame. They won't let her off with house arrest this time."

I looked from Aunt Lauren to the dead guard.

Mrs. Enright laughed. "You're thinking of raising him, aren't you? Such a resourceful girl. I suppose we have you to thank for all this." She waved her free hand at the cracks in the walls. "That's what I like about you. Resourceful, clever, and, apparently"—she motioned at the guard again—"getting more confident in your powers each time we meet. I'd almost like to let you raise him, just to see what you'd do."

"Let us go or—"

"I'm the one with the gun, Chloe. Your weapon takes longer to activate. If he so much as twitches, it's good-bye to Aunt Lauren. Any bargains come from me, and I'm still quite willing to deal with you. I think we could—"

A dark shape leaped on her back. As she fell, she twisted to see a huge black wolf pinning her. She opened her mouth to cast, but Derek grabbed her by the back of the shirt and whipped her against the wall. She recovered, rolling aside and reciting words in a foreign language. He grabbed her and flung her again. She hit with a crack, then lay still.

I raced forward.

"Chloe!" Aunt Lauren shouted, freed from her binding spell.

"It's Derek," I said.

"I know. Don't—"

I was already there, dropping beside him as he panted, flanks heaving, fighting for control. I grabbed handfuls of fur and buried my face against him, tears threatening.

"You're okay," I said. "I was so worried."

"You weren't the only one," said a voice.

I glanced up to see Liz and smiled. "Thank you."

"I just went along for the ride. After that happened—" She waved at Derek. "You know how blind people need Seeing Eye dogs? Well, apparently werewolves could really use Opening Door poltergeists."

Derek rumbled deep in his chest and bumped me.

"We need to go. I know."

I started getting to my feet, but he leaned against me. I could feel his racing heart. He pressed his nose against my neck, breathed deeply, shuddered, and his heart slowed. When he sniffed again, his nose went to the back of my neck, finding the blood and grumbling with concern.

"It's just a bump," I said. "I'm fine."

I wrapped my hands in his fur one last time, holding him tight, then pushed to my feet. I turned to Aunt Lauren. She stood there, staring. Just staring.

"We have to go," I said.

Her gaze lifted to mine and she stared some more, like seeing someone she didn't recognize.

"Liz is here," I said. "She'll scout the way."

"Liz . . ." She swallowed, then nodded. "All right."

I gestured at Tori's mom. "Is she . . . ?"

"Still alive, but it was a hard blow. She should be out for a while."

"Good. Derek? We need to get Tori and Simon. Follow

me. Liz, can you go ahead and make sure the way is clear?"

She smiled. "Yes, boss."

I took a few steps, then realized Aunt Lauren wasn't following. I turned. She was still staring.

"I'm okay," I said.

"You are," she said softly. Then firmer, "You really are."

We set out.

forty-six

WE COLLECTED TORI AND Simon just as they were heading out to rescue *me*. After a very brief explanation about the earthquake and the wolf by my side, I asked if Simon had gotten hold of his dad. His face darkened, telling me the answer wasn't good.

"Voice mail," he said.

"Seriously?"

"It said he was unavailable and switched to voice mail. I left a message. He could have been out of range or on the phone or . . ."

He didn't finish, but we all knew what he meant. *Unavailable* could mean a lot of things, not all of them as innocent as being stuck between cell towers.

"We'll call again as soon as we're out," Aunt Lauren said. "Which should be soon."

We headed for the nearest exit. We'd gone about twenty feet before Liz came racing over.

"Three of them," she said. "Coming this way."

"Guns?" I asked.

She nodded.

If it was three unarmed staff—even with supernatural powers—I'd be willing to take them on. But guns were another thing. I told the others.

"There's an unused wing to the west," Aunt Lauren said. "They won't guard that exit because it's through a secured door."

I followed her and used the key card to get us into the wing. As soon as we were through, Derek stopped short, the hair on his back rising, lips curling in a silent growl.

"Do you smell someone?" I whispered.

He shook his head sharply, with a grunt, as if to say *sorry*, and we started forward again, but he was wary now, gaze flicking from side to side.

"I know this place," Simon murmured. "I've been here."

"Your dad used to bring you to work sometimes when you were little," Aunt Lauren said.

"Yeah, I know, but this place . . ." He looked around, then he rubbed the back of his neck. "Creeps me out, whatever it is."

"The exit is around the corner and down at the end," Aunt Lauren said, ushering us on. "It leads into a yard. We'll need to climb the wall, but that's another reason they won't guard it."

We continued along. Simon and Derek weren't the only ones getting chills. It was so quiet. An empty, dead place. Shadows hunkered along the walls, out of reach of the security lights. It stunk, too, reeking of antiseptic soaked right into the floors, like an abandoned hospital.

I glanced in the first open door and stopped short. Desks. Four tiny desks. A wall of faded posters of alphabet animals. A blackboard, still showing the ghosts of numbers. I blinked, certain I was seeing wrong.

Derek nudged my legs, telling me to get moving. I looked at him, and I looked at the classroom.

This was where Derek had grown up. Four tiny desks. Four little boys. Four young werewolves.

For a second, I could see them—three boys working at the three clustered desks, Derek alone at the fourth, pushed slightly away, hunched over his work, trying to ignore the others.

Derek nudged me again, whining softly, and I looked down to see him eyeing the room, every hair on his neck on end, anxious to get away from this place. I murmured an apology and followed the others. We passed two more doors, then Liz came running back.

"Someone's coming."

"What?" Aunt Lauren said when I relayed it. "From

down there? That can't be. It's—"

The clomp of footsteps cut her off. She looked each way, then waved to the nearest door.

"The key card, Chloe, quickly!"

I opened it and we all tumbled inside. As I closed the door behind us, the lock whirred shut. I looked around, squinting to see with only the glow of an emergency light.

We were in a huge storage room packed with boxes.

"Lots of places to hide," I whispered. "I suggest we find one."

We split up as footsteps echoed down the hall. I turned, nearly tripping over Derek. He hadn't moved, just stared into the room, fur bristling.

I looked around. I saw boxes, lots of boxes, but over along the far wall, something else—four beds.

"T-this was—" I began.

"Where is everyone?" boomed a voice from the hall.

Derek snapped out of it, grabbed my sleeve between his teeth, and tugged me deep into the sea of boxes. We found a spot in the back corner where boxes were piled three high, leaving a small space for us to hide. Derek nudged me toward it. I whispered for the others as he went back to gather them up.

In a minute, we were all wedged in that space, crouched or sitting. Derek stood at the opening, guarding it, ears swiveling. As the steps drew closer, I didn't need his hearing to pick up the voices.

"Scientists." A man snorted. "They think they can hire a few rent-a-cop half-demons and they're ready for something like this. Arrogant sons of . . ." His mutters trailed off. "How close is Mr. St. Cloud?"

"His flight will arrive in seventy-five minutes, sir."

"Then we have an hour to clean this mess up. How many kids was it again? Four?"

"Three were recaptured. The fourth—the were-wolf—wasn't, but there was a report that he'd entered the building."

"Great. Just great." Their footsteps sounded outside the door. "All right, here's the plan. I need two survivors. If you can get me two, Mr. St. Cloud will be happy. And that doesn't include the werewolf."

"Naturally, sir."

"We need a place to set up a base of operations. The team will be here in five minutes."

"It doesn't look as if they use this wing, sir." A door creaked. "This room even has desks and a blackboard."

"Good. Start setting up and get Davidoff on the radio. I want him down here now."

I waved for Liz to go check things out.

We all strained to listen, praying they'd find some problem with the room or be offered a better one. It didn't happen.

"At least they're on the other side of our escape route," Tori said.

"It doesn't matter," Simon said. "We've got a Cabal SWAT

team setting up down the hall. We're screwed."

Liz came running back in. "There are two guys in suits and one wearing what looks like a soldier's uniform. Plus four more like him marching up the hall."

The clomping of boots echoed her words.

"We'll hold tight," I said. "They'll send those guys searching—hopefully somewhere else. When we get a chance, we'll run."

Derek chuffed and slid in behind me, letting me rest against him, so warm and comfortable that I started to relax, and when I did, so did he, muscles softening, heart rate slowing.

"So you two came on your own?" I said to Liz. "How?"

"Drove."

"But Derek doesn't have his license."

Simon laughed. "Doesn't mean we don't know how to drive. Dad let us start last year, bombing around empty parking lots."

"That's a few minutes at the mall, not eight hours on the highway."

Derek grunted, as if to say it'd been no big deal, though I'm sure it couldn't have been easy.

"We took Andrew's truck," Liz said. "After we found . . . After Derek found his . . . Well, you know. We probably weren't far behind you. I helped navigate."

"How'd you communicate?"

"Paper and pen. Amazing inventions. Anyway, once we were in Buffalo, I led him here. We couldn't figure out a way in and he got stressed and apparently that"—she waved at him—"is what happens when a werewolf gets stressed. By then, the garage door was open, some staff guy bringing in a car. He took one look at Derek and decided it was time for a new job."

Noises sounded in the hall. Liz went to check it out. Behind me, Derek's flank twitched. I rubbed it absently, the muscle jumping under my fingers. Then I asked the question I'd been dreading since Aunt Lauren first found me.

"Rae's dead, isn't she?" I said. "Dr. Davidoff said she was transferred, but I know what that means. The same thing it meant with Liz and Brady."

The look on Aunt Lauren's face at that moment . . . I can't describe it, but if I had any doubt about how much she regretted the role she'd played in all this, I saw it as I mentioned their names. For a second she said nothing. Then she jumped, like she'd been startled.

"Rae? No. Rae isn't dead. Someone broke in and took her. They think it was her mother."

"Her adoptive mom?"

Aunt Lauren shook her head. "Her birth mother. Jacinda."

"But Dr. Davidoff said she was dead."

"We said a lot of things, Chloe. Told a lot of lies, telling ourselves it was better for you all, but really, just because it was easier. If Rae thought her mother was dead, she wouldn't ask for her. From everything I heard, though, they think that's who—"

Derek's flank twitched again. I glanced down to see a muscle spasming. Another started in his shoulder. When he caught me looking, he growled, telling me it was nothing, just ignore him and pay attention.

As Aunt Lauren talked, I rubbed the muscle in Derek's shoulder and he leaned against my hand, relaxing. I knew it wouldn't help. He was ready to Change.

"We need to get going," I said. "I'm going to call Liz."

She raced through the boxes before I even finished summoning her. Tori's mom had joined the SWAT team in the next room. Apparently, Derek hadn't hurt her as much as I might have hoped. She was nursing a killer headache . . . and a killer grudge. Derek was to be shot on sight—shot dead, not tranquilized.

Reinforcements from a Cabal satellite office were on the way to help sweep the building with manpower and spell power. They were determined to find us before this St. Cloud guy arrived.

"We're going to have to make a run for it," I said. "As soon as it's quiet—"

Derek convulsed, nearly throwing me off him.

"Someone doesn't like your plan," Tori said. "And just when I was thinking how nice it was that he doesn't have a voice. Won't keep him from arguing apparently."

"That's not it," I said as Derek convulsed again. "He's Changing back."

"Can it wait, because—?"

Derek's whole body spasmed, all four legs shooting out, a back claw nicking Simon, a front paw swatting Tori. They both leaped out of the way.

"I think that's a no," Simon said.

"We need to clear out," I said. "As you can tell, this requires room. And it might not be something you want to see."

"Tell them I second that," Liz said. "I caught a glimpse, and that was enough." She made a face and shuddered.

I shooed them out, then turned to Derek, lying on his side, panting. "You've done this alone now, so I guess you don't need—"

He caught my jeans leg between his teeth, pulling gently, his eyes asking me to stay. I told the others I was, and said if they heard any sign that the SWAT team was searching this hall, they were to get out—all of them.

"We aren't leaving you two," Simon said.

Derek growled.

"He's agreeing with me," I said. "For once. You have to go. With any luck, they'll presume that means Derek and I are someplace else."

Simon didn't like it, but he only grumbled for Derek to hurry.

Aunt Lauren stayed after they'd gone. "If anything happens, you're coming with us, Chloe. Derek can look after—"

"No, he can't. Not like this. He needs me."

"I don't care."

"I do. He needs me. So I stay."

We locked gazes. Again, a look passed through her eyes, surprise and maybe a little bit of grief. I wasn't her little Chloe anymore. I never would be again.

I walked over and hugged her. "I'm fine."

"I know." She hugged me back, fierce and tight, then left to join the others.

forty-seven

DEREK'S CHANGE CAME FASTER now and maybe a bit easier—no vomiting this time. Finally it was over, and he fell onto his side, panting, shaking, and shivering. Then he reached for my hand, holding it tight, and I entwined my fingers with his, shifting closer and using my free hand to brush sweaty hair from his face.

"Whoa," a voice said, making both of us jump. Simon stood in the entrance to our corner, a pile of fabric in his hands. "You really need to get dressed before you start that."

"I'm not starting anything," Derek said.

"Still . . ." He held out the stack in his hands. "Dr. Fellows dug up some hospital greens for you. Get dressed and then . . . whatever."

"We weren't—" I began.

"Have you still got my note?"

I nodded.

"Give it to him."

I pulled the folded page from my pocket and handed it to Derek. When he was busy with it, Simon let the smile fall from his face as he studied his brother.

"Is he okay?" he mouthed.

I nodded. I passed Derek the scrubs as he refolded the note, then turned away to let him dress.

"We good?" Simon asked.

"Yeah." Derek lowered his voice.

A squeak of shoes as Simon turned to go. Derek called him back, grunting with effort as he rose, his bare feet padding over. A short, murmured conversation. Then the slap of Simon smacking Derek's back, and his footsteps retreated.

A whisper of fabric as Derek dressed. Then a hand on my waist, a light touch, tentative. I turned and Derek was right there, his face above mine, hands sliding around me as I tilted my face up—

"What the—?"

We both jumped—again. Tori stood there, staring at us, Simon behind her, grabbing her arm.

"I told you not to—" Simon began.

"Yeah, but you didn't say why. I sure didn't expect . . ." She shook her head. "Am I the last one to know everything around here?"

Liz raced in. "What's going on?"

"Derek's ready," I said. "We need to move."

We had one gun, one werewolf, one poltergeist, one super-charged spell-caster, one not-so-supercharged spell-caster, and one perfectly useless necromancer, though Liz was quick to remind me that she needed me to relay her words.

Our plan, though, involved something much simpler than a supernatural showdown. We were falling back on the advice Derek's dad had given him for dealing with a significantly stronger opponent: run like hell.

While Liz watched the operations room, we'd try to make it to the exit door. If we failed? That's when the gun, werewolf, poltergeist, and spell-casters would come into play.

According to Liz, there were five people in that room—Mrs. Enright, Dr. Davidoff, the head suit, his assistant, and one SWAT guard. They seemed to be staying put, manning the war room while the employees searched. Every now and then, one of those employees would pop in for an update or orders. We just had to pray that didn't happen during the few minutes it'd take us to get to the door.

As we coordinated a what-if plan of attack, Derek stood beside me. Aunt Lauren kept giving us weird looks. We weren't doing anything to earn them, but she kept glancing over and frowning.

Finally she said, "Derek? Can I speak to you?"

He stiffened and glanced at me, as if to say, *What does she want?*

"W-we don't have time to—" I began.

"It'll just take a second. Derek? Please?"

She waved him across the room. Tori and Simon were arguing about spells and Liz was in the hall, so no one else noticed. Aunt Lauren said something to Derek. Whatever it was, he didn't like it, his gaze shooting to me as he scowled and shook his head.

Was she telling him to stay away from me? I could hope that today she'd seen he wasn't dangerous, maybe even seen how I felt about him, but I guess that was too much to hope for.

I wanted to march over and interrupt, but before I could, Derek stopped arguing. He eased back, head bent, hair hanging forward, deep in thought. Then he gave a slow nod. She reached out and took his arm, leaning in to say more, her face taut with urgency. He kept his gaze down, nodding. I told myself he was just saying whatever she wanted to hear so we could get out of here, but I'll admit I felt a lot better when he walked straight to me, rumbling, "You ready?"

We stepped aside as Aunt Lauren got Simon and Tori.

"Was she telling you to stay away from me?" I asked.

He paused, then said, "Yeah." He squeezed my hand out of Aunt Lauren's sight. "It's okay. We're good."

We headed for the hall.

* * *

Our biggest worry had been the loud click of the door lock, but Derek listened and motioned for me to open it while the men were talking. Then Derek took the lead, in case anyone came in through the exit door. I was behind him, Simon behind me, Tori and Aunt Lauren following.

Those thirty feet seemed like thirty miles. I longed to bolt for the door, throw it open, and be gone; but we had to move silently, which meant excruciatingly slowly.

We'd gone about ten feet when someone in the war room said, "We have a breach, sir. A perimeter spell."

"Where?"

Derek picked up speed, just a little.

"Hold on," the man said. "It seems to be right outside—"

"Chloe?" Aunt Lauren's loud whisper floated through the halls.

I spun to see her jogging the other way—toward the room where the Edison team and the Cabal guys were. She called my name again, like she was searching for me.

My mouth opened. A hand clamped over it, an arm going around my chest, holding me still, Derek's voice in my ear, whispering, "I'm sorry."

"I think I hear them," Dr. Davidoff said.

"Chloe?" Aunt Lauren ran full out now, shoes slapping the linoleum. "Chloe?"

She wheeled into their room and let out a yelp.

"Hello, Lauren," Tori's mom said. "Lost your niece

again?" She cast a binding spell, freezing my aunt. "I see you still have that gun. Let me take that, before you kill someone else."

As I struggled, Derek waved for the others to keep going. I vaguely saw Simon and Tori pass me as Derek scooped me up and started for the exit, and I knew *this* was what Aunt Lauren had told him to do, what he'd tried to argue against. If there was trouble, she'd sacrifice herself to save us. His job was to get me out of there.

I twisted my head to see Mrs. Enright holding the gun on Aunt Lauren, still frozen.

"Time to rid ourselves of a very inconvenient—"

"A gun, Diane?" a man's voice called. "Guess your charm isn't the only power you underestimate."

A man stepped around the corner. He was about my dad's age, a couple of inches shorter than Mrs. Enright, slender, with silvering black hair. He was smiling—and it was a smile I knew well, even if I'd never seen this man before.

"Dad!" Simon shouted, skidding to a halt.

forty-eight

M R. BAE LIFTED A hand, waving casually, like he'd walked in on us sitting around chatting. I struggled and Derek released me.

"Hello, Kit," Mrs. Enright said. She turned the gun on him.

He tsk-tsked. "Is that really the impression you want to make, Diane? Prove to everyone here that a witch needs a gun to fight a sorcerer?"

She lowered the gun and raised her hand instead, fingers sparking.

"There," he said. "That's better. Now come on over and show me how much you missed me."

She cast an energy bolt. Mr. Bae's hand flew out and her bolt stopped short, exploding in midair. The guard advanced on Aunt Lauren, gun pointed, now that the binding spell on her was broken.

Simon lunged forward, but his father motioned for him to run. Simon kept going. Derek caught his shoulder. He looked down at me, then from the door to his father, caught between the impulse to protect him or protect us.

"Fight," I whispered, and it was all I needed to say. Derek released Simon and pushed me toward the door. Tori locked the guard in a binding spell and yelled for Aunt Lauren to follow me. My aunt sprang up and grabbed the guard's gun and hit him in the head with it as Derek plowed into Dr. Davidoff, sending him flying.

Tori cast another spell, then another. I don't know what they were, only that the walls started to shake. The cracks from earlier yawned wider. Plaster rained down.

I wanted to do something, anything, but Derek saw me and shouted for me to get back. Then one of the men in a suit hit him with a spell, knocking him forward before his dad slammed an energy bolt into the guy. I stayed where I was, knowing that as much as I wanted to help, I'd only put everyone else in danger trying to protect me.

The building continued to shake, weakened walls and ceiling cracking. White dust rained down, enveloping everyone, and I could catch only glimpses through it, snapshots of the action.

Tori facing off with her mom.

Liz running toward Mrs. Enright, a broken plank in her hand.

The guard lying unconscious under everyone's feet.

Derek tackling the main suit, his dad and Simon taking on the other.

Aunt Lauren standing over Dr. Davidoff, gun at the back of his head.

Then, with an earsplitting crack, the ceiling gave way. Huge chunks of plaster and broken wood crashed down. Boxes and crates and filing cabinets toppled through from the attic. The ceiling kept ripping and cracking, and I looked up to see it splitting right over my head. Derek shouted. He hit me, knocking me to the floor and pinning me beneath him as the rest of the ceiling collapsed.

When the hall finally stopped rumbling, I heard Mr. Bae calling for Derek.

"Here," Derek said. "With Chloe."

He moved off me and helped me up. I rose, coughing and blinking. I could make out Simon and Mr. Bae safe in the room where we'd hidden earlier.

"Tori?" I heard Liz saying. "Tori!"

I squinted and moved toward her voice; Derek still gripped my arm, staying close. Liz was hunched over Tori.

"Tori!" I yelled.

She lifted her head, brushing a hand over her face. "I-I'm okay."

As she got up, I looked around frantically for Aunt Lauren. Then I saw her, stirring under a pile of rubble between me and Tori. I leaped forward, but Derek pulled me back.

"Stay there, guys," Mr. Bae said. "Tori—" He paused and when I looked over, he was staring at her, like he'd only just seen her now, *really* seen her.

"Dad?" Simon said.

Mr. Bae shook off the surprise and said, slowly, "Tori? Head toward me. That ceiling doesn't look good."

I glanced up. Broken timbers and huge pieces of plaster swayed overhead. Boxes teetered on the edge.

Tori looked around. The guard and two guys in suits were almost buried under the rubble. Dr. Davidoff lay on his stomach, not moving. Beside her lay another body—her mother, her eyes open, staring up.

"Ding-dong, the witch is dead," Tori said. She swayed. Then she made a weird, strangled hiccupping noise, shoulders hunching. "Mom . . ."

"Tori? Hon?" Mr. Bae called. "I need you to come over here, okay?"

"Aunt Lauren," I said. "She's caught—"

"I've got it," Tori said, wiping her sleeve over her face. She bent and started pulling pieces off my aunt.

A plank flew up from the pile behind Tori. Dr. Davidoff's eyes were open, mentally guiding it. I opened my mouth to scream a warning and Liz raced to grab it, but it swung down, hitting Tori in the back of the head. She fell face-first to the rubble. Aunt Lauren scrambled up, pushing the last pieces of plaster aside. Then she stopped. Dr. Davidoff rose behind her, gun pressed to the back of her neck.

Liz grabbed the plank he'd hit Tori with, but he saw it move and said, "No, Elizabeth." He swung the gun toward Tori. "Not unless you'd like some company in the afterlife."

Liz dropped the wood.

Dr. Davidoff moved the gun back to Aunt Lauren. "Pick that board up again, please, Elizabeth, and move in front of me, so I can see where you are."

She did.

"Now, Kit, I'm going to give you five minutes to take your boys and go. The modifications appear to have succeeded with Simon. As strong as Derek is, he seems normal for a werewolf. Another success. Chloe and Victoria are the problems, but I assure you, they'll be well cared for. Take your boys and—"

"I'm not going anywhere," Derek said. "Not without Chloe."

He stiffened, like he expected me to argue, but I barely heard them talking. My blood roared in my ears, stomach churning, knowing what I had to do, fighting to get past every instinct that screamed against it.

Dr. Davidoff's eyes lifted to Derek. He frowned, assessing, then nodded. "So be it. I won't turn down the opportunity to keep our only werewolf subject. Take your son, then, Kit."

"I'll take *both* my sons," Mr. Bae said. "And Victoria and Chloe and Lauren."

Dr. Davidoff chuckled. "Still don't know when to cut your losses, do you? I'd think ten years on the run would have taught you a lesson. Think of everything you gave up, just because I wanted Derek back. I'm sure Simon would have been a lot happier if you hadn't been so stubborn."

"Stubborn's good," Simon said. "And it runs in the family. I'm not leaving until you give them up, too."

Derek rubbed the back of my shoulders, mistaking the tightness for fear, not concentration. Simon cast an anxious glance my way as sweat poured down my face. I closed my eyes and focused.

"Go, Chloe," Aunt Lauren said. "Just go."

"That's not how it works," Dr. Davidoff said. "I can shoot you and Tori before Kit or Derek can take me down. Make up your mind, Kit. There's a Cabal team on the way, if they haven't already arrived. Cut your losses and go."

A shape rose behind Dr. Davidoff. Derek sucked in a breath, then slowly released it and whispered under his breath, encouraging me. Simon and Mr. Bae quickly looked away so Dr. Davidoff wouldn't turn around.

"You only have a few minutes, Kit," Dr. Davidoff said.

"Pick up the gun," I said.

He laughed. "Your aunt knows better than to dive for a gun ten feet away, Chloe."

"Dr. Davidoff," I said.

"Yes?"

"Shoot him."

He frowned, mouth opening. Mrs. Enright's corpse swayed. Her eyes met mine, rage-filled eyes.

"I said—"

She fired. Dr. Davidoff hung there, mouth working, hole through his chest. Then he dropped. I squeezed my eyes shut and released Mrs. Enright's soul. When I opened them, Aunt Lauren was crouched beside Dr. Davidoff, fingers to his neck. His ghost stood beside her, staring, confused.

"He's gone," I said. "I—I see his spirit."

Someone shouted. Boots clomped in the distance.

"We have to go," Mr. Bae said. "Lauren—"

"I'm fine."

"Derek, grab Tori and follow me."

We raced out the door just as shouts echoed behind us. Mr. Bae yelled for Simon and Aunt Lauren to get over the wall, as he boosted me and Derek carried Tori. I got to the top, then crouched beside Simon, the two of us helping Derek as Liz ran ahead, shouting the all clear.

As we climbed down, Mr. Bae stood atop the wall, ready to shoot spells at anyone who came out. But no one did—the rubble and the bodies slowed them down long enough for us to get away. By then, Tori was conscious and we ran, all of us, as far and as fast as we could.

forty-nine

M R. BAE'S VAN WAS parked a mile away in a shopping mall. He'd bought it a month ago, using faked paperwork, so it couldn't be traced back to him, and it looked like he'd been living in it. He threw his sleeping bag and a cooler into the back, and we all climbed in.

I don't know where we ended up. Pennsylvania, I think. No one asked. No one cared. It was a really long, really quiet drive. I was in the back with Aunt Lauren, and even though I noticed Derek glancing back at me anxiously every now and then, I soon fell asleep to the murmur of Simon and his dad in the front seat.

I woke up when Mr. Bae pulled into a roadside motel. He got two rooms and we split up, guys going in one, girls in the other. Mr. Bae said he'd order pizza for us all and then we'd talk. Aunt Lauren said not to rush. No one was hungry, and

I'm sure the guys wanted some alone time with their dad.

Liz and Tori seemed to figure I needed alone time with Aunt Lauren, too. Liz took off, saying she was going to wander and she'd be back by morning. Tori said her stomach was queasy from the long drive, so she was going to sit outside for a while to get some fresh air. Aunt Lauren asked her to go behind our unit, so no one driving past could see her.

That's when it really hit me: we weren't going home, not yet anyway. And we'd have to get used to always thinking about stuff like that, about who might be watching.

I sat beside Aunt Lauren on the bed, and she put her arm around my shoulders.

"How are you doing?" she asked.

"Okay."

"What happened back there . . . At the lab . . ."

She didn't finish. I knew what she meant—killing Dr. Davidoff. And I knew that if I mentioned it, she'd tell me I hadn't actually killed him. But I had. I wasn't sure how I felt about that, only that Aunt Lauren wouldn't be the person I'd talk to about it, because she'd only try to make me feel better, not help me work through it. For that, I'd need Derek, so I just said, "I'm okay." Then, "I know I can't go home right now, but I want Dad to know I'm okay."

"I'm not sure that's—"

"He has to know. Even if he can't know about the necromancer stuff and the Edison Group stuff. He has to know I'm safe."

She wavered for a moment, but seeing my expression, she finally nodded. "We'll find a way."

When I found Tori out back, she was just sitting there, like that night at the warehouse when her dad betrayed her. Sitting there, staring into space, hugging her knees.

This had to be so hard for her. The guys got their dad back, I got Aunt Lauren back. And Tori? She'd watched her mother die. No matter how horrible Mrs. Enright had been, no matter how much Tori had come to hate her, she'd still been her mother.

Tori wasn't alone here. She still had a parent, a biological one anyway, but I was sure Mr. Bae wouldn't be too quick to tell her. That would be too weird, like saying, "Sorry you lost one parent, but here's a replacement."

I sat down beside her.

"I'm sorry about your mom," I said.

A short, bitter laugh. "Why? She was an evil, murdering bitch."

"But she was *your* evil, murdering bitch."

Tori gave a choked laugh, then nodded. A tear slid down her cheek. I wanted to put my arm around her, but I knew she'd hate that, so I just moved closer, bumping against her. She tensed and I thought she was going to move away, but then she relaxed, leaning against me. I could feel her body shaking as she cried. She didn't make a sound, though, not even a whimper.

A huge shadow rounded the corner. Derek stepped out, head tilted to catch the wind. His lips twitched when he saw me, curving into a crooked smile.

"Hey," he said. "I thought I—"

Tori lifted her head and wiped her eyes on her sleeve, and Derek shut up.

"Sorry," he said gruffly and started to retreat.

"That's okay," she said, getting to her feet. "My pity session is over. You can have her now."

As she walked away from us back to our room, Derek stood there, looking uncertain again. Anxious again. I waved for him to sit beside me, but he shook his head.

"Can't right now," he said. "Dad sent me to find you."

I went to get up, but my foot was asleep and I stumbled a bit. Derek caught me and didn't let go. He bent, like he was going to kiss me, then stopped.

Was he always going to do that? I almost teased him about it, but he looked so serious, I didn't dare.

"Your aunt," he said. "Did she say anything about your plans?"

"No."

Once more he leaned down to me, then stopped again.

"Didn't she say *anything*? Like whether you're going home or not?"

"I'm not. As long as that Cabal is still out there, we can't. I suppose we'll stay with you guys, if that's what your dad has in mind. Probably safest."

He exhaled, like he'd been holding his breath, and I finally understood why he was so anxious. Now that we'd escaped the Edison Group and were back with our families, he thought that meant we'd go our separate ways.

"I'm definitely *hoping* we'll stay with you guys," I said.

"Me, too."

I slid closer, feeling his arms close around me, tightening. Our lips touched—

"Derek?" his dad called. "Chloe?"

Derek let out a growl. I laughed and backed up.

"We seem to get a lot of that, don't we?" I said.

"Too much. After we eat, we're going for a walk. A *long* walk. Far from every possible interruption."

I grinned up at him. "Sounds like a plan."

Speaking of plans, Mr. Bae had plenty. Over pizza he confirmed what I expected—we needed to go on the run again, this time from the Cabal.

"So everything we did back there, at the lab . . . it didn't do any good?" I said.

"Probably only pissed the Cabal off," Tori muttered.

"No, it helped," Mr. Bae said. "The Edison Group won't recover from this anytime soon, and it'll take some time for the Cabal to sort through everything and plan a search. Fortunately, being a Cabal, they've got a lot on their to-do list, and we won't be at the top. You're valuable, and they'll want you back, but we'll have some breathing room." He glanced at my aunt. "Lauren? Living on the run may not be what you had in mind, but I'm going to strongly suggest you and Chloe come with us. We should stick together."

Derek looked at me, tensing, like he was ready to jump in with arguments if Aunt Lauren disagreed. When she said, "That would be best," he relaxed. So did I. Simon grinned and shot me a thumbs-up. I looked over at Tori. She seemed to be holding herself as still as she could, her face rigid, not giving anything away.

"And Tori will come with us, right?" I said.

"Of course." Mr. Bae smiled at her. "I suppose I should make sure that's okay with her, though. Will you stay with us, Tori?"

She nodded, and slid a half smile my way.

"We'll need to lie low for a while," Mr. Bae said. "I have a few ideas of places we can go. Simon says Tori got a list of the other subjects. We'll make contact with them. They have to know what was going on . . . and what happened. We'll look for Rae, too. If she's with her mom, that's good, but we'll want to make sure of that. We don't want anyone left behind."

It was overwhelming, but it felt weirdly good, too, knowing we weren't alone, knowing we could help the others. We had a lot of work ahead of us, but a lot of adventures, too. I was sure of that.

*　　*　　*

Derek and I went out for our walk after dinner. Alone.

There was an open field behind the motel and we headed there. Finally, when we were far enough from the motel, Derek led me into a little patch of woods. He hesitated then, unsure, still just holding my hand. When I stepped in front of him, though, his free hand went around my waist.

"So," I said. "Seems you're going to be stuck with me for a while."

He smiled. A real smile that lit up his whole face.

"Good," he said.

He pulled me against him. Then he bent down, breath warming my lips. My pulse was racing so fast I could barely breathe. I was sure he'd stop again and I tensed, waiting for that hesitation, stomach twisting. His lips touched mine, and still I kept waiting for him to pull back.

His lips pressed against mine, then parted. And he kissed me. *Really* kissed me—arms tightening around me, mouth moving against mine, firm, like he'd made up his mind that this was what he wanted and he wasn't backing down again.

I slid my arms around his neck. His tightened around me and he scooped me up, lifting me off my feet, kissing me like he was never going to stop, and I kissed him back the same way, like I didn't *want* him to ever stop.

It was a perfect moment, one where nothing else mattered. All I could feel was him. All I could taste was his kiss. All I could hear was the pounding of his heart. All I could think about was him, and how much I wanted this, and how incredibly lucky I was to get it, and how tight I was going to hold onto it.

This was what I wanted. This guy. This life. This *me*. I was never getting my old life back, and I didn't care. I was happy. I was safe. I was right where I wanted to be.